A Very Vi

Where love can b

Whittleston-on-the-Water is a quaint village
on the banks of the Thames, now under the
ownership of the new Lord Hockley. Far from the
Mayfair ballrooms, life still bustles and buzzes
with scandalous gossip, simmering passion
and unexpected love...

Read Sophie and Rafe's story in
The Earl's Inconvenient Houseguest

Isobel and Ned's story in
His Maddening Matchmaker

And Rose and Sam's story in
A Wedding to Stop a Scandal

All available now!

Author Note

I am going to let you in on a secret. Whittleston-on-the-Water, the location of my Very Village Scandal series, isn't entirely fictitious. It is basically what I imagine my little corner of Essex would have been like back in the 1800s. Like my hometown, Whittleston is within spitting distance of the River Thames estuary and just twenty-one miles from London. The long lane that leads into the fictional village is where I actually walk my dog, Trevor. It's twisty and narrow and covered in places in a dense canopy of trees. Picture-perfect and relatively busy during the day but quiet and slightly scary at night, so I've often thought about casting it in a story somewhere. Preferably involving someone getting stranded and obviously in bad weather. Fortunately, Dr. Sam Able, Miss Rose Healy, an unusual emergency and a rogue blizzard close to Christmas gave me the perfect opportunity...

VIRGINIA HEATH

—

A Wedding to
Stop a Scandal

HARLEQUIN
HISTORICAL

HARLEQUIN®
HISTORICAL™

Recycling programs
for this product may
not exist in your area.

ISBN-13: 978-1-335-59588-1

A Wedding to Stop a Scandal

Harlequin Enterprises ULC
22 Adelaide St. West, 41st Floor
Toronto, Ontario M5H 4E3, Canada
www.Harlequin.com

Printed in U.S.A.

When **Virginia Heath** was a little girl, it took her ages to fall asleep, so she made up stories in her head to help pass the time while she was staring at the ceiling. As she got older, the stories became more complicated, sometimes taking weeks to get to the happy ending. Then one day, she decided to embrace the insomnia and start writing them down. Over twenty books and three Romantic Novel of the Year Award nominations later, and it still takes her forever to fall asleep.

For Judy Johnsen

Who started out as one of my readers
and is now a trusted friend.

Chapter One

November 1818

'Aunt—I really must go!' Rose shouted that up the stairs in the vain hope that it would chivvy her relative into coming down them. 'The poor coachman is freezing up on his perch thanks to all the snow!'

'One moment, dear!' Some crashing and banging came from above. 'It has to be in this last box.'

Although why her Aunt Agatha suddenly needed to send her brother and Rose's father an old book about farming was beyond her when her papa would certainly have no interest in it. Here was a progressive farmer keen to experiment with new ideas and Papa wasn't one for reading at the best of times unless it was about one of those new ideas. All it would do in their house in Suffolk was languish on a shelf there, unloved and gathering dust, just as it was here. Which, she supposed, so would she when she returned. A depressing prospect she wanted to be at peace with but wasn't.

Yet.

There was some more crashing and banging and then a whoop of triumph. 'I've found it!'

'Hallelujah,' muttered Rose under her breath as she signalled to the clearly irritated coachman that she would be with him in one minute. 'Finally.'

Not that she was particularly keen to leave Whittleston-on-the-Water either, but she had rather run out of excuses to linger longer. She had only come to stay with her aunt to escape watching her former fiancé become a parent with the woman he had jilted her for and originally only planned to stay for the summer. But then she had extended things so that she could be still here when her new friend Sophie had her baby—as well as to put off facing heading back to her own village for a bit longer. Now Sophie's little girl had not only been born, little Lillibet had been christened so she could not even use the excuse of that to dally any longer, despite wishing she could.

Aside from the inescapable fact that she was still too wounded by her former fiancé's very public betrayal to want to be confronted by him again, especially when he had left her for another woman almost a year to the day, she rather liked Whittleston-on-the-Water. Nobody pitied her here. That was likely because very few people here knew she had been jilted back in Suffolk, and those that did didn't judge her for it nor did they ever bring it up, which suited Rose just fine. She was able to function so much better in blissful denial that she had loved and lost while never being loved reciprocally in return. It was the latter that hurt the most now because she should have seen it coming sooner. Especially when it came to light that most of the village knew of her fiancé's affair long before she did. That was the undeniable downside of life in a close-knit community. Everybody knew everybody else's business and that was all well and good until it was your business that fuelled all the local gossip!

And her feckless former fiancé's betrayal had, for the longest while, been a gift to the inhabitants of her little corner of Suffolk, where little occurred and scandal was thin on the ground. Because not only had he absconded to Gretna Green at Christmas, without making any mention of it to her, he had shamelessly returned in the New Year with his new wife, who within a few more months was already so pregnant it showed. Not that the pair tried to hide it at all. Or disguise their delight at the impending birth nor hide how besotted they were with each other. In fact, to further rub salt into Rose's humiliated, gaping wound, they became the most tactile couple her village had ever seen! Always holding hands and gazing at one another with soppy, lovesick expressions on their duplicitous faces while she just had to grin and bear it until her bludgeoned heart bled and her teeth hurt!

Why on earth would any sane person be in a hurry to return to that?

But not wanting to face them again wasn't the only reason Rose would rather stay here. Nor was avoiding returning to all the brutal gossip she had been subjected to for months after her jilting. She had made some wonderful friends here too, all of whom she would miss. Sophie and Rafe, Ned and Isobel. Archie and the irrepressible Mrs Fitzherbert. She would probably miss her twice-weekly teas at that old lady's house almost as much as she would miss her aunt. Yes, Agatha Outhwaite was a judgmental, slightly pompous busybody with affectations of grandeur—but her heart was in the right place. At least as far as her family were concerned.

She was a bit of a harridan towards everyone else! But
for all her flaws, she had treated Rose as if she were her
own daughter these last six months and she owed her a
huge debt of gratitude for taking her in and giving her
a safe place to lick her wounds in private. Even if she
had sent her half mad with her constant meddling and
moaning in the process.

And then there was the enigmatic Dr Able, who she
would be sorrier to leave than perhaps was wise, given
recent events. But as birds of a feather flocked together,
she and the handsome doctor had hit it off straight away
and had, almost immediately too, formed a pact to fend
off all the rampant matchmakers who were rife here in
Whittleston. As two single people both actively avoiding any romantic attachments whatsoever, they had
spent the last six months chatting together at every
social occasion to ensure neither of them had to chat
to anyone eligible foisted upon them. She had no clue
why he was so against potentially romantic liaisons—
because they were, by tacit agreement, more convenient
friends than confidantes—but thanks to her feckless fiancé's treachery, she had sworn off men for life.

Rose's heart had mended—after a fashion and albeit
with deep and indelible scars that had left her jaded, un-
trusting and cynical—and her father and mother missed
her dreadfully. And her brother Daniel was coming
home on leave from the army at Christmas and he too
would expect to see her—so it was time to go. It was
also time to face her past, put all the hurt and all the
cruel gossip behind her and try to formulate her future.
Whittleston-on-the-Water had been a marvellous distraction when she had needed one, but it was still limbo.

A transient and convenient sanctuary rather than a permanent home. More was the pity.

'I knew I had kept it!' Her aunt appeared at the top of the stairs heaving a giant, thick volume that was bigger than the altar Bible at St Hildreth's and which must have been at least fifty years old. 'My father, God rest him, swore by this book and I dread to think how my brother has coped all this time without—' She stumbled a third of the way down the staircase.

'Let me help you, Aunt.'

As she waved her niece away she tottered momentarily, fighting for balance. Before Rose could get to her, the heavy book flew out of her aunt's hands, missing her by a whisker before her flailing relative fell forward.

Rose tried to stop her and take the bulk of the impact, but when that failed they rolled head over heels until they hit the hard hall floor together with a thud.

Pain shot up Rose's knee and she yelped.

Despite withstanding a similar impact, her aunt, however, was ominously silent.

Even as she untangled their entwined limbs and sat up to shake her the older woman was motionless. 'Aunt Agatha…?' No response. 'Are you all right?' She gently prodded her and still heard nothing.

The commotion had brought both the maid and the waiting coachman scurrying in. Unlike the young and startled maid, the coachman rushed forward to assist as Rose tried to arrange her aunt into a less awkward position on the floorboards so she could check to see if she was still breathing.

She was, thankfully, but there was a deep cut on her forehead that was oozing blood and her eyes had rolled back into her head. Enough to make the wide-eyed maid whimper in fear.

'Go and fetch the physician!' Rose barked out that order and all the panicked maid did was blink. 'Mary!' She snapped her fingers. 'Get Dr Able! Now!'

The final command galvanised the girl into action and she ran out through the door while Rose prayed that the good doctor was home. He might only live a few yards across the market square, but he was a busy man who served all the villages hereabouts.

Unsure whether attempting to move her aunt would cause more harm than good, she instead shuffled her bottom to sit closer to the older woman's head and did her best to soothe her as she stroked her hair. 'It's all right Aunt.' She sincerely hoped it was, although all the blood said different. Her aunt's usually ruddy face was ashen and slack. 'Help is on its way.'

'Urgh...' The mumbled groan simultaneously flooded Rose with relief and fear. 'Hurts...'

'Where does it hurt, Aunt?'

'Back...head...' She tried to lift her head and collapsed again. 'Dizzy.'

'Shh. Rest. The doctor will be here soon.'

Above her, the coachman held out a handkerchief, and in the absence of anything else practical to do, Rose used it to stem the flow of blood still leaking from the deep cut on her aunt's head.

'Want me to go and check on him?'

She nodded. 'Please. If he's out on his rounds take the carriage to find him. And send someone to fetch my uncle from the newspaper office.' Uncle William would want to be here. He and Aunt Agatha weren't only devoted to one another, they were all that each other had. Especially if this was serious and...

Rose swallowed past that negative and unhelpful thought, annoyed that her mind had lapsed back into cynicism rather than the practical here and now where it was most needed. 'Can you move your fingers, Aunt?' With some concerted effort, it turned out that she could. 'And your toes?' Two feet wiggled slightly, giving her some hope that her poor aunt wasn't paralysed.

'What happened?'

She did sag in relief when Dr Able rushed in, glad to be able to hand over all medical duties to the supremely competent physician who had been trained in such things. Thanks to years of being her father's right hand on the farm, Rose knew how to alleviate a horse's sprain or how to treat milk feather in a cow, but her knowledge of human anatomy and remedies left a lot to be desired.

'She fell down most of the stairs. Knocked herself out but she's conscious again now.' A pointless thing to say when her aunt was staring directly at him and the wide-eyed Archie Peel, who was clutching the physician's medical bag.

'That's a nasty cut you have on your head, Mrs Outhwaite.' He knelt beside them to examine it. 'One which I fear will need a stitch or two to close it.' He turned to his self-appointed assistant, who worshiped him like a hero. 'Prepare me a suture, Archie, and ready the iodine.'

The lord of the manor's young brother immediately complied, and did so with surprising competency. Surprising on two counts. Firstly, because despite his one and twenty years, Archie had been born with a condition which rendered him childlike for ever—a boy trapped inside a man's body—so having the ability to prepare a suture was impressive. And secondly, because the kind-hearted physician had clearly spent hours training Archie to do the task for no other reason than to make the lad feel useful whenever he decided to follow him around like he had today. Knowledge that did odd things to Rose's insides.

Satisfied that the head wound wasn't life-threatening, Dr Able moved to Aunt Agatha's torso. 'Tell me if you feel any pain.' With a competent and calm briskness that was reassuring, the doctor began to run his big hands gently down her limbs while he searched for broken bones. He flexed her arm at the left elbow first and then rotated her shoulder. That made her aunt wince. 'Do you have pain in your shoulder?'

'No.' Her aunt's voice was small, her face ashen. 'My back.'

'Let me just check your legs.'

As he examined them, Rose tried to be helpful. 'She can move her hands and feet.'

'That is a good sign.' He smiled at her and then at his patient. 'There are no signs of breakages so far, but where backs are involved its always best to err on the side of caution so I need you to lie here until I can find enough stretcher bearers to get you upstairs.' He gestured to the Archie to go and find some burly villagers who could assist. 'Miss Healy, if I could ask you to fetch a cushion or pillow while we await them?'

'Of course.' She winced herself as she stood, and of course he noticed that.

'My apologies, Miss Healy, I did not realise that you had been hurt too.' He went to stand to assist her and she waved him away.

'It's nothing. Just a sprain.' To prove it was just a sprain, she gritted her teeth and tried to ignore the pain in her knee and walk to the parlour as normally as she could. A task that became almost impossible as she carried the cushion back and caught him glaring at her.

'Go and sit before you do more damage to yourself,' he barked, pointing to the narrow settle in the hall, 'and I'll see to you once I have finished with your aunt.'

'There really is no need.'

He responded with a scowl that could curdle milk. 'If you don't mind, I shall be the judge of that on this particular occasion, Miss Healy. I am the trained medical professional after all.'

She did mind, but she decided not to argue until he had dealt with her aunt.

She minded because something about Dr Able had always unsettled her, and it wasn't just the thought of his competent hands exploring under her skirts that suddenly made her feel…all peculiar. It was because she had always considered herself excellent at reading people—her cheating former fiancé aside—and despite liking him a great deal, she couldn't quite work him out, no matter how hard she tried. Often he was affable, occasionally he was charming and worryingly disarming. Then sometimes, like now, he could be brusque and no-nonsense. He was, however, no matter which of those versions of himself he chose to be, depending on his whim during a particular day or situation, always inscrutable.

Sophie and Isobel had mentioned that was because he preferred to keep himself to himself, although neither knew quite why when she had asked. He had been married once, though, and his wife had died. Information Ned had managed to prise out of him one night after they had both partaken of one too many ales. All they knew beyond that was that he had arrived in the village three years ago after he had left the army and taken over the previous aged physician's practice when he retired. Since then, apart from all the extensive doctoring he did here, he kept his private life very private and himself politely aloof. An important, central part of this close-knit community but not quite part of it at the same time.

In other words, a complete and quite frustrating conundrum—but one she could not help liking. Or empathising with. How he had lost his wife was nobody else's business, so she did not blame him for keeping that secret—unless he had murdered her, of course, which seemed highly improbable, given both his profession and character. If he had chosen to keep that part of his life hidden it suggested he had come here to escape all those constant reminders of a love lost.

She knew from bitter experience how awful it was for an entire community to publicly witness an intensely private heartbreak. All the well-intentioned pitying looks and expressions of sympathy alongside the hurtful speculation as to the real cause of her cheating fiancé's rapid abandonment ensured you never got a chance to forget things or move past things. The constant, optimistic advice was even worse. Always unprompted and never welcomed, it only served as a constant reminder of what you had lost and wouldn't get back.

'Agatha!' Uncle William dashed in in a blind panic. 'What have you done to yourself?'

Hot on his heels came Archie, with the butcher and the baker, and all were briskly pressed into service by Dr

Able. Within moments, they were using a thick blanket as a stretcher and with the minimum of disruption to their patient's comfort, her aunt was transported up the stairs.

As Uncle William insisted on being by his wife's side, Rose could do nothing beyond wait outside their bedchamber with Archie, who had helped her limp up the stairs, then insisted on holding her hand for support, while the doctor finished his examination. He was so thorough he took over half an hour before he emerged.

'She has a minor concussion, a bruised coccyx and likely has ruptured a disc in her back. She will need constant observation until the morning for the first problem and several weeks of bedrest for the second until all the swelling has gone down, but she should make a full and complete recovery.'

'I told you not to worry,' said Archie with a devoted smile at the doctor. 'Dr Able is the best physician in the world.'

'I wouldn't go that far, Archie.' Amusement danced in the doctor's hazel eyes. 'But I will concede that I am definitely the most *able* physician in Whittleston-on-the-Water.'

'That's because you are the only physician in Whittleston-on-the-Water!' Archie laughed. then promptly stopped. 'What's a coccyx and ruptured disc, Sam?'

'I'll explain it later.' Dr Able gently pushed him away. 'In the meantime, make yourself useful and fetch Mrs Outhwaite a nice cup of tea to help calm her nerves after her nasty fall.'

'What *is* a ruptured disc?' Only once Archie was gone did Rose repeat his question.

As if he was expecting it, he explained in uncomplicated layman's terms. 'Between each vertebra in the spine is a small, disc-shaped cushion of cartilage that prevents the bones from scraping together. Sometimes, and usually as a result of an injury, one dislodges slightly so the cushion is no longer there.'

'Hence the pain, because her vertebrae are rubbing together?'

He nodded, not even slightly patronising, his whole demeanour so calm and matter-of-fact it was reassuring. 'It could just as feasibly be the bruising as it is a popped disc, of course, because she'd got an impressive one at the base of her spine already, but the treatment is still the same. Bedrest until either the disc finds its way back to whence it came or the swelling goes down. Often those two things are linked anyway, and she has full feeling in all her limbs so there is no sign the damage is permanent.'

'That is good news.' For the first time since the accident had happened, the knot in Rose's throat loosened. 'What can be done to aid her recovery?'

'In the short term, I've given her the tiniest bit of laudanum to help with the pain for now and we'll be able to increase that once she stops seeing stars. I shall give her some more if I am happy with her progress in the morning.' He smiled. 'But after that, the dosage will need to be carefully monitored as laudanum often does more harm than good in the long run and a patient can easily become addicted. I would heartily recommend that that medicine be kept under lock and key rather than be left on Mrs Outhwaite's nightstand for her to administer to herself. People in pain will do whatever it takes to stop it and laudanum is infamous for causing confusion—and for killing those who take too much.'

'I've read about that so I will ensure that it is safely stored downstairs where she cannot get at it.'

'Other than that, there really isn't much you can do apart from see to her needs, give her plenty of willow bark tea, a twice-daily cold poultice to ease the swelling and let nature takes its course.' He held out his hand and she took it without thinking, allowing him to help her up. 'Now, which of these bedchambers is yours, Miss Healy?'

'I beg your pardon?'

He slanted her a withering glance. 'I've not forgotten that you were injured too and now I need to examine you.'

'Trust me, Dr Able, it is nothing. Just a twang. A slight sprain. Nothing worth making a fuss over.'

Her uncle chose that exact moment to poke his head around the door. 'Thank you for all your help, Dr Able. And thank you especially for your supreme patience with my wife just now. Agatha has never been a particularly good patient and always thinks that she knows best.'

'That is a trait that clearly runs in the family, Mr Outhwaite, as her niece has also been injured and is trying to avoid being treated too.' He flicked her an irritated glance. 'Because clearly she knows best and that overrides all my years of medical practice.'

'Oh, for goodness' sake, Rose! Not you too!' Her uncle shook his head. 'Go with the good doctor immediately and let him do his job!'

As he disappeared back to tend to his wife, Dr Able offered Rose a smug smile. 'You heard what your uncle said, and if that isn't encouragement enough to do the right thing, know that I am not leaving your side until I am satisfied that it *is* just a sprain. Know, too, that you are not the most stubborn person currently standing on this landing, Miss Healy.' He gestured with his medical bag. 'So which one of these rooms is yours?'

Chapter Two

Sam regretted his insistence on examining Miss Healy
in her bedchamber the second he escorted her into it.
At the time it had seemed like the most sensible option, because she had been visibly limping while trying
to pretend not to be in any pain and he didn't want to
cause her more pain by dragging her back downstairs.
He had tried not to give passing thought to the fact that
his patient was Miss Healy.

Miss *Rose* Healy, with the beguiling green eyes and
mischievous conversation. The woman who had, for
some inexplicable reason, become his regular partner
during the weekly post-church whist tournament up at
Hockley Hall. The woman he cheerfully spent hours
conversing with at the monthly assemblies while they
both avoided having to have dancing partners thrust
upon them by all the local matchmakers. The Miss Rose
Healy he might have had three or four very errant, very
vivid and highly improper dreams about in the last few
months. Dreams that he had rolled his eyes at and put
down to the annoying remnants of his manly urges,
which had refused to die when the love of his life had,

and then hastily dismissed because he had no place in his life for such dangerous attachments any more.

Not one of those things had rung glaring alarm bells when she had needed medical attention because why would they? He was not only a physician to his core but healing his patients here in the environs around Whittleston was his only reason for being nowadays. Besides, it wasn't as though he didn't examine women all the time in their bedchambers and was always proudly professional and dispassionate while he did so, so he had no reason to expect examining her to be any different.

Except now that they were all alone in her bedchamber and she was lying atop the mattress, blinking up at him as warily as he suspected he was blinking down at her, it did not feel quite as dispassionate as it should have. It felt…awkward…and oddly intimate in both a physical and cerebral sense. Which was terrifying when intimacy in all its forms was something he actively avoided nowadays. You couldn't keep a person at arm's length if they were in your head!

Why the hell was she suddenly in his when he hadn't thought of any woman like that in years?

Not since the love of his life had died in his arms and he had as good as ceased living himself.

As the walls of the tiny room contracted, cocooning them in loaded discomfort, he tried to focus on her as his patient and not as the only woman who had piqued his masculine interest in four comfortably numb years. 'Where does it hurt?'

'Just my knee.' Her smile was apologetic. 'I am sure it is nothing.'

'Do you mind if I…?'

Oh, good grief, he was going to have to feel her leg!

Lift up her skirts, peel off her stocking and touch actual skin! Soft, sensual, feminine skin!

'Not at all.'

Rather than groan aloud at the prospect, he faked an unbothered brusqueness he did not feel as he balanced his backside on the mattress beside her. He took half a second to give himself a stern talking-to, reminded himself that he was dead inside, then grasped the hem of her very fetching green dress. He slid it upward, almost groaning aloud again because, of course, she had a splendid pair of legs, being taller than the average woman. They were long and as shapely as her fine pert and feminine figure. To torture him further, her ivory stockings were made of the finest gauge of wool imaginable. Slightly thicker than silk but only by a whisker. The garters, however, were silk, and the couple of inches of creamy skin above them was divine.

Heaven help him.

'If you could just…um…undo those and expose your knee?' Sam used the urgent need to rummage in his medical bag as an excuse not to undress her. Then panicked when he realised there really wasn't a damn thing in his bag which was necessary for a physical examination. In desperation, he grabbed a bandage and some iodine while he prayed her injury was indeed a sprain so he could use the liquid on the bruises before binding them.

He turned and almost choked on his own tongue as he caught the erotic sight of her rolling the stocking down and entirely exposing the whole of her left leg to his gaze. The flesh on her calf was smooth alabaster, married by just one freckle the size of a ladybird which sat like an old-fashioned beauty spot above her ankle. He wrenched his suddenly hungry gaze from it to stare at her knee and only then, as he forcibly pushed the un-welcome and wholly unexpected surge of lust from his mind, did he remember that he was a doctor.

'It's very swollen.'

Willing his mind to focus on his job, he sucked in a calming breath and probed the area with his finger-tips. Except his fingertips refused to react in the way a dispassionate doctor's should and heated as they ex-amined, and while they categorically did not touch her inappropriately, they flatly refused not to want to. That was a new and worrying development after so many years of blissfully feeling nothing.

'Unfortunately, that knee bore the brunt of my fall.'

Her eyes focussed on the wall rather him and that suited Sam just fine. The last thing he needed was to accidentally show how off-kilter he was by his body's sudden reawakening. It was bad enough watching her chew her bottom lip, drawing the plump flesh through her teeth as he tried and failed to focus on her injury.

'But I can still move it, so it is probably something muscular rather than any actual damage to the joint.'

'Remind me again where it was that you did your medical training?' He wasn't entirely sure why his sar-casm came out sounding a tad too flirtatious for his lik-ing. Or why he was smiling, but it made her giggle and that went some way towards breaking the ice.

'I've dealt with many a horse's sprained muscles on my father's farm and we Healys have famously strong bones. I cannot think of a single family member who has ever broken one so… I am presuming, Dr Able.'

'A decent physician works on facts and not presump-tions, so if you don't mind…'

'Pray continue, Doctor.' She laughed again. 'And I shall try not to be presumptuous.'

Every nerve-ending seemed to fizz with unprofessional awareness as he touched her again, his fingers fumbling during the brisk and supremely self-conscious examination while she tortured him by chewing her bottom lip some more. Before he groaned aloud, he sat back and huffed as he reached for the iodine.

'Much to my chagrin, it appears that you are right and it is just a sprain.'

He dabbed the chemical on the bruise, then managed to wrap the bandage around her knee in record time. A small miracle when something about her leg in his hands made his heart race.

'I prescribe plenty of ice, tea and a couple of days of sitting in a chair with your foot elevated and you'll be back to avoiding waltzing with all the undesirables in time for the next dreary Whittleston assembly.'

He shot her a grin, glad that that was safer and more familiar ground for them both, because avoiding well-intentioned but ill-considered matchmaking was what they usually did together. However, Sam also experienced a simultaneous flash of regret alongside the relief as he returned her skirts to an appropriately modest level. When a part of him, the part that was supposed to be dead and buried and devoid of all human emotions, wanted to lift them higher.

'I am afraid you are going to have to find another conspirator to help you to evade all the matchmaking in future as I shan't be there, Dr Able.' When he frowned, baffled, she chuckled. 'Clearly you have forgotten that I am finally returning to my home in Suffolk?' She gestured to her attire. 'Hence the travelling dress and the waiting coachman.'

'You are leaving *today*?'

That news really unsettled him although he couldn't put his finger on why. Obviously, he had noticed the travelling dress. The green wool caressed her enticing curves like a lover, and he might well be dead inside, but he wasn't blind! He had also known she was going at some point. It was one of the main reasons why he had lowered some of his guard and allowed himself to enjoy her company at all the social events the local physician was obligated to attend. He preferred transience to permanence. Transience required little emotional investment and a very little was all he was prepared to risk nowadays. Losing everyone who mattered to you did that to a person.

'That came around fast.'

He had been so blasted busy of late he had clearly missed that her departure was more imminent than he realised. Or he had realised but had avoided thinking about it because he had been making a concerted effort this last month not to think of her at all, thanks to all the erotic dreams she had featured in of late. He probably should be glad she was going—especially now that his errant eyes, as well as his nocturnal thoughts, regarded her as an attractive woman rather than a patient—but he wasn't.

And that was beyond worrying!

'Actually, it came around much slower than originally planned.' She rolled her eyes at his continued bafflement. 'I know that you're a busy man, Dr Able, but surely even you noticed that I was meant to leave at the end of August and in two weeks it will be December?'

He shrugged, sheepish. 'I truly *am* a busy man.'
Which he was, by design. His work was his everything
now that his everything was gone.

It was the only reason he got out of bed each morning. He made sure to fill every waking hour with medical purpose, because if he didn't misery swamped him
and he was nought but an embittered and broken husk
again, in constant pain. With genuine purpose he was
able to lock all the heartbreak and hopelessness in a
box in his mind which he rarely reopened as that was
safest. That was why he never turned down a patient.
The more he had, the merrier he was. And by merrier,
he actually meant sane. Functioning.

However, he had also developed a habit of pushing
certain other, uncomfortable things to the back of his
mind too, rather than think about them, and Miss Healy
was one of those things. Had he purposely avoided
thinking about her because she called to him? Not on
a heart and soul level—he did not have it in him to do
that again, nor any heart left to do it with—but he liked
her. And liking a woman in *that way* was a danger to his
hard-won equilibrium that he wasn't prepared to risk.

As if she read his mind, she huffed. 'I would say try
not to miss me, but I can see that you won't.'

She nudged him playfully and, still not quite over
the visceral impact of her shapely leg, his stupid body
felt it everywhere.

'Some friend you have turned out to be!'

In an equally teasing tone, he parried, despite the
strange panic going on internally, 'I've always thought
of us as more acquaintances than friends.'

Which was also true. Acquaintances were safe, because they could be kept at arm's length and friends

couldn't. He avoided the emotional attachment of friends too nowadays as it was simpler.

He'd had plenty back in his early army days, before he'd watched too many of them die to feel any incentive to replace them. Witnessing death was an integral part of a doctor's life and he had felt too many too keenly— and one in particular—not to be conscious of the enormous toll it took on you.

Now he supposed he had a few trusted acquaintances who did not try to get too close. They were people he respected and could count on in crisis but who knew how to mind their own business and give him his space. People like the gruff local farmer Ned Parker, who Sam was more than happy to drink a pint of ale alongside at the pub, or Rafe, the new lord of the manor here in Whittleston, who had fought Napoleon too and really didn't want to talk about it either. Or even Archie, Rafe's younger brother, who was a man trapped in a child's body, who followed him around asking constant questions and didn't mind being put to work if the need arose. Those were his almost friends now— almost but not.

'Acquaintances!' She pushed him from her mattress in faux disgust. 'I take back what I just said about you needing to find a new conspirator to help you fend off all the husband-hunters as you clearly do not need my help to get rid of them. All you need to do is use that unique charm you just used so effectively on me, and they'll all avoid you like the plague.'

She went to stand and he gently pushed her back.

'Might I remind you, madam, that you need to keep your weight off your knee and your foot elevated?'

'Which I shall do for the entire, arduous six-and-a-half-hour carriage ride back to my father's house in Suffolk. But before I do, I need to check on my Aunt and then say my goodbyes to her.' She stood again and sailed past him like a limping but regal duchess. 'Goodbye to you too, Dr Able. I would like to say that it has been a pleasure being your acquaintance…' she shot him a saucy smile that was as devastating to his equilibrium as her damn legs were '…but I'd be lying as I daresay I'll fail to remember you five miles down the road. Such is my lack of interest in you.'

Chapter Three

'I couldn't, in all good conscience, leave her dependent on the servants for the next few weeks. Not after everything that she has done for me.'

Like all news in a small English village, gossip of her aunt's accident yesterday had spread like wildfire around Whittleston. That was why it was barely nine in the morning and Mrs Fitzherbert, Sophie and Isobel were all currently sipping tea with Rose in Aunt Agatha's much too ostentatious parlour.

'Besides it is only for a few more weeks, so it is hardly a hardship as I will still be back in Suffolk for Christmas.'

'Of course you had to stay,' said Sophie, in complete sympathy for that partial truth. 'There is nothing worse than being tended to by anyone other than your nearest and dearest when you are at your most vulnerable. It was very decent of you to put off your trip to nurse her.'

'Never mind that Agatha's clumsiness gave you the perfect excuse not to leave, young lady.' Never one to mince her words, Mrs Fitzherbert eyed Rose dubiously over the rim of her teacup. 'You've been looking for a good enough reason to avoid that scoundrel in Suffolk for weeks.'

She was about to argue when the old lady's cane came down on the floor with a thud.

'Or are you going to barefaced lie to us all—your three closest and most loyal confidantes here? Claim that you are perfectly at ease returning to a village where your former fiancée is raising a family with the woman he impregnated and then left you for? Because I do not believe for one second that you could be at ease with it. I certainly wouldn't be and I have thrice the bravado of all of you combined.'

'If my poor aunt hadn't fallen down the stairs, I would be in Suffolk now! My trunks were loaded and my gloves were on!'

'I did not say that you weren't intending to go, Rose.' Mrs Fitzherbert sniffed. 'Only that you were relieved by the reprieve—because we both know that it was a reprieve, young lady. One that I should imagine felt like a king's pardon as soon as you realised Agatha was conveniently invalided enough to require your help.'

'It would be uncharitable to find any joy in my poor aunt's recent misfortune and I resent the implication.'

She tried to summon all her bravado to maintain some pious indignation at that accusation as, to her great shame, she had quickly not only seen the benefits that came from her poor aunt's injury, she had seized them with both hands. No sooner had her uncle declared that he would close his newspaper for the duration of Aunt Agatha's convalescence so he could nurse her through it himself Rose was reminding him of his civic duty to ensure the *South Essex Gazette* continued to be the twice-weekly honest beacon of news all its legions of readers deserved. When the truth was they could just as easily read the daily copies of *The London Times* which arrived only a day late on the mail coach.

But no! Just as Mrs Fitzherbert had accused, she had finally found an excuse to stay for at least another month. She'd immediately had her baggage unloaded and the coachman despatched back to Suffolk with a hastily written letter to her parents. A letter that, to her further shame, over-embellished the extent of her aunt's incapacity. She had promised that she would be home in Suffolk for Christmas come hell or high water, though, to appease her parents, so it was still more of a reprieve than a pardon.

'Besides, I am not entirely sure how effective you will be as a nurse,' continued Mrs Fitzherbert, unrepentant, 'when you are injured too.' She used her cane to prod Rose's raised foot.

'My injury will be healed in mere days—hers will take weeks.'

Was it wrong to pray for months to avoid having to face all her scandal and her treacherous fiancé in Suffolk just a little bit longer? Of course it was. She was a dreadful niece. A dreadful person *and* a coward.

'My uncle has stepped into the breach for the first few days but he cannot do so indefinitely when he still has a business to run. Who better to relieve him of one of those tasks than me?'

'If you say so.' That came from the highly amused Isobel, who had so far remained quiet but who was also as blatantly unconvinced as Mrs Fitzherbert. 'Let's dress your latest avoidance up as benevolence.'

'It is benevolent,' said Sophie coming to her defence, 'and staying to look after Mrs Outhwaite an admirable thing to do. That it also saves poor Rose the awfulness of facing the wretch who broke her heart for a little longer is simply a bonus. As is the fact that we all get to enjoy the company of our friend for a little while longer, so you can both stop trying to rile her when not three days ago you were both plotting to find an excuse to keep her here longer.' She glared at Mrs Fitzherbert.

Mrs Fitzherbert went to argue, but instead pressed her lips together because they suddenly, and much too stealthily, had a visitor.

One who had lifted Rose's skirts and touched her naked legs without stockings! And one who had given her body all manner of improper yearnings as a result!

Oh, good heavens above, she wasn't anywhere near ready to face him yet!

Not when he must have heard her sharp intake of breath when he had first touched her! And perhaps even felt her pulse quicken beneath his much too talented and intoxicating fingertips.

'I thought you had left for Suffolk?'

Rose's cheeks began to heat. Partly because she didn't want to be challenged again by Mrs Fitzherbert in front of someone who knew nothing about her unfortunate jilting but more because her flesh tingled from the memory of his unsettling caresses.

'I had a last-minute change of plan.'

'She's staying to take care of her aunt,' said Sophie loyally, with a veiled warning towards Whittleston's most incorrigible and only nonagenarian in case she threw any doubt on that. 'Once she is back on her own feet, of course.'

'I'm glad to see that you are actually following doctor's orders, Miss Healy, because when I left you yesterday there was a little too much rebellion against them for my liking.'

And just like that Dr Able was coming towards her smiling.

'How is the knee this morning?'

'Much better.' It was actually worse now that the swelling had taken hold, but she wasn't going to admit that in case he insisted on investigating. 'It's clearly the mildest of sprains. Milder than mildest in fact.'

Please don't say I'll be the judge of that!

'I'll be the judge of that.'

Fiddlesticks!

'And I might as well take a look at it now before I see your aunt.'

Double fiddlesticks!

To her horror, he gently lifted her foot from the footrest so that he could perch on it, then rested her foot in his lap.

'How is your aunt this morning?'

Rather than hoist up her skirts while in polite company, his hands delved under them to feel the injury above her stockings and that was somehow worse. It seemed clandestine. Felt naughty.

Naughty but, to her body and to her utter mortification, oh, so nice.

The sublime warmth of his hands burned through her thin stockings and awakened the tender flesh beneath again. Instantly her pulse ratcheted and for a moment emptied her mind of everything else—including his question. It was only when his fingers paused that she remembered he had asked it and that it still hung in the ether.

'She had a fractious night.'

Because Rose had never been one of those women who blushed prettily, she willed the ugly blotches from blooming on her face but they refused to listen. Heat suffused her neck as the dratted things multiplied.

'And struggled to get comfortable.'

Which was the politest way she could think of of saying that her Aunt Agatha had run her poor husband and the maid ragged with her constant demands.

'The first night is always the worst.'

Dr Able's hands made one devastating final sweep over her leg that left her breathless before he withdrew them.

'Just as the first day after a sprain is always the worst.'

Thankfully, he took her shoeless foot from his lap and removed himself from her footstool so that she could breathe again.

'Your knee is very swollen today. Try to wrap it in a cold compress every couple of hours until it subsides.'

'I will, Doctor.'

'Splendid. Then I shall leave you to your tea, ladies, and attend to Mrs Outhwaite.' He grabbed his bag and inclined his head.

He had barely climbed half the staircase when Isobel's teacup clattered into her saucer and she grinned. 'Well, if that wasn't conclusive proof, I do not know what is!'

As both the smugly smiling Sophie and Mrs Fitzherbert were also clearly convinced of something too, Rose felt left out. 'Conclusive proof of what?'

'The palpable attraction you have for Whittleston's inscrutable local physician is deliciously mutual.'

'I'm sorry?' Rose blinked while her entire face exploded in a blush so ferocious it scorched her ears.

'Didn't I tell you that she had a *tendre* for him?'

Ignoring Rose's outrage completely, Isobel leaned closer to the others and they all began to discuss her as if she wasn't there.

'They always find a way to have a private little moment at every social event, and they both have that same look in their eyes whenever they look at one another.' Her friend smouldered at Mrs Fitzherbert to illustrate, and the old woman smouldered back. 'We all might have been invisible just now as Dr Able only had eyes for Rose too.'

'That frisson between them was indeed *palpable*. Especially when his hands disappeared beneath her petticoats.' Sophie fanned herself with her hand. 'For a moment I didn't quite know where to look.'

'I know.' Isobel again. 'I felt like a voyeur, watching them.'

'Well, I didn't,' said Mrs Fitzherbert. 'At my age, I have to live vicariously through you young girls and that display really was everything a good bit of unfulfilled lust and longing should be. I thought Rose, especially, did an outrageously poor job of disguising her desires.'

'I have no desires for Dr Able!'

'You went as red as beetroot when he examined you.'

'That, Isobel, is because I am not accustomed to allowing a man to touch my legs!'

'You also bit your lip as he touched them,' added Sophie, drawing her own lips seductively through her teeth in a manner that, if Rose had been guilty of it, basically would have made her a shameless wanton. 'And your bosoms heaved as you breathed.'

'They did not!'

'There was some definite heaving.' Isobel stared at

her chest pointedly. 'I would also be prepared to wager that there was some fizzing and tingling going on beneath your ribs too, because your voice came out all breathy and strained when you finally managed to answer to him.' Then, to rub salt into the wound, she mimicked and exaggerated Rose's strangulated sentence. '"My aunt h-had a f-f-fractious night, Doctor…and so did I. I couldn't stop thinking about your manly hands exploring my needy flesh."'

While Mrs Fitzherbert threw her head back and laughed, Sophie fanned herself again and that was the final straw.

'Have you all gone mad?' Rose's face was on fire. Her heart was hammering and yet she knew she had to nip this much-to-close-to-the-bone teasing in the bud now or her three incorrigible friends would never stop. 'Do you all seriously think that a woman who has only just had her heart publicly broken would seriously be on the market for another man?'

'We aren't suggesting that you want to marry him, Rose,' said Isobel with a suggestive wiggle of her eyebrows, 'more that you wouldn't mind having your wicked way with him.'

'I would if I were you.' Mrs Fitzherbert's brows also began to wiggle. 'Nothing makes you forget a disappointing man faster than one who doesn't disappoint in the slightest, and what better way to regain your shattered confidence with the opposite sex than a passionate affair with a handsome gentleman like him? Who is a doctor, to boot, so one would hope he has an extensive and thorough knowledge of a woman's *particular* anatomy and an innate eagerness to want to make it *feel better.*'

Rose's jaw gaped in shock and remained hanging for several seconds until she regained control of it to hiss her outrage. 'That is even worse!' If her dratted knee had been up to it, now would have been the precise time that she'd have stormed out. 'As if I would ever behave so…so…scandalously.'

'It would only be a scandal if it were public, and I can attest that even here in Whittleston it is possible to take a discreet lover without causing any gossip. None of us would tell anyone outside of this room.'

That came from Sophie. Sophie—who was supposed to be the most rational and sensible of her three friends. Not to mention, as the new lady of the manor, supposedly the most respectable!

'Indeed it is! I've enjoyed many over the years and at least half have been a complete secret.' Miss Fitzherbert sighed at the memories. 'There is something quite invigorating about a covert liaison. I highly recommend it, Rose. It is exactly what you need right now to raise your spirits. Then you can leave here feeling like a beautiful temptress and not one idiot's leavings.'

'But you had been widowed! Such behaviour is politely ignored if one is a widow!' Rose couldn't believe what she was hearing. 'And I haven't yet been married!' As that irrefutable logic did not seem to permeate their thick skulls she added to it. In panic. 'I am all done with men and still not over being jilted—but if I did change my mind in the future, how would I explain my lack of chasteness to my husband on our wedding night if I did take the doctor as a secret lover?' Even as she said it, she knew it was the wrong thing to say as all three faces lit up. 'Not that I will ever want Dr Able as my lover! You are all wrong on that score. So wrong I cannot even begin to tell you.' She attempted a laugh which she feared only dug a deeper hole for herself.

'I blamed all the horse riding I did in my youth for the lack of my maidenhead.' Mrs Fitzherbert cackled with delight at that admission. 'Only on my first wedding night, of course. It was rather a moot point for all the others. Although, to be fair to all three of my husbands, I don't think they cared overmuch about who I had been with before them—they were more interested in me *being with them* in the moment! I've always been very adventurous in the bedchamber.'

'You could do worse than have a fling with our intriguing local physician, Rose.'

Isobel was like a dog with a bone. They all were. And she was a sitting target thanks to her knee.

'You never know, what starts as a fling could well become more. Isn't that right, Sophie?'

'It is indeed. Rafe started out as just a fling and look at us now.' She wiggled her wedding ring finger. 'From little acorns…'

'You see…' Isobel ignored her horrified expression to continue. 'Something wonderful might come of it and, for what it is worth, I think you and he would make a *wonderful* couple. The attraction is already there…'

'Oh, for pity's sake!' Rose surged to her feet, swallowing the pain. Bad knee or no bad knee, she wasn't going to entertain this a second longer. 'I wish I had returned to Suffolk yesterday as I think I would much prefer having to face him than listen to your nonsense!' She limped to the door, but before she stormed through it she turned to wag a warning finger at all of them.

'Kindly get it into your meddling heads that I do not currently need a lover to raise my spirits!'

She spun and marched straight into a warm and solid wall.

She scrunched her eyes closed rather than look up. The unwelcome fizzing and tingling beneath her ribs confirmed it was the doctor before he spoke.

'You do, however, need to raise your foot to keep your weight off that knee, Miss Healy, so kindly sit back down.'

Chapter Four

Sam had avoided visiting Mrs Outhwaite for a few days. He had blamed medical business, which was easy to do when he was the only physician in a five-mile radius and everyone seemed to be suffering from the same persistent winter cough that was doing the rounds. But it wasn't only business that had made him reluctant to darken the Outhwaites' door—it was Miss Healy.

For reasons best known to his usually level and dispassionate head, she had laid siege on it and given it all manner of inappropriate ideas that a doctor really shouldn't have for one of his patients. Especially a doctor who was dead inside and no longer had the inclination or the capacity for that sort of yearning.

He wanted to blame her legs, because they were a particularly striking pair, but it wasn't just those that had haunted his dreams these past three nights, it was apparently all of her. Her eyes. Her skin. Her voice. Her effervescent and mischievous character. Her humour. All those things suddenly called to him on a visceral and worrying level and he couldn't silence that call no matter how much he tried.

And he had tried!

Tried everything from keeping himself extra busy to a chilly sluicing at the pump before bed and none of them made a blind bit of difference. Something unwelcome within had risen from the dead and it was unsettling beyond measure.

Of course, it did not help that he was convinced he had inadvertently walked in on her friends trying to matchmake the pair of them, any more than it helped that Miss Healy clearly hadn't been impressed by the prospect.

When Isobel and Mrs Fitzherbert got their teeth into a notion, nothing short of a miracle was going to stop it. Isobel had certainly cornered him when he had made the grave mistake of going into her shop to buy some boot polish yesterday, and then found himself stuck in a never-ending circular conversation about how marvellous it was that Rose was staying longer, albeit under the most unfortunate of circumstances and wasn't she looking lovely lately.

Thankfully, he hadn't seen Mrs Fitzherbert since, but was dreading the collision as she was unlikely to be as subtle as Isobel and, knowing her, had likely already opened a book on them. Because here in Whittleston-on-the-Water, wagering on gossip was almost as rife as the gossip itself. He had certainly put a few shillings on Rafe and Sophie getting together when that book had opened, and he had almost won the pot on Ned and Isobel.

Almost.

Until Mrs Fitzherbert had practically cheated to get the pair married at record speed. He had no desire, however, to give the gossips any fodder concerning him or to encourage the interminable meddling which went hand in hand with all the speculation. By its very nature, speculation involved prying and prying involved inter-action, and he preferred to keep an impersonal distance between himself and other people nowadays. It might be a lonely way to live, and frankly he likely deserved no less after he had failed his wife so catastrophically, but it was less messy. Less complicated. Now that he had been hollowed out by grief and rendered a blissfully empty emotional shell, he didn't have the care about anyone beyond the superficial or the professional—and vice versa. That way, when they eventually succumbed to whatever malaise destiny inevitably chose for them, he wouldn't have to feel it. At least in any way more than any physician should feel the inevitable demise of a pa-tient he couldn't save.

He could like them before that happened, of course, just not too much. Enjoy a little of their company, but not too much in case he formed an attachment. And he certainly did not want the added complication of at-traction in that mix. Yet he was undeniably attracted to her, enjoyed her company immensely and liked her more than he had allowed himself to like anyone since his wife. Therefore, avoiding Miss Healy was not only prudent in his current unsettled state, it was necessary. At least until his emotions settled and he was back to being fully dead inside, as he preferred.

But there was no avoiding her now. Mr Outhwaite's urgent note this morning about his wife's continued pain and the need to increase her laudanum meant he had no option but to make the call he had been putting off.

He brushed the snow from his shoulders before he steeled them and knocked the door.

The maid answered and immediately showed him

upstairs to her mistress's bedchamber. Mr Outhwaite, who had summoned him, was nowhere to be seen.

'Thank you for coming, Doctor.' Miss Healy rose, all smiles until Mrs Outhwaite started to speak.

'It's about time too, as I could have died in the time it has taken you to return!'

Sam dealt with that politely, too used to Mrs Outhwaite's acid tongue and theatrical tendencies to take any issue with her pithy tone. 'My apologies, but I have many sick people under my care, most much sicker than you, and I must prioritise them according to need. Especially in November, when the deadliest chills and influenza are rife. Little Ramstead has been hit particularly hard and at least half of that village is presently unwell.'

An answer his grouchy patient did not like. 'Why are you wasting your time in Little Ramstead when your practice is here? It is not good enough, Dr Able!'

'Now, Aunt,' said Miss Healy, shooting him a pointed but exasperated look, 'that is unfair...'

'Of course it is fair! Little Ramstead should employ their own doctor rather than stealing ours, and priority should be given to the patients who live closest!'

'It is the pain talking.' Miss Healy was clearly mortified by her crochety relative's outburst. 'My aunt does not mean to offend you.'

He waved that away with a wry smile at his patient, who was propped up in bed rather than lying flat as instructed. 'She does mean to offend me, and yet she still hasn't.' He reached for Mrs Outhwaite's wrist to take her pulse. 'That is because I am very aware that your aunt's bark is worse than her bite and that she has always been a foul-tempered and ungracious patient who would try the patience of a saint.' The older woman went to argue, but he cut her off. 'Anger is not good for healing, Mrs Outhwaite, and you know better than to try to browbeat me into submission. Have you been taking your medicines?' Sam stared blandly at the cold cup of willow bark tea on the nightstand. 'Or are you doing your usual and refusing like a petulant child because they don't taste nice?'

'Well… I…er…'

'I shall take that as a no.' He shook his head. 'I don't suppose you have even bothered with the poultice.'

'It's cold and slimy and smells—'

Sam sighed. 'In summation, you haven't taken any of the medications, you refuse to do anything that might lessen the swelling and insist on sitting upright on an unsupportive mattress rather than a chair, when you know full well that that puts undue pressure on the injured disc because I explained that to you.'

That was met with pursed lips and folded arms. 'I am bored stiff lying flat, have no time for your quack cures, and I *do* take my laudanum as that is the only thing that works on the pain and allows me any sleep!'

'She wants more of it, Doctor,' said Miss Healy wringing her hands, 'and refuses to heed all your warnings about its prolonged use. In fact…' She gave her aunt a chiding look. 'She has browbeaten my uncle into going to the apothecary to fetch more—which is why I insisted that he also summon you. In view of your dire warnings, I didn't want my aunt taking more without your approval if it will harm her, and already I think that she has been taking too much.'

So it had been Miss Healy who had sent for him?

Good for her! Mr Outhwaite had never been able to stand up to his wife.

'Thank goodness someone in this family has some common sense as you are quite right, Miss Healy. Laudanum is dangerous. It is highly addictive and turns the brains of addicts to mush. To be honest, if I had any sway over the government, I would ban its sale in apothecaries tomorrow and make it a medicine that could only be administered under the strict supervision of a physician. However, seeing as Mrs Outhwaite's flatly refuses to heed any of my advice, if she has decreed that only laudanum will aid her recovery then I suggest we both leave her to it.'

'What?' exclaimed both women in unison.

'Indeed. Let us wash our hands of her. You can head back to Suffolk safe in the knowledge that you tried your best, and I have too many patients on my books as it is. Mrs Outhwaite has always been one of my most troublesome, so I'll be glad to be shot of her. I am also certain the village will enjoy gossiping about her rapid decline into a drooling, incoherent, opium-fuelled stupor. They do so love a scandal here in Whittleston. Especially when I inform them that she brought it all on herself because she knew best. There is nothing like hubris to turn an upstanding member of the community into a pitiable laughing stock.'

He couldn't resist tapping his chin, as if pondering her decline, to rile his current most ornery patient.

'I can only imagine how vicious all the gossip will get then as, in my experience, people have little sympathy for opium eaters.' Sam reached for his bag, snapped it closed, then stood. 'However, kindly take note that when the hallucinations render her nonsensical, incontinence sets in and her poor, nagged husband begs me to do something to save her from a slow, painful and drooling death, I won't. There will be nothing I *could* do for her by that point.' He shrugged, enjoying himself. 'Except put her out of her misery by smothering her with a pillow, and I'm afraid the Hippocratic Oath prevents me from doing that.'

As Mrs Outhwaite stared, open-mouthed, her mischievous niece stifled a smile and decided to play along. 'Will it really turn her brain to mush, Doctor?'

'I am afraid it will. Rapidly and irretrievably so. Brains do not heal like a cut or a graze. When a part of it is damaged, it dies. Withers like a grape on the vine. Of course, the decline usually begins with impaired reasoning and erratic behaviour. I've known patients dance naked in public after increasing their dose.'

Mrs Outhwaite's face blanched.

'There was one poor chap in the army who not only stripped himself naked, he became convinced he was a chicken and wandered around the camp flapping his imaginary wings and pecking in the dirt looking for corn. We had to lock him up for his own safety, but even after we gradually weaned him from the drug he still pecked at his food and tried to lay eggs.'

Maybe he was over-egging things now, but his lie was making Miss Healy's fine brown eyes twinkle with amusement, so he didn't care.

'The poor man. What became of him?'

'There are only so many times you can fail to lay an egg, Miss Healy, before the spirit shatters for good.' How he said that with a straight face he had no clue, but it seemed to be doing the trick because Mrs Outhwaite was scared. Scared enough to grab his arm.

'But if a patient has only taken one or two doses more of it than was prescribed, surely that isn't catastrophic?'

'In the short term, no. But prolonged use at such high levels over more than three days or four days…' he pretended to pluck that number from his extensive medical knowledge rather than his imagination '…and the rot sets in. That's when the laudanum starts to control the taker, so I would always advise alternative treatments in the long term that are equally as effective but nowhere near as dangerous…' He allowed his voice to tail off as heard Mr Outhwaite's arrival in the hall below, doubtless with enough blasted laudanum to knock out a horse. 'But obviously you do not have to listen to my advice now that you are no longer my patient.'

'But of course I am still your patient!' Outrage mixed with the fear. 'At least as far as I am concerned. You are the one who made idle threats, Dr Able. And to a defenceless sick woman too.'

That last bit was said for her husband's benefit as he had just climbed the stairs—clutching a much too large bottle of the drug.

'Oh, they weren't idle, madam. If you continue refuse to follow my precise instructions, persist in your stubborn insistence that only laudanum will work and try to bully your husband or your niece into giving you more of the stuff, I *will* wash my hands of you.'

That brought her up short and she bristled. 'Physicians are supposed to have a kind and sympathetic bedside manner and you, Dr Able, are nothing but mean.'

'My job is to heal the sick, Mrs Outhwaite, not pander to them.' He took the offending bottle from Mr Outhwaite's hand. 'Now, if you will excuse me, I have some very sick people to attend to in Little Ramstead. I shall return to check on your progress in a few days, when I shall expect to see that you have followed my treatment plan to the letter. This is no longer on it.' He pocketed the bottle. 'Henceforth, it is willow bark only for the pain, and I will send over a sleeping draught to help with your insomnia. And if you must sit, then do so sparingly in a proper chair for no more than a half an hour at a time. Do I make myself clear?'

'Crystal, Doctor.' It was Miss Healy who answered. 'I shall show you out.' As soon as they were alone, she grinned. 'Thank you for that. My uncle struggles to say no to her and she needed...'

'A swift kick up the backside?' Sam smiled back before he could stop it. 'You were right to send for me, but I fear it will not be the only intervention you will need to make to get her to see reason. Your aunt truly is one of the most infuriating patients I have ever come across. When she broke her wrist two summers ago, she was so outrageously demanding I honestly came close to telling Hippocrates and the Royal College of Physicians that they could go to hell and smothering her with a pillow to put myself out of *my* misery.'

She laughed as she started down the stairs and instantly he felt taller and lighter. Which was another worry when he was content to remain dead inside.

'Aunt Agatha can be a difficult character, to be sure, but her heart is mostly in the right place.'

'She needs standing up to.'

'I can do that. Perhaps not quite as assertively or as entertainingly as you just did, but I have my own methods. Getting rid of Uncle William will help, and I fully intend to march him back to his newspaper tomorrow as he is honestly more hindrance than any use in the sickroom. He will do whatever it takes to have a quiet life, whereas I am not so easily—'

'Trampled over by Mrs Outhwaite's iron will?'

'I was going to say rankled, but I suppose your version is more apt. I suspect the next few weeks are going to be much harder work than I anticipated.'

With perfect timing, Mrs Outhwaite began to wail from above in exaggerated agony as her henpecked husband tried to assist her.

'No good deed goes unpunished, Miss Healy, and your first mistake was not getting on that carriage bound for Suffolk once you learned her wounds weren't fatal.'

'In my defence, she has allowed me to hide here these past six months so it felt like the right thing to do.'

'Hide?' Ned had mentioned to him a while back that she had had her heart broken, but Sam did not know the details. Nor had he wanted to, because probing too deep into a person's private life wasn't the most prudent way to keep them at arm's length. Yet all of a sudden he wanted to know all about her. 'From what?'

She pulled a face, clearly regretting her choice of words, then shrugged. 'If you think the gossip and meddling here in Whittleston is vicious, it is double that in my village. Much like your chicken man, there are only so many times a woman can be pitied for remaining unmarried before it shatters the spirit.' She lingered on the bottom step, her chin defiant and proud. 'And in case you are now terrified that that was an unsubtle hint that I am in the market for a husband, Dr Able, as I am sure that you must be after you overheard my friends' unsubtle attempts to matchmake the other day, please don't be. Without going into unseemly details, I have recently had quite enough of men to last a lifetime, and irrespective of how convinced my friends are of our suitability, I am quite content to remain without the disappointment of one for the foreseeable future.' She shot him a wry grin filled with sarcasm as she marched to the door. 'Try not to be offended by that bitter blow.'

He was, oddly, but didn't want to analyse why because he knew he wouldn't like the answer. Instead, he decided to focus on the fact that he respected her for tackling the great unsaid head-on when the easiest thing would have been to leave it hanging. Yet in one fell, direct and courageous swoop, she had demolished any need for further awkwardness between them.

'I shall do my best to get over it quickly. Although I daresay the village won't. If Mrs Fitzherbert is involved, then there will be a book on us half filled with bets already as to when we will succumb.'

'Isn't there always?' She chuckled, unperturbed. 'It is their money to waste.'

'I suppose it is.'

It would be easier being the subject of unwelcome matchmaking gossip now that he knew there was no substance to it. Miss Healy wasn't the slightest bit interested in him in that way, thank goodness, so he could put all that to the back of his mind again where it belonged.

Thank goodness!

He gestured to her leg with his bag to change the subject. 'You're walking better.' Only the barest limp remained.

'I am indeed now that the swelling has subsided. The enormous, purple bruise it has left in its wake, however, is quite something to behold.'

He wanted to behold it. However, as his reasons for wanting to see it were probably more to do with her splendid legs than any legitimate medical reason, he decided to let sleeping dogs lie and opened the door to leave.

'Bruising is a good sign. It means the body is doing its best to fix the problem. But still, you should take things easy on it for at least the rest of the week. If, that is, your demanding aunt allows you to.'

'Are we still on for whist on Sunday afternoon or would you feel more comfortable with a different partner now that you know Sophie, Isobel and Mrs Fitzherbert fancy the pair of us for Whittleston's next bride and groom?'

She really was one for grabbing the bull by the horns and looked him square in the eye as if daring him to be the one with less mettle.

'Forewarned is always forearmed, and you are too competent a whist player to lose on the back of a silly piece of idle gossip.' He inclined his head politely, for some reason smiling again. 'While we continue to trounce them all and steal their money, we can watch all their machinations safe in the superior knowledge that we are immune to them.'

'I do so love to feel superior.' The glint of mischief was back in her eyes. 'Perhaps we should find a way to put a sly, anonymous bet on the outcome too? If we are going to be subjected to no end of machinations between now and my departure, then we should at least benefit from it. I'd be in for half a guinea that I leave here before Christmas Eve without a ring on my finger.'

It was another dare, but one he happily took as it cemented their new accord.

'I'll match that stake and, if you are truly game, I'll find someone to place the bet anonymously for us.'

'You could do that?'

'I am the most *able* physician in Whittleston-on-the-Water and I am owed quite a few favours hereabouts.'

'Then I insist that you call one in and look forward to counting our joint winnings.'

He inclined his head, suddenly glad that they had cleared the air. 'Until Friday, Miss Healy.'

Chapter Five

They'd cleared up at the whist tournament on Sunday afternoon. At Dr Able's insistence, the usual stakes had been doubled, and after a spirited final game they'd won the pot, which Rose had found most satisfying.

It was almost as satisfying as all the amusement they had mutually found in the subtle but shameless match-making they'd been subjected to that night. Made all the sweeter by the fact that he had been true to his word and had placed a bet through the local constable on them *not* getting married, when nobody else had. Which meant the odds they'd got were phenomenal. She didn't need the money, any more than she suspected he did, but she was determined to win it and enjoy it regardless.

Therefore, as it made financial sense to make the villagers think there was a frisson between her and the handsome doctor, she had playfully flirted with him over the card table. With some cajoling he had almost flirted back, and that had had a profound effect on everyone watching. Eyebrows had arched and eyes had slanted sideways and the amount of people whispering, obviously about them, had been very satisfying to see.

Then they had laughed about their evil plan as they had split their winnings after Mrs Fitzherbert insisted that he had to escort her home in his curricle—seeing as they were both going the same way and it was broad daylight.

That short trip had sent the local gossip into a frenzy, because everyone had seen them sitting side by side in the close confines of his curricle, laughing away, which in turn, meant more people bet on their union and the prize pot they weren't supposed to know about, let alone be part of, became increasingly more worth winning.

For her own amusement Rose had stirred the pot a bit more by acting all distracted and dreamy at the Friday Sewing Circle, even pretending to blush when she was accused again of fancying the doctor around that crowded table, where she'd issued a half-hearted denial.

After all, if they were all going to think it anyway, she and her new partner in crime might as well profit from it.

Tonight was the night of the local assembly, and for once Rose was looking forward to it. Not only would it give her a welcome few hours' respite from her demanding aunt, but it would fan the flames of gossip further if she and Dr Able played their cards right.

To that end, she had put on a wholly inappropriate gown. The deep crimson silk wasn't particularly revealing, but the colour was bold and it was the sort of gown a woman wore when she wanted to make a special effort for someone. She hoped that the village hall would be as stuffy as it usually was during this well-attended gathering, as silk and short sleeves were a ludicrous combination when it was freezing outside.

'You look very fetching this evening.' Uncle William beamed with approval over the newspaper he was reading as she poked her head around the bedchamber door. 'I sincerely hope that a certain learned gentleman appreciates all the effort you have gone to.' He flicked a knowing glance at his wife.

'Of course he will appreciate it.' Aunt Agatha smiled smugly. 'Our Rose is quite the catch. The rate things are progressing, I wouldn't be at all surprised if Dr Able makes a formal declaration of interest soon and then they can start officially courting. Perhaps we should insist he stays for tea the next time he visits to help expedite matters?'

The word expedite set alarm bells ringing, as did the mutually wiggling brows.

'Or should we invite him to dinner instead, seeing as we only have until Christmas?'

'I don't think that either is wise.'

Rose wasn't surprised that her own kith and kin had also put a bet on her and the local physician as her aunt had been dropping unsubtle hints for days. But she didn't want them to either build their hopes up or lose too much money on her. She also found herself not wanting to build her own hopes up either. For some reason, the idea of a bit of romance between her and her handsome co-conspirator was no longer being quite as unappealing as it should be. Was her heart mended? Mending? Or just plain hopeless?

'I am nowhere near ready to think about courting again.' The mere thought of courting again, trusting again and laying herself open to more humiliation again should surely make her panic?

Her aunt waved that away. 'Never say never, dear, and remember while he might not have a title, he is a *doctor.*' Her aunt had always been obsessed with status. 'A well-respected one at that.'

'Even so, I am still not interested.'

Maybe, sometime in the distant future, she might be tempted to dip her toe back into those murky waters again. If someone truly worthy and genuinely trustworthy came along. But her faith in mankind—with the emphasis on the *man*—needed to have been fully restored first. It still bled inside her chest from time to time and she still felt humiliated.

'I know the entire village is abuzz with rumours and speculations after the last card game, but you are two of the few people who know the fraught circumstances which brought me here to Whittleston and how deeply it all affected me.'

Hers had been such a brutal and public humiliation. Made unbearable by the pathetic fact that she had been utterly in love with her fiancé and completely blindsided by his callous betrayal. But there was no point attempting to deliver that pessimistic prediction when her entire family hoped that she would not only recover from the mighty blow she had been dealt but would move on. And the sooner the better too.

'Therefore, I feel that I can be completely honest with you and say that while I like Dr Able as an acquaintance, and maybe even as a friend, I really do not have any desire to know him on any other level.'

'Yes, but—'

'In short—' Rose gave them both a pointed look of her own '—what I am really saying is do not waste your hard-earned money wagering on me and Dr Able skipping off into the sunset together as it isn't going to happen.' While her aunt pouted at that disappointing news, Rose bent and kissed her on the forehead. 'I have to go.'

'Do you need your uncle to escort you to St Hildreth's?'

'No need. I shall be constantly under the watchful eyes of Mrs Fitzherbert, Sophie and Isobel.' Who would all be hoping to see some spark of confirmation that their futile quest was working. 'And I have an escort. He should be here any moment.'

'He?' Another knowing look passed between husband and wife. 'I don't suppose *he* would happen to be a besotted doctor, would he?'

'He wouldn't.' She rolled her eyes with a smile. 'Archie is my escort.'

'Archie!' Aunt Agatha flung her head back on the pillow in exasperation. 'Did Dr Able not even ask?'

'Have you taken your sleeping draught?'

'We both have.' That came from her uncle, who had clearly reached the end of his tether too and needed oblivion.

'Then goodnight.' Rose grinned as she exited the bedchamber. 'Don't wait up, Uncle. You both need your rest and I shan't be too late.'

She was tying the ribbons of her bonnet when her dashing escort arrived. Typically, the younger brother of the new lord of the manor was grinning from ear to ear as she opened the door.

'Look, Rose! It's snowing again.' He held out his gloved palm to display the smattering of flakes he had caught. 'I hope it settles so that I can go sledding again down the hill!'

Archie might well be knocking on the door of two and twenty in actual years but, thanks to his condition, he was half that inside and always would be. Bizarrely, it was part of his unique charm and she, like everyone else in Whittleston-on-the-Water, absolutely adored him. He was as exuberant as he was inquisitive, as kind as he was irrepressible, stubborn, frequently unreasonable, always insisted on an intricately tied cravat to go with whichever bold waistcoat he decided to wear and never failed to make you smile no matter how low your spirits.

'You can come with us again if you want to.'

'Not after last time, thank you.'

She still wasn't fully over that last time, a fortnight ago, when she had agreed to it, assuming that Archie actually possessed a proper sled. The sort she was used to with a seat and some sort of mechanism to steer it. Instead, he had produced an enormous metal tea tray which he had cajoled her onto and then almost killed her on it.

'I shall stick to throwing snowballs at you—if it settles.' She caught a few flakes of powder and watched it melt on her skin. 'Which I sincerely doubt it will when the roads are still so wet from the last flurry we had.'

Thank goodness. It had been nothing but alternating treacherous ice and filthy slush for weeks now.

'It's going to settle,' said Archie, with all the confidence of a terminal optimist. 'It will be six feet deep by the time we leave the assembly. Mark my words.'

He held out his arm like a proper gentleman, then kept up a constant stream of excited chatter for the entire five-minute stroll to the village hall behind St Hildreth's, then quickly abandoned her the second they walked through the door.

Rather than hunt about for company, Rose lingered in an alcove while she took in the familiar scene, grateful that she had one more assembly in this quirky little village. Whittleston had been both her sanctuary and her salvation. A reminder that life went on and bad times faded. She was no longer a broken, defeated mess. She was battle-scarred and battle-hardened, but she looked forward to getting up in the mornings again and had finally found her smile.

She was smiling at all the revelry when the hairs on the nape of her neck danced with awareness.

'I have it on the highest authority that the book is now worth a healthy seven guineas in total and only us two have betted against ourselves falling into the parson's trap before the end of Advent.'

She turned to see the doctor holding two cups of what the Reverend Spears insisted on calling punch.

He passed one to her and toasted her with his cup. 'Here's to our guaranteed win.'

She clinked her cup to his. 'Three and a half guineas each isn't to be sniffed at, so well done us.' A woman could buy a lot with that, and she was resolute that the first thing she would treat herself to was the daring off-the-shoulder evening gown she had found in the fashion plates in Isobel's haberdasher's, and which her talented seamstress friend had promised her that she would make before she left. She would wear her outrageously bold new gown at the Suffolk assembly on New Year's Eve. An assembly where she intended to dance every dance, laugh in the face of adversity and show her feckless former fiancé once and for all that she was over him.

And perhaps she finally was? Rose certainly no longer felt as weighed down by his rejection as she had been and that was progress. He also didn't cross her mind as often as he had either—unlike her charming companion tonight, who had rather taken root in it.

'I reckon it will be closer to four by the time you leave.' Dr Able quirked one dark brow towards the on-lookers. 'Just look at the way they are all pretending not to watch us. Can you believe that the odds currently stand at three to one for a Christmas Eve wedding? How trite and sentimental is that?' He pulled a face, then took a sip, then pulled a worse one. 'Good grief, this is more dreadful than usual!'

Rose took a tentative taste herself, then winced. 'I think the wine is off.'

'This isn't wine, Miss Healy, it's vinegar. Maybe even acid.'

'It's a travesty, that is what it is.' Mrs Fitzherbert made them both jump. 'Give those cups to me to dispose of while you two go and dance.' She winked at them. 'The first waltz is next.'

'I c-can't,' stuttered Rose as she panicked over how much the old lady had heard, and panicked more at how much the prospect of waltzing with him suddenly appealed. 'I have a bad knee.'

'Which she must still keep her weight off.'

Dr Able offered her his arm. It was solid and strong beneath her fingertips. The solid muscle would give the most vigorous farm labourer some competition. How on earth did a village physician develop such an athletic physique? And he was so lovely and warm. Enough that she, in her stupid short sleeves, wanted to burrow against him to absorb it.

'Let us find a chair.'

The sight of her holding his elbow caused everyone to stare. Only some did so surreptitiously; the rest did it with such glee it was shameful. Almost as shameful as her improper enjoyment of the feel of his bicep.

'Do you think she heard us talking about our bet?'

'If she had, she would have made her presence known sooner.'

He helped her into the chair even though she needed no help, but the solicitous way that he did it sent the gossiping villagers into a frenzy. Almost as much of a frenzy as the gentle weight of his palm on her back affected her bouncing nerves.

'But if she did, it will make no difference. Knowing the ladies of this parish, any resistance would be seen as a challenge. A giant gauntlet thrown down which will simply result in them all redoubling their efforts to push us together. Thankfully we know that it won't work.'

'It most definitely won't.'

'Because you are sworn off men for the foreseeable future and I am incapable of ever loving again.'

He meant that as a throwaway line, but it sparked Rose's interest exponentially—while simultaneously and inexplicably disappointing her. 'Incapable? Am I allowed to enquire why? Or does that break the unwritten rules of acquaintanceship.'

His lips flattened and for the longest moment she thought he would say no, but instead he sighed. 'That part of me died with Catherine. I could never...' He stopped himself, then huffed. 'Take it from me, hearts don't heal, Miss Healy.' He smiled without humour at his unintentional pun. 'They might pump blood effectively after being broken, but that is all they will do.'

Which did not bode well for hers stitching itself back together any time soon.

'How did she die?'

Again, he was silent for so long she did not think he
would answer, but he did. After another huff. 'Typhus.
I'd been posted to Lisbon and had been at the main camp
there for over a year. But as there were no signs of the
war ending and I was nowhere near the front at the time
she wanted to be with me. I, as I am sure you can imagine, was adamant that she should stay home, where it
was safe, not just from the war but from all the horrors
that come with it.'

He swallowed and never had one instinctive swallow
conveyed so much pain and regret.

'But because Catherine was stubborn to her core
when she set her mind to something, and because other
soldiers' wives followed the regiment from camp to
camp as a matter of course, she thought I was being
unreasonable. Behind my back, she managed to convince the Colonel of the Essex regiment to allow her to
travel with the new recruits to Portugal and surprised
me there in the middle of an epidemic. Before I could
get her on the next boat home she caught it.' His eyes
were suddenly haunted. 'And that was that.'

'I am so sorry.' And she was. It must have been awful
for him—a doctor—not to be able to save her. 'I cannot
imagine how painful that must have been for you.'

The haunted eyes shuttered. 'I daresay it was more
painful for her. Typhus is a brutal disease.'

Something tragic and desolate skittered momentarily
across his pinched features before he pushed them away.
The supreme effort that took was visible for barely a
moment before he changed the subject.

'Am I allowed to enquire how your heart got broken?'

'What makes you think it was broken?'

'It takes one to know one.'

'I was jilted, Dr Able, almost a year ago to the day.'

He clearly hadn't expected that and his expression widened with shock before the inevitable pity manifested.

'The irony is that I was supposed to have a "trite and sentimental" Christmas Eve wedding—but it never happened.'

He winced. 'My apologies for putting my big foot in it. When I said that a Christmas wedding was trite...' His words trailed off when he saw her wry smile. 'I'm sorry.'

'So am I, but what can you do?'

As always, tears of humiliation pricked her eyes but she refused to acknowledge them. She had cried enough for a wretch who, frankly, did not deserve her efforts, then for a bunch of malicious gossips who had made her life a misery afterwards. It was better to channel all her sadness and humiliation into anger. Perhaps not healthier but it hurt less.

'His absconding the month before wasn't the worst of it. Everyone back in my village saw it coming long before I did and yet none of them told me. They were so busy trying to spare my feelings that they inadvertently had a hand in crushing them to pulp.'

'How so?' His gaze was sympathetic.

'I suppose all the clues were there the first time he postponed our nuptials, six months after his proposal, because it was obvious then that he wasn't in a hurry to spend eternity with me. But, alas, love is blind and pathetically forgiving. I believed all his nonsense about wanting to prove himself worthy out of his father's shadow and even found it romantic that he wanted to stand on his own two feet when he walked me up the aisle. I even believed it the second time too, which

I suppose makes me as dim as a pauper's candle...'
The wry smile faltered a little. 'But as he was making
some half-hearted attempts with the stock market, I let
it slide. When his attempts failed and he seemed depressed about it all I didn't push for another wedding
date for at least six months.'

'How long were you engaged?'

She could see that even the frowning physician had
worked out that all those delays didn't bode well.

'Two and a half glorious years, Doctor. So long that
it—and by "it" I mean me—was becoming a bit of a
joke in Suffolk. But of course being a foolish optimist
back then, I gave him more of the benefit of the doubt
and blithely looked forward to my extra-special Christmas wedding. However, while I was busy organising
my wedding trousseau, and eagerly counting down the
hours till our nuptials, he was busy conducting a rather
torrid affair with a young widow whom I'd believed
to be my friend. Such a good friend that I even sipped
tea with her in her parlour the day before the pair of
them eloped to Gretna Green. Where she allowed me to
waffle on about how excited I was for my future. And
I brought her a cake which I had thoughtfully baked
myself.'

Her duplicitous friend had nibbled at it in near silence while Rose had made cringing enquiries about
what to expect on her wedding night, because her prudish mother had not been able to bring herself to have
that conversation. Entirely unaware that the woman
was more familiar with the intimate workings of her
philandering fiancé's body than she could have possibly imagined.

'That's awful.'

'Isn't it? She let me leave, still thinking she would be my bridesmaid, and he didn't even have the decency of informing me that the wedding was off until he remembered to post me a letter ten days later—from the Highlands, where he was on honeymoon. It was a curt missive too.'

Rose was purposely flippant. Ever hopeful that if she could pretend to the world that it didn't matter then it would stop mattering to her.

'Only six lines, but straight to the point. He wanted me to know that he had never intended falling in love with another woman, but now that he had he was relieved.'

'*Relieved?*'

Dr Able was shaking his head, outraged for her, while she inwardly cringed some more. Despite burning that letter within minutes of reading it, every cruel word had been engraved on her broken heart.

'Indeed. Without any attempt at apology, he stated that he realised he wouldn't have strayed in the first place if he truly had loved me, and that he should never have proposed to me when he knew, deep down, that marrying me would have been the biggest mistake of his life.' Rose always experienced a violent surge of anger whenever she recalled that part of his letter. 'Which was *lovely* to hear.'

'Ouch.'

Clearly unthinking, he reached for her hand and that somehow meant the world.

'I would say that you are undoubtedly better off without him and that there are plenty more fish in the sea, but I won't as that most definitely would be trite. I daresay you've had enough well-meaning people offer you those empty platitudes and, as previously discussed, it wouldn't help your poor heart any. For some of us, there was only ever meant to be one fish.'

'I thought I was the only one who had developed an aversion to fishing.'

'I surrendered my net and rod when I put Catherine in the ground.'

One of the busybodies from the sewing circle scuttled past, then stopped dead when she spied them holding hands. As he tried to pull his hand away, Rose tightened her grasp and winked as she stared deep into his eyes. Only when the woman had dashed off to spread that delicious new piece of gossip, did she let go. Shocked to her core because, thanks to the stormy depths of his gaze and the potency of his touch, something had shifted within her.

He was cautiously amused but definitely wary. Hardly a surprise when the way he had stiffened at her touch wasn't the slightest bit flattering. Especially when her entire body had done the exact opposite and had positively melted instead.

'And what, pray tell, was that about, Miss Healy?'

Off-kilter, she flapped her fan while she stared at the dancers rather than into his wit-scrambling eyes. 'I was merely adding a little more fuel to the fire. Gilding the lily to ensure that we both make a pretty penny once Whittleston's latest matchmaking debacle is over.'

That was her story and she was going to stick to it.

She forced her gaze to flick back to his, amused rather than unsettled. 'Now that we are partners in crime, you really need to make more of an effort to look enamoured of me too, if you want to be assured of four guineas apiece. You did agree to our ruse, after all.'

'I agreed to place a bet for us, Miss Healy, not fabricate a romance.'

'Spoilsport.' She nudged him with her elbow. 'With some acting and some judicious flirting, I think we might even be able to get that pot up to five apiece. Or have you always been no fun?'

'I used to be fun.' His smile was wistful. 'I also used to be a dreadful flirt too. Before…'

She knew exactly how he felt. 'It's funny, isn't it, how one tragedy can so fundamentally change you?' It was actually quite refreshing to be allowed to feel hopeless alongside someone who empathised. 'I used to be a sunny optimist, with effusively romantic notions, and now I am an embittered and distrusting cynic.'

Albeit one who was having some effusively romantic notions right now.

'You do not act like a cynic.'

'I am flirting with a man for no other reason than to win a bet—if that is not cynicism, Dr Able, I do not know what is. But when you have nothing but despair and more regret to look forward to, I see no reason why we irrevocably damaged souls cannot take whatever amusement we can if the opportunity presents itself.' She twirled a finger in her hair and batted her eyelashes like a coquette. 'I am twisted like that. Bitter and twisted—it is a classic combination. And, take it from me, the twisted part makes life the tiniest bit more bearable. It also helps that I am gifted with a warped sense of humour and find amusement at the most inappropriate times. For example, in full grip of my heartbreak, I had the most marvellous time pretending to be besotted with Ned last summer to make Isobel jealous. Only a tiny part of that was because I could see they were both in denial about being head over heels in love. The rest was all selfish self-amusement.'

'I suppose you do have an exemplary record of fooling people.'

'Which bodes exceedingly well for us winning our bet. People never imagine that lightning can strike twice, therefore the entire village will believe our faux flirting is real.' She took the tiniest sip of her foul drink to glance coquettishly over it. 'Just look at Mrs Fitzherbert and Isobel over there.' They were watching them like excited hawks while doing their utmost to pretend not to. 'They are completely fooled by my superb performance already.'

He was silent again for the longest time, staring aimlessly at all the dancers. When they stopped and a fresh crop began to regroup he nudged her. 'How is this for twisted, then? I bet we could push the pot to reward us with six guineas apiece if we dance both the first and the last waltz together tonight.'

Unaware that his suggestion had both thrilled her and unsettled her in equal measure, he slanted her a sinful glance that suited him too much.

'I am game if you are, Dr Able.'

She held out her hand in readiness, her foolish, misguided heart jumping for joy while her wayward body rejoiced at the opportunity to press itself against his.

'Welcome to the dark side.'

Chapter Six

As always, the final waltz signalled the end of Whittleston-on-the-Water's monthly assembly. Normally, Sam would have escaped long before in case he got pressganged into that torture, but tonight he had not only stayed, he had also danced it. And at his own instigation too. A situation which would have been unthinkable only a few hours ago.

That he'd remembered the steps was a bloody miracle as he hadn't danced it since his honeymoon six years ago. There had never been much call for waltzing while Napoleon had been at large and even if there had, he had been too besotted with his pretty wife at home to want to. The waltz was the dance of love after all, and he had been so hopelessly in love with her that it would have felt wrong to perform it with another. A betrayal of his vows almost. But it was hardly a betrayal when those vows had died with Catherine.

He'd expected to be riddled with guilt because it was Miss Healy he was holding in his arms instead, but he hadn't been. Maybe that was because they were partners in crime on a joint quest to amuse themselves by winning a bet? Or maybe it was because he knew the dance meant nothing because they were both irrevocably damaged souls? Whatever the reason, twirling around the floor with the most beautiful woman in the room while the other single men looked on with envy had felt marvellous.

And there was no doubt that she was the most beautiful woman in the room.

While Sam might want to remain immune to her feminine charms, from the moment he had first set eyes upon her tonight he had not been able to help noticing that the deep red gown suited her. The cut displayed a womanly figure that drew male stares like bears to honey—including his. It contrasted perfectly with her chestnut hair, and the bold colour and the confident style matched her slightly irreverent, slightly mischievous character.

Thanks to her witty observations and tendency towards sarcasm, she was as entertaining on the dance floor as she was off it and they both found amusement in all the gawping spectators. Despite all the dangerous and distracting ideas holding her in his arms was giving his body, waltzing with her had been *fun*, exactly as she had promised. More astonishing was that, during it, he had even forgotten to feel dead inside and that had been…oddly liberating when he was usually grateful to be numb.

No doubt he would pay for it in guilt later, when he tried to sleep and the images of Catherine's last moments haunted his dreams to remind him of all his failings, but for now he was content to enjoy the feeling of lightness just a little while longer. Therefore, conscious that they were still being scrutinised, and enjoying the ruse immensely, he insisted with helping her on with her cloak before he handed her over to Archie, who was waiting impatiently to walk her home.

Why Archie was her designated escort when he lived at Hockley Hall, almost a mile away in the wrong direction, when Sam and Miss Healy were practically neighbours he did not know. Beyond that it simply wasn't done for a single gentleman to escort a single lady home on foot in the dark. Archie, although undeniably technically a single gentleman himself, was deemed safe because he was Archie, whereas Sam was obviously a potential despoiler. Which was laughable when he'd had to examine her in her bedchamber unchaperoned and nobody had even thought he might despoil her then despite his wanting to! But dark deeds were apparently only done in darkness, and even in this parochial little enclave of Essex where the strictures of society were mostly ignored some improprieties were unforgivable.

Therefore, despite them heading in exactly the same way, out of respect for that ludicrous propriety, he had to hang back on some pretence. Then leave a respectable five minutes later than the woman he had spent the entire evening with because that was the done thing.

Except the moment he stepped out onto the pavement, he saw Miss Healy and Archie were still there. As was the Hockley carriage, from which Archie's elder brother was frowning while pointing to the ground, where large, robust flakes of snow were now falling with a vengeance and settling fast.

'No, Archie.' From the set of his little brother's jaw, Rafe was arguing with him. 'You will get into this carriage now so that I can drive Rose home. I am not letting you wander all the way back to the hall alone in a blizzard!'

It was nowhere near a blizzard, but Sam understood why Rafe did not want his brother out alone in this. If Archie got confused and lost his way—a very real possibility when Whittleston was a blanket of fresh white and the younger Peel had the faculties of a boy prone to panic—it could be dangerous.

'He's right.' Miss Healy laid a hand on Archie's arm as she tried to be gentle. 'I would never forgive myself if you got lost, so you must get in the carriage with your family.' Then she smiled at Rafe. 'But as the snow is already deep enough to cause you issues too, I can honestly walk myself home faster than you can drive me, and I don't want to be the cause of you getting stuck.'

'But it isn't proper for you to walk home alone in the dark and I promised to protect you!' Archie stamped his foot. 'A gentleman's word is his bond.'

'You would still be escorting Rose home if we take her in the carriage!' Poor Rafe was clearly at his wits' end. 'Therefore, I would appreciate it if you would stop arguing and get in this blasted coach quick-sharp before all this snow makes the roads impassable.'

'Your big brother is right.'

Sam decided this was as good a time as any to announce his presence. Archie listened to him. Sometimes. He had always been in awe of the fact that Sam was a doctor, as if that alone meant his word was gospel.

'The lane up to Hockley Hall is steep and prone to snowdrifts that block it. The sooner your brother tackles it, the more chance you all have of getting home tonight. If you are worried about Miss Healy, you can appoint me as your second to fulfil your promise to protect her. Surely you trust me to get her home safely?'

He did his best impression of a man about to be wounded as he knew Archie hated to upset people.

'Well… I…' The lad blinked, wavering. 'Of course I trust you, Dr Able, but…'

'Then that is the perfect solution!' Before Archie's legendary stubborn streak came to the fore again, Miss Healy pushed her intractable escort towards the carriage. 'You go home with Rafe before the road becomes blocked and I'll walk home with Dr Able.' With surprising strength, she shoved him into the seat next to his sister-in-law. 'Goodnight, Archie.'

She slammed the door closed with a wink at Rafe, and the carriage lurched forward.

'I honestly thought we would be standing here all night arguing.' She grinned, making her fine eyes sparkle. 'Thank you for stepping into the breach.'

'It was hardly any trouble when we are practically neighbours. I would have risked the dreadful scandal and offered before, but Archie was adamant that you specifically asked him to do it.'

'Only because I did not want to inconvenience my uncle—who also would have insisted on escorting me the short five minutes home too if I didn't have a trustworthy alternative in place. Which is ridiculous when this is sleepy Whittleston-on-the-Water and I would be perfectly safe. But no. I must be wrapped in cotton wool for the sake of my fragile reputation! Being a woman is so irritating sometimes.'

Sam chuckled at her perfectly logical complaint. 'For what it's worth, in my professional experience women are always the stronger rather than the weaker sex as we are always told. They seem to work twice as hard and bear everything with more fortitude and grace than most men do.'

'That is very forward-thinking of you.'

'One can be bitter and twisted and forward-thinking, Miss Healy. They are not mutually exclusive.'

That comment made her laugh—until she skidded on the snow. She grabbed his arm to stay upright and when she let go wobbled some more, so he naturally offered it to keep her upright. Then regretted it when she took it, because her touch awoke something primal.

'It turns out that dancing slippers have absolutely no traction.' She scowled at her inappropriate footwear, then shivered. 'They are not particularly warm either. I knew I should have changed into my walking boots the second I saw the weather, but I didn't because they wouldn't have gone with my gown. That will teach me to put vanity over practicality.'

'At least it is only a short walk back.'

Something he was suddenly grateful for, because her arm in his felt nicer than he was comfortable with. Thanks to Archie's protracted altercation with his brother and the snow, all the other revellers had dissipated, so they had the path from St Hildreth's to the village square to themselves. The snow had muted all the usual sounds of the night and the lack of stars above made the world suddenly seem more intimate. As if they were the only two people in it. Something that made the shrivelled husk of his heart race.

'You will be back with your aunt and uncle well before frostbite sets in.'

'On the subject of my aunt and uncle, you should probably know that they might have also placed a bet on us getting together—despite all my protestations to the contrary—so there is a high chance you will get an impromptu invitation to take tea with us, or dinner, so have your excuse ready. It is unlikely tonight, as they both decided to partake of your sleeping draught, but forewarned is always forearmed. My aunt, especially, has been desperate to find me a replacement fiancé since the scoundrel I was engaged to replaced me.'

Despite the flippant tone, hurt shimmered briefly in her eyes and he experienced the overwhelming urge to throttle that scoundrel for his callous treatment. To his surprise, his fist had even clenched, so Sam flexed his fingers and tried to make light of it for her sake— because that was what she always did.

'I am surprised Mrs Outhwaite considers me good enough when she fancies herself a cut above all of us here.' He blurted that before he had the good sense to censor it and instantly regretted it. Mrs Outhwaite was still her aunt, and blood was always thicker than water. 'That was unkind and uncalled-for, and I apologise.'

She sighed, unoffended. 'I adore my aunt, as she has been nothing but kind to me at a time when I need to be reminded that not all in the world is bad, but I am not blind to her shortcomings. She and my uncle were never blessed with children, and I suppose, in the absence of a family of her own to love and respect her, my aunt overcompensates by trying to command the respect of everyone here in Whittleston instead. Unfortunately, she has gone about that entirely the wrong way. She puts too much stock in nonsense like status and doesn't possess the…*diplomacy*…necessary to correct that. Of course—' she tugged his arm playfully '—it doesn't help that she is prone to theatrics and has no understanding of the concept of tolerance. You should be flattered that she is prepared to tolerate you, Dr Able, as that is a rare accolade.'

'Then I suppose I should be honoured that she considers me tolerable enough for her beloved niece and will endeavour to keep my uncharitable opinions about her to myself going forward.'

'Do not flatter yourself too much, though, Dr Able, as in the same breath she did say that beggars could not be choosers.' There was that infectious glimmer of mischief in her eyes again as they turned onto the square. 'I sincerely doubt she would tolerate you at all if she didn't fear her scandalously jilted niece was doomed for a life gathering dust on the shelf. As being jilted does, ironically, render a woman rather unweddable. No man wants another man's cast-offs at the best of times, and they all will now wonder what it was about me that sent him running to the hills in the first place. Especially since he and his new wife and adorable baby have ingratiated themselves back into my village.'

'They didn't have the good grace to move away?' Her story just got worse and worse.

'His father is the wealthiest landowner and biggest landlord in my village, and nobody wants to upset the man they pay their rent to—even if they genuinely do think that his son is scoundrel. Forgiveness has been surprisingly forthcoming despite their despicable treachery —aided, no doubt, by some rather salacious rumours which have cast doubts upon my character and given some of the more stupid or most intimidated some sympathy for the wretch. Which is marvellous for my former fiancé, because he gets to go about his life unchallenged, but not so marvellous for me.'

'What sort of doubts?' He had the inexplicable urge to avenge them all.

'Fabricated nonsense that nobody sensible believed for a minute.' She waved it away with a sunny smile that did not quite touch her eyes. 'But it still was a blow to my self-esteem.'

She flicked him a wry glance intended to convey that she was over it, except her acting skills weren't quite good enough.

'Not much goes on in Suffolk, so it was all anyone talked about for far too long. Especially after the pair of Judases returned and his father got involved. The only viable solution to the awkward problem of our enforced proximity and the continued speculation, as far as my family are concerned, is for me to marry. And the sooner the better. Their desire to get the job done—alongside the impending birth of the adorable child those two back-stabbers created—was the reason I came here. Hoping to escape it all. Except, like my misguided and well-meaning parents, my usually picky aunt would rather I shackled myself to a nobody, like you, Dr Able, than remain a pitied and infamously discarded spinster for ever.'

He wanted to hug her, but instead continued in the same droll, sarcastic tone. 'A *nobody*? Thank you very much. Some friend you are.'

She could not resist another dig. 'Friends? I thought we were merely acquaintan—'

'Dr Able! Thank God!' Ted Dewhurst, the son of one of the tenant farmers from Little Ramstead suddenly appeared out of the snow. 'One of my father's mares has been foaling all day. The babe is still stuck fast and she's in such a bad way now he thinks we might lose them both!'

'I am not an animal doctor, Ted. I know absolutely nothing about mares and foals.'

'It's November—are you sure she is foaling?' That came from Miss Healy. 'She could have colic.'

'Positive,' came the lad's response. 'She's the size of a house and you can see the babe moving inside of her. Her season has always been odd because it's near constant. Her last foal came in January. That was a big one too.'

'Last January? So recent?'

'Aye, miss. It came as a surprise to us too that it had happened again so fast, but she had no problems then so we assumed it would be all right. But this time...' Ted turned to plead with Sam. 'You need to come, Doc! It's stuck and you're our last hope.'

'I'm really not sure what help I can be.' It wasn't in his nature to allow anything to suffer, but he didn't relish the prospect of shooting a horse to put it out of its misery. 'If it was a human baby—'

'Oh, for goodness' sake, Dr Able, surely the basic principles of a birth are the same? Go and fetch your equipment and curricle this instant!' Miss Healy pointed to his door like an exasperated schoolmistress. 'Humans and horses are both mammals, after all.'

'With very different anatomies! I barely know which end of a horse is which!'

'Then it is lucky for you that this farmer's daughter does, isn't it?' She turned to Ted, her suddenly snippy tone gone. 'You go home and we'll be with you as soon as we can. Tell your father to get plenty of straw and rope ready. If it's a large foal we might need it, and if it is large and also breach, as I suspect it is, we will definitely need it.'

Intrigued and slightly peeved by the way she had taken charge with such confidence and forced his hand, Sam made short work of readying his curricle, and by the time he had fetched his equipment, she was already seated in it, huddled inside her cloak like a monk to stave off the cold. Snow had settled on her hood.

'This weather is worsening, and this could take hours. You go home and I'll go alone.'

'Because you know so much about horses that you are confident you can save her?' Her jaw set stubbornly and she did not budge.

'Because of propriety, Miss Healy! Because it isn't the done thing for a single man and woman to walk home alone in the dark together after an evening of public waltzing and flirting, let alone ride off into the night in a curricle together!'

'Oh, stop being so silly. Little Ramstead is less than five miles away and we will likely be back before anyone misses us.'

'Being ruined isn't silly, Miss Healy, and despite the unfairness of it all a woman's reputation *is* fragile!'

'It will be a cold day in hell before I put my already tarnished reputation before what is right! I have the knowledge to save that foal and I am going to use it, even if I have to find another horse and ride by myself to Little Ramstead!'

'Please—be reasonable.' Sam spread his hands and tried to temper his tone. 'If your aunt or uncle are waiting up for you then this could be catastrophic for both of us.'

She pointed towards their house. 'Can you see a lamp burning anywhere but on the porch?'

She had him there as all the windows were dark. The

downstairs ones were devoid of curtains too, no doubt so the outrageous gossip Mrs Outhwaite could keep a close eye on the comings and goings in the square, so it was plain to see that nobody was awake.

'They both sleep like the dead so I can assure you that neither will notice me arriving home a little later than usual! My aunt is the lighter sleeper and thanks to your sleeping draught she has been practically unconscious between the hours of ten and ten.'

'Still, this isn't wise, nor proper, and—' Sam found himself talking to a raised palm.

'A horse is more than a conveyance to a farmer, Doctor. It is an intrinsic part of his livelihood and the loss of one can have dire repercussions. Especially if the farmer happens to live from hand to mouth as I suspect Ted's father does.'

He might have known this canny minx would spot the patches and holes in the lad's clothes.

'I will not see a family starve because you think that my helping them is improper and I sincerely doubt anyone in this village will think it the least bit improper if they ever find out the circumstances. This is prime farming country and when a crisis happens the people in these close-knit villages rally round and happily forgive the odd bit of impropriety if it is necessary. I've visited countless farmers in the middle of the night when a neighbour needed help and still retained my reputation.'

She folded her arms and glared at him from the perch.

'So stop being silly and let's go. You might be the one with the medical degree, but I'll wager I've brought more foals into this world than you have.'

'On your own head be it, then.'

He would have argued more fervently, but she was right, damn her. Sam had no clue how to birth a foal and he wasn't confident he could save the mare. Knowing his luck, he'd kill the mother and the child. Ted's father had been struggling to keep his head above water for years and he didn't want that on his conscience.

Conscious of her inappropriate evening gown and slippers, he made a quick about-turn to retrieve an additional blanket from inside and tossed it to her, then climbed up beside her. Thankfully, to prove her right, despite it being barely after ten, Whittleston-on-the-Water was as silent as the grave when they set off, as everyone else had had the great good sense to weather the storm in their beds. Not a single lamp burned in any window in the square, which was just as well. There was gossip and there was gossip, and two single people suddenly disappearing together at midnight, no matter how innocent or necessary, was bound to put the fox amongst the hens. Especially after the two waltzes they had foolishly engaged in to pique all the busybodies' interest.

'Seeing as you are the expert, and I am apparently your assistant in this endeavour, you should probably tell me what you need me to do when we get there.'

'Pull, Dr Able.' She smiled. 'Pull on the rope like your life depends on it. That is your role tonight.'

'And yours is?'

'To attach the rope to the foal's hooves.' She held up one gloved palm. 'My hands are smaller than a man's and therefore can manoeuvre themselves into tighter crevices. It won't be pretty but I daresay you've seen worse.'

Miss Healy took immediate charge when they arrived at the farm, insisting on more light, more straw, some cooking fat and a bucket of hot water. Then she examined the horse, whispering soothing words to the struggling beast as she massaged around her tummy.

'How long has she been lying down?'

'Three hours now,' said the farmer. 'She had a few spirited goes at pushing but all to no avail.'

'Let's see what's wrong.'

She cooed this to the mare, then stripped off her cloak. Her fine crimson silk gown was incongruous with her surroundings, but she was oblivious of that. Instead, she smeared her arms to the elbow in the fat, dropped to her knees and gently inserted one hand beneath the mare's tail.

When she next spoke, it was to no one in particular. 'It's not breech, thank goodness, but it's upside down.' For the benefit of those who barely knew one end of a horse from another, she elaborated. 'It's lying on its back in her uterus, which means every time she pushes its hooves are pushed into her intestines rather than the birth canal. I need to turn it.'

With that, she went to war within the mare, rolling about on the bloody straw as she wrestled with the foal.

After an eternity, which involved a great deal of grunting from the woman and the expectant mother, she finally gave them some hope. 'It's finally moving!'

There was more wrestling. More grunting. And then Miss Healy withdrew her arms and collapsed on the straw. 'The foal is in a better position but not ideal. It's also huge. Much bigger than average. And she's exhausted so I don't think she can push it out without assistance.'

Sam stripped out of his coat. 'Is it time for the rope?'

'I'm afraid it is.'

Miss Healy talked him through making a retractable loop while she caught her breath, and then visibly braced herself as he passed it to her.

'Once I get this around the hooves, plant your feet and give it all you've got. This will be a battle. Big foals have an annoying tendency to get sucked back inside if the line isn't taut, so whatever you do, don't stop pulling once you start. Once the feet are out, grab one.' She glanced at his cream evening waistcoat with a frown. 'I'm afraid this next part is going to get very messy.'

'I've seen worse.' He rolled up his sleeves. 'And I am ready when you are.'

Miss Healy managed to get the rope looped around the foal's feet with surprising speed but she was right about it being a battle. For the first few minutes all his pulling seemed to be for nought, until suddenly it wasn't. Sam staggered backwards and all at once, there were the hooves. Two slimy black beacons of hope still trapped inside the birthing sac. Miss Healy tore it open with her bare hands and shouted at him to pull harder, which he did with a growl. Quick as a flash, she wrapped her hands tight around one of the feet and heaved. Once he was certain she had a firm enough hold he did the same, and they tugged together until the legs were followed by a nose, then a head, and then, like a slippery bar of soap in the bath, the rest slithered out in one messy brown lump.

A lump that did not move.

The farmer and Ted set about clearing the foal's airway and rubbing it down with straw while Sam held his breath. Beside him, he could tell Miss Healy was doing the same. They both let it out in a whoosh when the foal finally came to life. It twitched its feet, wiggled its head and, as his exhausted mother used the last of her strength to lick him, wobbled precariously to his feet while still attached to the umbilical cord.

'Do we cut it?' For reasons best known to himself, Sam was grinning at the miracle of this birth. The relief and sense of achievement was so palpable he could almost taste it.

Miss Healy shook her head and then collapsed back onto the straw, the definition of a spent but elated force. 'Not yet. It should snap on its own once the placenta comes out and she tries to stand.'

Which, it turned out, was exactly what happened not ten minutes later, while they both gratefully sipped hot cups of tea after the coldest wash known to man.

Chapter Seven

Rose tossed her bundle of soiled clothes into the curricle. The stays and petticoats might still be salvageable, but the gown was so beyond hope she had left it with the farmer's wife to dispose of, supremely grateful for the warm dress the woman had lent her despite all its patches.

Dr Able helped her up, stowed the basket of eggs the farmer had insisted on giving them as payment because he couldn't afford otherwise, and then hauled himself in beside her.

'We did it.' She beamed at him, proud of them both, supremely thankful the mare and her foal would both live to fight another day.

'You did it. I just pulled.' He offered her a wry smile. 'I am impressed, Miss Healy. Not only at your superior knowledge of equine anatomy, but with your calm and level head in a crisis. You would make an excellent physician.'

High praise indeed, because he was an excellent physician.

'Aside from the outrageous fact that women aren't allowed to be doctors, I would be a terrible physician as the sheer responsibility would weigh me down and I would take every failure all too personally.'

Her gut told her, now that she had been allowed a small window into his soul, that he did too, and that perhaps the tragedy which had befallen his wife and left him devastated explained why he kept the world at a distance.

'I'd be distraught if we'd failed. An inconsolable, weeping mess.'

For a moment she thought that she had touched a nerve, until he pulled a face. 'Thank the Lord we succeeded, then, as I do not have the requisite bedside manner to deal with a weeping mess. I'd simply hand you the reins and jump from the curricle. No matter what speed it was travelling at.'

'Would you really?' It was difficult to imagine a man so capable being felled by a few tears. 'Even in this atrocious weather?'

'If you're asking if would I choose hypothermia over hysteria? Of course I would! I'm a man of science and science is always logical, even when our limitations in understanding it defeats us. There are books I could read on hypothermia. Effective tried and tested treatments I could administer that might work. There is no rhyme or reason to a woman's tears, no medical books on the subject, and certainly no logic. Worse, the only treatment is a handkerchief, and that's not guaranteed to be effective, or platitudes, which I am atrocious at.' He shuddered for effect as they turned back onto the lane. 'I think I'd actually dive headfirst into a raging flood to avoid floods of tears.'

'Have you always been a man of science?'

'I think so. I cannot recall a time when it did not intrigue me. But then my father was a physician, so I suppose it's in my blood.'

'Was he? Where?' Seeing as the tight-lipped doctor was finally in the mood to open up, Rose decided to take advantage of that.

'Here—in Essex. About forty miles north-east, to be exact. I grew up in Witham. Do you know it?'

'I know it well. It's on the road to Long Melford, where I grew up. Do you still have family there?'

He shook his head, frowning more at the worsening weather and deep snowdrifts on the road ahead than at the question. 'My father passed several years ago and I sadly have no memories of my mother, who died when I was still in leading strings. I was their only child and left the town to join the army a decade ago, so I have no ties to Witham now.'

'You weren't tempted to return there when you took up private practice?'

'No.' His expression shuttered again, so abruptly it shocked her. She had definitely unwittingly hit a very raw nerve this time. Had his wife come from Witham too?

Should she ask?

While she deliberated the wind whipped up and sent the falling snow swirling. Within moments the visibility went from passable to non-existent, and the need for further conversation became redundant as he struggled to see the road ahead.

The wheel clipped something, then slid sideways, and the horse began to panic, bucking his head and dancing on the spot, not keen to venture blindly into the abyss. Rose didn't blame him. The snow was so violent now each flake bit into her skin and burned her eyes, and she was bundled up in a protective cloak. All the poor horse had was blinkers, and they wouldn't protect him.

She didn't need to tell Dr Able to stop the curricle. He had already decided attempting to continue was suicide until the blizzard subsided, and was carefully manoeuvring off the lane and into a gap beneath a canopy of trees. The bare tangle of branches above didn't give them much protection, but afforded enough to calm the horse at least.

'I fear we are going to have to wait it out.'

She nodded.

'Hopefully, seeing as this wind has whipped up quickly, it will pass quickly.'

As if it had heard him mention it, a frigid gust blasted their way with such force it rendered the canopy above useless. Hard pinpricks of ice stung Rose's cheeks while the gale stole her hood and sent it billowing backwards.

'If you can turn the curricle to face away from the wind and push it closer to the trees, I'll find somewhere less exposed nearby to tie up your horse.'

Rose grabbed the blanket from her legs and gingerly slid off her seat. The snow came to her knees and the relentless south-westerly found every hole in the tatty borrowed dress to chill her skin, apparently now determined to get worse before it got better. Together they battled the elements to unhitch the animal, and while he attempted to use the other blanket to fashion a makeshift cover to shield the open front of his curricle, she led the horse several yards into the calmer woods.

Fortunately, it did not take long to find a spot so filled with trees that the whistling wind carried hardly any snow. It was still bitter, though, so she draped him from ears to tail in the blanket, and in the absence of anything else to secure it to the horse's body used several hairpins like wire laces under his belly and at his neck. Only when she was convinced his new woolly coat was secure did she tie him to a low-hanging branch, then retrace her steps.

Dr Able, in a misplaced display of gentlemanliness, was waiting for her outside the curricle, stamping his feet, shivering. His greatcoat was so covered in snow it was white. Somehow he'd secured the blanket to the canopy tightly enough that it flexed around the perch but refused to budge, no matter how hard the wind slapped it. He insisted on helping her into their emergency camp, then quickly followed.

Impenetrable darkness engulfed them as he knotted the only gap in the blanket shut.

Even in their cocoon it was bitterly cold. So cold that there really was no choice but to snuggle together to share each other's warmth—which did nothing for her equilibrium at all. Her bosoms, especially, were misbehaving wildly against the solid wall of him. She had never been so aware of her wretched nipples in her life, thanks to all the cold and the need puckering them!

While her body was busy conjuring all manner of improper scenarios that wound her tighter than a spring, his was undeniably tense. Unflatteringly so—as if he couldn't imagine a worse possible scenario—which only served to make Rose feel more self-conscious. Awkwardness hung in the confined space like a shroud. So intense it almost overtook her scandalous awareness of her own bosoms.

She tried to ignore it for as long as she could, but when her toes began to curl inside her cramped slippers, from cringing more than from the cold, she had to break the uncomfortable tension. Maybe some conversation would help take her mind off *things*?

'Perhaps, with hindsight, you were right and I should have gone straight home after the assembly.'

'I did warn you on your own head be it.'

She didn't need to see his droll expression to picture it. He was the king of the I-told-you-so glare.

'You could be curled up in bed right now, a fire roaring in the grate, safe in the arms of Morpheus. But instead you are stranded for goodness knows how long in the middle of nowhere. Both of us stinking of the stable and with no supplies beyond some foul-tasting medicines and a dozen raw eggs.'

'But at least I am not still draped in inappropriate silk, Dr Able, so every cloud...' She couldn't help finding that tiny consolation funny. Hilarious, in fact. Although she had no earthly idea why when there was a very real possibility of them both freezing to death here in the middle of nowhere in the middle of the night.

'You really do have a warped sense of humour, don't you, Miss Healy?'

But because laughter was infectious, he was now chuckling too.

'Laugh and the world laughs with you, Dr Able. Cry and you cry alone.'

It was an ethereal grey inside the curricle when Rose awoke with a start. At some point after their breath had banished most of the chill from inside their cocoon they both must have nodded off. Then clearly she had snuggled closer to keep warm, as her head was resting on his chest and his arm was draped around her shoulders, the gentle heat of his big palm resting on the flare of her hip. Her own hand had burrowed into his great-coat and had settled on his heart. The steady, slow beat beneath her fingers suggested he was still fast asleep.

She stealthily tried to extricate herself from his embrace, but he stirred with her first movement, muttering nonsense. His arm then tightened around her as he buried his nose in her hair. He sighed contentedly—then stiffened to granite when he realised with whom he was so intimately entwined.

Rather than have that awkward conversation, Rose briskly sat up to open the blanket. As her eyes adjusted to the change she was alarmed to see it was neither dark nor light outside, but at least the wind had gone. Dawn hovered dangerously close, which meant they must have slept for hours, but was still a little while away, thank goodness! The last thing either of them needed was returning to the village in daylight. It was one thing to be irrevocably tarnished by a jilting, another entirely to be compromised into complete ruination.

'The good news is that the blizzard has stopped.' She stretched some of the aches out of her body rather than look at him. 'It's still snowing, but not enough to prevent us getting home. The bad news is that it's almost dawn.'

'Oh, good grief! It's blasted market day!'

It was obvious from his tone and the haste with which he ripped the blanket from the canopy that he had also realised their situation was precarious. The square was a flurry of activity on market days.

It seemed to take for ever to get the curricle back onto the lane, and thanks to hours and hours of snow which had settled thick the short journey back to Whittleston was hard yards. Both in effort and atmosphere.

The easy-going man she had laughed with only hours before had disappeared and was now replaced with one who was implacable and worried. His dark brows were furrowed as he steered them ever closer to the village.

'What time is it?'

The orange-purple hue on the edge of the horizon warned the night was near its end, but the soaring spire of St Hildreth's against it reassured her that their journey was almost over.

He fumbled beneath his greatcoat for his pocket watch, then squinted at the dial in the stingy light. 'A quarter to six.'

'Then all is not lost.' She reached over to touch his sleeve and retracted it immediately when his arm stiffened. 'We have at least half an hour before the first market traders start arriving. We should both be safely home by then.'

'Unless your aunt and uncle have raised the alarm and sent out a search party!'

'Don't be silly!' Such was her confidence in that, she laughed. 'Neither are early risers. They sleep like the dead, remember, and both took your sleeping draught.' A fact that she hoped she could rely on. 'But to be on the safe side, once we reach the outskirts I shall get out and use the back alley. I can sneak in through the kitchen door without setting a single foot in the square where anyone might see us together, whereas nobody will bat an eyelid and think that you have been out on a call.'

'And if your aunt and uncle hear you returning and demand an explanation?'

'Then I shall tell them the truth.' Panicking for no reason now was pointless.

'Telling them we spent the night together is bound to end well!'

'We helped a farmer with his horse, got caught in a blizzard and had to wait for it to pass! We did nothing wrong, Dr Able, beyond helping a family in need, and they would not dream of telling anyone if I asked them not to. My aunt might live for other people's gossip, but she would do anything to avoid being tainted by a scandal herself.'

He didn't look convinced. Instead, he stared straight ahead with a surly, tight expression as he snapped the reins. Maybe it was his anxiousness rather than a premonition, but the nearer they got to the village, the more uneasy she became too. No matter how much Rose tried to reassure herself that they were unlikely to see a soul this early, last night's blizzard complicated things. People would have to get up sooner to inspect the damage and shovel paths from their front doors or would set off early to go about their business to ensure they did not arrive late.

Before they turned onto the main road into Whittleston she was so unsettled she had to listen to her gut. 'Drop me here and I'll take the longer way home through the fields on foot.'

The fact that he immediately steered his curricle to the side of the lane told her he was panicking too. 'If you're sure.'

'It's the safest option. Nobody will raise an eyebrow if you return to the square at dawn. They will raise merry hell if I am beside you.'

She was several yards through the drifts before he called her back. 'You forgot your things!'

As they were her most intimate things, she was grateful for the reminder. The last thing she wanted was him finding the parcel in the footwell later and inadvertently seeing her unmentionables. She held out her arms and he tossed the loosely tied bundle. To humiliate her, a frigid gust of wind came from out of the blue, unravelling the bundle in mid-air and sending her unmentionables everywhere.

She waved him away, wanting him long gone for two reasons now, and not just her ruination, but he was up and out of the curricle before she could stop him, in hot pursuit of her stays which were now splayed across the spiky bare twigs of a dead piece of hedge. He clearly had no clue what he'd been chasing until he retrieved it, then quickly bundled it into his fist once he did.

Mortified, she grabbed one limp stocking from the snow as she watched him bend for the other. She'd gone to grab the intimate garments from his outstretched hand when her foot found a hole and she fell forward. He lunged to catch her and must have found the same void beneath the snow, because they slammed together. Being bigger, and heavier, gravity was on his side, sending her backwards before he landed atop her.

The collision winded them both. Enough that neither could move for several seconds after the impact. When they did, it was in a tangle of arms, legs and her evening cloak, until they both froze as they were suddenly bathed in light.

A light which was quickly extinguished by its wide-eyed bearer—Ned Parker. But not quickly enough for the group behind him not to have witnessed the pair of them rolling around in the snow together as they all raised their own lamps, illuminating them again.

'I told you they were probably off having a tryst!'

The accusation which came out of the dark was from Whittleston's postmaster.

'Now, George…' Ned spoke, his arms outstretched to hold everyone back, while Rose and the doctor scrambled to their feet and she righted her skirts. 'I am sure there is a perfectly reasonable explanation…thanks to the blizzard and all.'

'There is!' Dr Able was in a panic. 'The Dewhursts had trouble with a horse and Miss Healy accompanied me to help birth a foal who was stuck. She's a farmer's daughter and—'

It was her Uncle William who pushed passed Ned and stayed him with a growl. In the lantern's dim light Rose could see he was quaking with anger.

'You left the Dewhursts' at midnight!' He prodded the doctor in the chest. 'I know that for a fact because I've just came from the Dewhursts myself! What the blazes have you been doing with my niece in the hours since? And while you are about it, you opportunistic scoundrel, explain to me why you didn't bring her home directly after the assembly, as you were apparently tasked to do?'

'We got caught in the storm as soon as we left and had to shelter from it!'

'The blizzard had stopped by two.' By the look of Reverend Spears as he approached, he was already concerned for their immortal souls. 'We know because we've been searching high and low for Rose since Mr Outhwaite raised the alarm that she was missing at midnight. That leaves a lot of unaccounted-for hours, young man. A lot of unaccounted-for and unchaperoned hours.'

'Where did you seek shelter?' Uncle William's eyes

had narrowed to slits. 'And, for the love of God, pray tell with whom?'

'In Dr Able's curricle, Uncle.' Rose tried to pour oil on troubled waters by reaching for her relative, who had slumped at that news. 'On the edge of the lane between the two villages.'

'If that is the case, why did Lord Hockley and I not see you? Nor did anyone else who's been searching for you for the last several hours! Because there's not a single person between here and Hornchurch who has seen hide nor hair of you, and between us all we've knocked on every door and checked every outbuilding. Nobody except for the Dewhursts—who have also been out searching for you since we woke them up at half-past two!'

'The snow must have camouflaged us.'

'Did it render the pair of you deaf too? You must have heard us approach and pass. Twice! Heard us calling for you? And you didn't think to flag us down? Or were the pair of you too occupied with *other things* after all your waltzing to notice?'

'Now, Mr Outhwaite...' Rafe stepped into the fray, all reasonableness. 'You know snow dampens sound, and if the curricle was covered in it it's unlikely we would have seen them.'

'That doesn't explain why they didn't head back to the village the moment the blizzard stopped!' Her uncle prodded the doctor again. 'What the bloody hell were you doing with my niece for all those hours?'

'Nothing untoward, if that is your implication! We waited for a good hour to no avail before we fell asleep and—'

'A likely story.' Uncle William held the lamp directly

in front of Dr Able's face so he could look him in the eyes. 'When we all saw the way you were fawning over her at the assembly!'

'He's definitely had his beady eyes on your Rose for a while now,' said the postmaster unhelpfully. 'Enough that we've all put a bet on them courting.'

'Courting involves doing things above-board and respectfully!' Uncle William invaded the doctor's space again, snarling. 'Not sneaking off to do dark deeds!'

'I trusted you, Dr Able!' Poor Archie was distraught and close to tears. 'I trusted you to get Rose home safe and you let me down!'

'I didn't, Archie. I promise. Miss Healy was practically home when Ted found us, and then…'

'I insisted on accompanying him to save the foal.' Rose addressed the whole crowd, seeing as they were all so whipped up they were baying for blood. 'Dr Able's knowledge of horses is limited and as a farmer's daughter I know more. Everything he has said is the truth. I swear it. He has been nothing but the perfect gentleman. The blizzard forced us off the road, and we both nodded off while we waited, but headed home as soon as we awoke.'

'Home is that way.' Uncle William jerked his lamp back towards the lane. 'So what were you doing in this field?'

'Well…' She could hardly say they'd been trying to avoid a scandal by sneaking home through the back fields as that would make it sound as if they weren't innocent. 'Um…'

Uncle William lifted the light to glare at the doctor again, and as he dropped it, it illuminated her stays, which were hanging from one of the buttons of his greatcoat.

'And why the blazes aren't those attached to your person?'

As all the onlookers gasped, her uncle's eyes widened like saucers.

'I can explain!'

But it was too late. Her uncle's fist was already flying towards Dr Able's chin. 'You filthy libertine!'

Chapter Eight

The lord of the manor placed a stiff brandy at his elbow and sighed. 'Whichever way you view it, it doesn't look good.'

Before Sam could be hung from the nearest tree by the angry mob, Rafe had bundled him and Rose into his carriage and driven them at speed to Hockley Hall while Ned did his best to calm everybody down. Which, of course, hadn't worked at all. Hence Ned was now at Hockley Hall too, braced for round two, and Sam was sitting with his head in his hands, his nose intermittently still bleeding.

'In the grand scheme of things, it doesn't really matter how innocently you came by Rose's stays. You still spent the entire night alone with her in your curricle while she wasn't wearing them. She's been comprised figuratively if not literally.'

'So now, despite being innocent of any wrongdoing whatsoever, I am expected to marry her? When I repeatedly cautioned her against coming with me for precisely that reason and she flatly refused to listen.'

Why had he allowed her to convince him?

Because he'd idiotically enjoyed her company and now he was paying the price!

'No,' said Ned with his typical gruffness. 'You could refuse to do the decent thing and she'll just have to suffer being ruined for life for, ironically, doing the decent thing by the Dewhursts. You'll have to move your entire practice elsewhere, of course, as no decent person within a fifty-mile radius will want anything to do with a libertine physician with no scruples nor morals. Especially if they have womenfolk to protect.'

'There was a bloody blizzard, for pity's sake, and I never laid a finger on her!' Although his fingers had itched to touch her when they had been all alone out there, snuggled together, and that scared the hell out him.

'Yet everyone saw her flat on her back, skirts around her waist, while you were fumbling on top of her.' Ned was matter-of-fact.

'Not to mention the stays swinging from your coat.' Rafe winced in sympathy. 'Or the silk stocking dangling from your fingers. People don't always believe what they see, Sam, but they always *see* what they believe, and apart from me and Ned here, they all *saw* a night of unbridled passion and seduction.'

'Never mind that any attempted seduction in all that snow would have likely left all my seduction equipment frostbitten and in real danger of dropping off!' Sam gestured to his groin, which had been annoyingly less dead than the rest of him of late because of her. Another reason why he had to get out of this. Miss Healy somehow called to a part of him that he had forgotten existed. 'It would make no sense for me to do the deed out in the elements in a field next to the village when I

could have done that more effectively and less dangerously within the curricle, hidden on the side of the lane!'

'Oh, they think you did that too,' said Rafe with another wince, 'which doubtless makes you an *insatiable*
libertine too, and is somehow worse.'

'Besides, everyone knows that when the passion is
mutual, the mood strikes and an opportunity presents itself…' Ned pulled a guilty face. 'Well, a bit of snow isn't
going to stop it, now, is it? It certainly wouldn't stop me.'

'Me neither,' said Rafe. 'And Whittleston-on-the-Water is blessed with a glut of similarly happily married
couples who will think much the same. After all, nothing gets the blood pumping and warms you up quicker
than a bit of—'

'Stop!' At this rate he'd be standing at the altar by
lunchtime! 'I do not want to marry Miss Healy.'

He couldn't marry. Not again.

Never again!

The very thought of the responsibility of another
wife—another life—was making him nauseous. He
was sweating like a pig, so dizzy he could barely lift
his head, and his shrivelled heart was racing so much
he genuinely feared an imminent heart attack! Or perhaps he was about to have a stroke? Certainly the loud,
ominous throb in his head wasn't normal.

'I can honestly think of nothing more abhorrent than
marrying Miss Healy.'

'That feeling is entirely mutual, I can assure you, Dr
Able! And rest assured I would not marry you if I had
a gun to my head and you were the last man on earth!
That is how abhorrent I find you!'

He managed to haul his spinning head up in time to

see her spin on her heel and march off while his two companions visibly cringed.

Sam glared at them, despite his roiling stomach. 'You might have mentioned she was behind me!'

'In our defence, we didn't realise she was until she spoke.' Rafe dropped his own head into his hands. 'Did you have to say abhorrent? Abhorrent is so... Good grief, poor Rose.'

'When I said abhorrent...'

How to explain why this was all so visceral and un-thinkable to him without opening the Pandora's box of hideous emotions he kept locked away to stay sane? If he didn't, then he risked the volcano erupting again, and if it did, who knew how many months it would take to cap it and end the madness?

'It was more about the situation than the woman.'

A lie—because it had a great deal to do with the woman too. Because she was leaving he had let his ironclad guard down enough that he had allowed him-self to like Miss Healy. Worse, he had allowed himself to enjoy their time together. He enjoyed their chats. He enjoyed her humour. Her irreverent take on things. He really enjoyed her mischievous side, perhaps because it felt so familiar and...appealing. He also, undeniably, found her physically appealing, so all in all she was a dangerous combination. Especially if she did not leave as he had been banking on her doing!

'I cannot marry again! Under any circumstances. It would...'

As the long-forgotten remnants of his dinner threat-ened to make an immediate reappearance, so too did Miss Healy's three friends. Sophie and Isobel looked ready to flail the skin from his bones, while Mrs Fitzherbert wielded her cane as if she fully intended to skewer his carcass on it once they were done with it.

'Excuse my language, Dr Able, but you are a cad!' Rafe's wife was quivering with indignation.

'He's worse than a cad.' Isobel's finger was wagging so fast it blurred. 'He's a scoundrel. An unconscionable, unfeeling, inhuman...'

'You are a callous bastard, Dr Able!' The tip of Mrs Fitzherbert's cane jabbed him hard in the ribs. 'Do you have no care at all for Rose's feelings?'

'When I said abhorrent...' Good Lord, but that really was an awful choice of word! 'I was referring to—'

'You didn't find her abhorrent when you waltzed with her last night!' The old lady's cane jabbed him again. 'Then you looked at her like a mouthwatering tart in the baker's window! What sort of despicable rogue makes a big show of fawning all over a woman, publicly beds her, and then refuses to do the right thing by her?'

'The sort who was only flirting with her to win the village pot, that's who!' As they all gaped in shock, he elaborated. 'It was Miss Healy's idea. We have an anonymised but substantial bet laid upon us *not* getting married and she thought we'd win more money if we were able to convince you all that we might.'

A devious plan that had been all hers and he now wished he'd had the good sense to have nothing to do with. He had allowed himself to be talked into her machinations, seduced by the thought of fun, and now he was expected to pay the ultimate price. For something that wasn't his fault! For something he had cautioned her against! Tried to stop her from doing! But she had blithely ignored his feelings, and now he was also supposed to ignore all his feelings to think of hers!

Like a wild animal caught in a trap, he was sorely tempted to gnaw his own foot off to escape it. 'Aside from waltzing with her, I've not laid a finger on her. We went to the Dewhursts to attend a horse, got caught in a blizzard, waited it out and then returned here as soon as we could. All facts which I am sure she will gladly corroborate if you ask her.'

'But you waited that blizzard out for several hours longer than you needed too, Sam, and it is those missing hours which are the crux of the matter.' Rafe was pacing now. 'What possessed you to take a last-minute detour into that field we found you on rather than brazenly driving into the village like two completely innocent people would have after such an ordeal?'

'I appreciate the field debacle looks bad, but…'

He was about to blame Miss Healy for that gross error of judgement too, but stopped himself because that wasn't fair. He'd been all for it at the time and, in her defence, if they hadn't got caught and she'd made it home through the back alley as she had intended, they wouldn't all be sitting here now.

'We knew people were likely to think the worst, and tried to mitigate against any gossip by splitting up so she could get home unseen.'

'Except you didn't split up and you were seen.' Ned punctuated the air with his finger. 'Seen doing things which would encourage anyone to think the worst.'

'I was helping her up after we both fell!'

'I'm sure you were.' Finally, Ned offered him one small concession. 'But it didn't look like that. In truth, I flung my lamp into the hedge because I was convinced we'd caught the pair of you at it. Her skirts were around her waist and you were between her legs.'

'For mere seconds.'

'For some exceptionally disappointing men seconds is all it needs.' Mrs Fitzherbert's disgusted shake of her head shocked them all, but she shrugged, unrepentant. 'It's not the length of time you were between Rose's legs that is the issue here, Doctor, it is the suspected length you slipped between them!'

'How many times do I have to tell you all the truth before you'll believe it?'

'I do believe it.' That also came from Mrs Fitzherbert. 'For truth is always stranger than fiction and your story matches Rose's completely.'

'Then, for the sake of reason and fairness, surely there has to be a compromise here?'

'The compromising has already been done!' Mrs Fitzherbert's cane thudded against the parquet. 'And what is done cannot be undone. It can only be atoned for!'

'Twenty people saw you atop her in the snow. Even if you can convince three-quarters of them that it was an accident, one quarter will always label you a shameless libertine and Rose a fallen woman.' Rafe stopped pacing and slumped into a chair with a huff. 'Mud sticks. The only way to unstick it and prevent your mutual ruination is to make yourselves respectable again by marrying. Like Ned did after he'd publicly ruined Isobel.'

'But Ned had actually ruined Isobel, in the literal as well as figurative sense, whereas I've not laid a finger on Miss Healy!'

'In view of last night's events, I think you should address her by her Christian name.' Sophie sat deflated beside her husband. 'You have been intimately entwined, after all. Albeit by accident.'

Despite his nausea, it was Sam's turn to pace. Waving his arms in the air in utter frustration to stop the walls from closing in. 'Surely the truth has to stand for something? Surely this village is capable of reason if the facts are laid out for all to scrutinise? Even a criminal is afforded a trial before a guilty verdict, and there is a glut of evidence that proves I am telling the truth. Or would they really rather watch two innocent people forced into the most miserable marriage imaginable purely for appearances' sake?'

'My lord…' Walpole, Hockley Hall's butler, made his presence known with a polite cough and a pained look towards Rafe. 'Mr Outhwaite is in the hallway and is demanding an immediate audience with Dr Able, while Miss Healy is donning her coat and demanding he take her home forthwith.'

'Then stop her and let him in.' Rafe didn't hesitate, despite Sam's groan. 'We need a definitive plan of action before anyone leaves.'

'Probably best to check he's not brought his pistols with him before you let him in, though,' added Ned unhelpfully. 'And maybe put a generous tot of brandy in Mr Outhwaite's tea to make him more amenable too, as the poor fellow isn't going to like what he is apparently going to hear from the doctor, who finds his niece abhorrent.'

It was said as a jibe, because Ned and Rose were good friends, and Sam took it as such.

'I am not going to be bullied down the aisle, Ned! Because I can assure that would be a massive mistake. One that would ruin her life!'

His was ruined anyway, and it had taken years to scrape enough of him together to function as well as he did. But he no longer functioned as he had. To keep going, to move forward, he'd had to close off all the vulnerable parts of himself. Banish all threat of the complicated and deep emotions which had ripped him apart. Husks didn't need to feel, they just needed to do until the doing was done. Sam was no longer capable of being a good husband. Or even of being a mediocre one. Wasn't capable of caring—not even slightly. He also wasn't willing to take on the responsibility of another person in his life. Couldn't! Wouldn't! His stomach churned again at the thought.

'In case it's escaped your notice, hers is already ruined, you selfish bastard!' Ned loomed, fists clenched. 'And she doesn't deserve that! If you are half the man we all hope you are, you'll step up and fix that!'

'She certainly doesn't deserve a future with me!' Sam's own fists clenched as his temper bubbled ominously. 'I wouldn't wish that living hell on anyone!'

Walpole reappeared again, looking anxious. 'I have put Miss Healy and her uncle in the morning room, where there is already shouting, my lord.'

Rafe stood to deal with that but Sam shook his head, forcing the anger back inside before years of pent-up fury and frustration escaped and consumed him again. 'This is my problem to sort. Mine and…hers.'

Although how they were going to sort it was a mystery when even the most reasonable residents of Whittleston clearly demanded a wedding. *Habeas corpus* certainly didn't seem to exist, because they had already been tried in the court of public opinion.

On leaden feet he left, and took a deep breath before knocking.

'Who is it?'

She sounded livid and he couldn't blame her.

'Me.'

He entered the room and closed the door behind him.

Mr Outhwaite was seated with a face like thunder. Miss Healy was standing, her hands clenched by her sides, her jaw set and her eyes red-rimmed. A sure sign that despite her defiant pride she had shed tears over their predicament—and perhaps his splendid misuse of the word abhorrent—but had wiped them away for this confrontation.

'My niece has informed me that a wedding is out of the question!'

'We did nothing wrong, sir.' Some deference seemed appropriate, despite the aggression in the older man's voice. 'Beyond attend to a distressed horse in the next village.'

'I beg to differ, sir!' Mr Outhwaite's eyes bulged. 'You were gone all night! Unchaperoned! Found intimately entwined!'

'And all those things have a perfectly reasonable explanation.'

There was no point shouting about it. Now that his anger was locked firmly back in its prison, where it belonged, Sam had enough of his wits left to know that oil needed to be poured on these troubled waters—fast— if they stood any chance of repairing the damage. Mr Outhwaite was one of the most important residents of the village, who needed to be convinced, so Sam sat.

'However, I do appreciate that we did, rather short-sightedly, behave recklessly when we went to attend the horse without a proper chaperon, and with hindsight we should have stayed with the Dewhursts until morning for exactly the same reason. As a result, we have now created an incorrect perception which we would beg you to help us change.'

He was being rather fast and lose with the 'we', but Rose didn't contradict him. Instead, without glancing his way she reiterated his point.

'I do not want to marry Dr Able, Uncle. Especially when all we are guilty of is being good Samaritans. As ill-considered as our unchaperoned trip to Little Ramstead was, it was done with the best intentions. I knew that I had the knowledge and skills necessary to birth the foal, so I argued with the doctor to take me there. I also threatened to go alone if he didn't, and then I panicked on the way home, insisting on leaving his conveyance in order to sneak around the back of the house. I was the one who fell and took him with me, and I convinced him to pretend to have some interest in me to win the bet, as I have just explained, so none of this is really his fault at all.'

'That's as maybe, but—'

She cut Mr Outhwaite off by kneeling before him and gripping his hand. 'Please try to help us get out of this! I cannot go from being jilted by one man who did not love me to being forced down the aisle with another who also doesn't. Have I not already suffered enough?'

'Well... I...'

'Dr Able and I are little more than acquaintances and totally incompatible. Expecting us to marry when my heart is still broken and he is still deeply in love with his dead wife is a recipe for disaster. Such a marriage is doomed from the outset to be miserable, and the only feelings that will flourish between us will be resentment and hatred. I know this is a dreadful scandal, Uncle, but scandals pass. This one will pass swiftly enough if we all hold our nerve and stick to the truth for the next few weeks, until Aunt Agatha is recovered enough for me to return to Suffolk.'

'And if the scandal follows you to Suffolk or, worse, beats you there? Then what, Rose?'

'Then we shall cross that bridge when we come to it. But I sincerely believe it will be little more than a ripple than a wave by the time it reaches there. Nothing more than a storm in a teacup.' Her forced smile was brave, if not reassuring. 'In less than three weeks I'll be gone anyway, so this will die a natural death here when I am out of sight and out of mind. We can all weather three weeks, surely?'

'Do you seriously think we can convince the entire village that what a significant number of reliable witnesses saw was completely innocent when it looked nothing of the sort?' Mr Outhwaite had gone from being angry to incredulous.

'Why not? Everyone under this roof believes us. You believe us. There's a newborn foal in the Dewhursts' stable that confirms at least half of the truth already. The constable will corroborate that we put a substantial bet on ourselves not marrying because he placed it for us, and it makes no sense that we would do that unless we meant it. Therefore, if Dr Able and I carry on as if nothing happened and we have nothing to be ashamed of beyond our lamentable disregard for society's rules, everyone will see that there is no attraction or romantic feelings between us. Isn't that right, Doctor?'

'It is certainly worth a try.'

While Sam was no longer capable of romantic feelings, it felt wrong to deny there was any attraction when he did feel that, regardless of how dead inside he wanted to be.

'It probably won't be easy to change minds—but it certainly isn't impossible. Especially if you lead the charge, sir.'

Like his wife, Mr Outhwaite was convinced he was widely respected. To be fair to him, as the proprietor of the *South Essex Gazette*, he was. He published a respectable paper filled with actual news and not salacious gossip, like the majority of the local rags did, and everybody hereabouts read it because of that.

'He's right, Uncle. If you appear wholly convinced of our innocence and swat away any criticism with good grace and humour, people might soon realise that Dr Able and I are as innocent as we claim.'

'We could try...' The older man wavered under his niece's pleading gaze, but his own gaze turned steely when it latched onto Sam's. 'But if it doesn't work I will expect you to step up, Doctor, and rectify this travesty in front of everyone in the church.'

'And I will.'

An affirmation that chilled Sam's blood and shocked Miss Healy enough that her mouth gaped.

'I am a man of honour and will not see your niece disgraced. However, I hope for her sake that this plan works as she deserves far better than I could ever give her.'

Before she left here, she also deserved to know why any union between them had to be a last resort. If the unthinkable happened and he had to walk her down the aisle, she had a right to know upfront what she was letting herself in for.

'I would be grateful, sir, if you would grant me a few minutes alone with your niece to apologise properly for what has happened?'

Chapter Nine

No sooner had her uncle left the room than the doctor's hazel eyes seemed to bore into her soul. There was a myriad of complex emotions swirling within them—all of them so sad she forgot to be angry at him for his cruel 'abhorrent' comment.

'I know this is all my fault, so if anyone should apologise for what has happened it is I.'

Rose was kicking herself at her own stupidity. Dr Able had tried to resist everything—from the bet to the fake flirting to the unchaperoned dash to save a horse—and she had trampled over his reluctance to do what she wanted instead.

'You did warn me on my own head be it, and you were right. You shouldn't have to pay for a mistake that was of all my making, so if the villagers here refuse to believe the truth I shall leave. Even if news of my stupidity reaches Suffolk, it will be less of a scandal there. It will all be hearsay, and such nonsense fades. Please do not worry that you will be stuck with me for all eternity, Dr Able, as I shall fix this.'

He didn't seem to find any reassurance in her words, and his expression became bleaker as he sat and gestured to her to do the same. Which she did, with a peculiar sense of unease.

'When I couldn't save Catherine I didn't want to live. There seemed no point in carrying on when she was my world. That same afternoon I drank two bottles of laudanum, lay down on the bed beside her and prayed that I wouldn't wake up.' He swallowed, his expression sad. 'Unfortunately, thanks to a much too good physician whom I have never forgiven, I did, and the army kept me under constant watch for two months to ensure that I couldn't find another way to join her in heaven. To thwart them, I applied for a transfer to the front, where I assured them that I would cope with my grief better if I could be kept busy. I was sent to follow Wellington, and immediately, rather than use them exclusively in the field hospital, I took my skills onto the battlefield. Preferring to treat the injured in the midst of the fray ostensibly to save more lives, but in reality simply to bring an end to mine.'

It was said so matter-of-factly, she realised he still regretted his end hadn't come.

'Each time I rushed in I prayed for a stray bullet or bayonet to find me and did nothing to save myself from any that came close. The sweet release of potential annihilation became the thing that kept me going, the only balm to the anger and pain which consumed me, and perversely I looked forward to every battle hoping that it would be my last. Sadly, fate continued to be cruel and kept me safe. For all my determined recklessness, I do not think that I even incurred a single scratch.'

His broad shoulders slumped, as if he still considered that a travesty, and Rose's heart bled for him.

She bit her tongue rather than tell him all the trite

things people said about grief. About time healing all
wounds and life going on, or that he clearly hadn't been
taken because fate knew he made a difference in the
world and clearly had other, hopefully less cruel plans
for him. Or even to take some comfort that his beloved
Catherine had gone to a better place. Better it allegedly
might be, but she was sure that if Catherine had loved
Dr Able as much as he clearly loved her, then she would
consider no place better than being by his side. How
wonderful and empowering it must be to be so adored…

Sadly, it was not something to which she could re-
late as, while she had loved with her whole heart, and
deeply, she understood now that it had not been recip-
rocated.

Rose also knew that while time probably—eventually
—did heal most things, there were some things a person just couldn't get over in mere months or years. Like
watching the centre of your universe die and not being
able to do a thing to stop it. There was no denying that
his wounds were so deep they made hers seem trifling.
It was almost inconceivable to contemplate what he'd
had to suffer.

Rather than resort to meaningless platitudes, she
reached across to stroke his hand, but he was so lost in
his own misery he did not appear to notice.

'When Waterloo failed to reward me with my last
chance to meet my maker, I briefly turned to drink to
numb my pain—except it didn't. Therefore I had to do
something more drastic. I had to kill that part of me
that feels. At least the part that feels anything beyond
the superficial. Being dead inside is the only way for
me to remain sane and…to continue.'

He twisted his palm up to hold her hand, sending

a jolt of awareness through her arm the moment their fingertips touched, then frowned down at it as if he had felt it too.

Although how could he if he were dead inside?

Perhaps the frown, like the devastation in his gaze, was merely further confirmation of his state of being. Perhaps he felt nothing, exactly as he claimed. And that felt like the saddest thing she had ever heard.

His attempt at a smile was more a tortured grimace, and even that seemed to take too much effort. It was then she realised that he was affording her a great privilege. He was allowing her to witness the real him, behind the façade of capable, no-nonsense, all-business doctor. It wasn't only his shoulders that had slumped…it was his entire being. The light in his eyes had dimmed. Deep lines of grief and guilt were etched upon his handsome face. Utter despondency and hopelessness manifested in physical form. So more intense and real than hers it made her ashamed for ever indulging in a moment of self-pity at the piffling inconvenience of being jilted.

She squeezed his hand tight, to give him some of her strength, because he appeared to need it in this tragic moment so much more than she did. 'There are many of us who are eternally grateful that you decided to continue. This village would be lost without you.'

'And I would be lost without this village. It gives me purpose—and that is all I have left nowadays.' His sigh was long and laboured. 'That is why I said that I can honestly think of nothing more abhorrent than marrying you. Because I am gratefully dead inside, Rose, and am not prepared to risk a resurrection under any circumstances. Catherine's death shattered me and scattered me into a million bloody pieces. I spent years in the most wretched, raging purgatory imaginable, trying to piece together enough of that mess to continue, and I do not have it in me to face anything like that again. You do not deserve being shackled to a man who cannot—nay, *will* not—care for you in any way beyond the superficial. I have no heart left to give you and no desire to imagine any sort of future, let alone one involving another. I live from day to day. Exist in the here and now. I left the best of me, the entire essence of me, in a sickroom in Lisbon, and all that is left now is genuinely what you see. A dry husk with a glut of medical skills that might save some and not save others, who uses them to pass the time and thus give himself some blessed relief from remembering.'

He stared into nothing for several, long seconds, then seemed to become self-conscious.

'Anyway… I wanted you to know why I would rather avoid ruining your life too. I am not, by nature, a cruel man, but fear I would be cruel with my determined indifference. There is nothing left inside me for more.'

He released her hand and moved to get up, but she touched his knee to stay him.

'Why couldn't you save her?'

It was a direct and intensely personal question, but one Rose needed to know the answer to. She suspected that he did too. It was obvious he was riddled with guilt and wanted to blame himself for her death. Maybe he deserved to? In his panic to heal her, maybe he had missed something? But she could not imagine that. He was too good at what he did not to have exhausted every possible avenue back in that sickroom in Lisbon, and his love was obviously so deep he would have moved heaven and earth to do so.

His nose wrinkled, and for a moment she thought he would seal up tighter than a drum. But he didn't. Instead, he took a deep, centring breath.

'Typhus is a contrary beast. It spreads with selective impunity and infects some more mildly than it does others. One hundred and fifty people were its victims back in Lisbon that summer. It did its worst, in varying degrees of severity, and spared a hundred and two. My darling wife was the final one of the forty-eight who perished. They kept telling me that there was no rhyme or reason to it and that we'd done all that we could—but how could it spare lesser individuals? Drunkards and layabouts lived to tell the tale and yet it took my Catherine. My effervescent and irrepressible girl. Who never did anything except spread sunshine and laughter and was never ill a day in her life before.'

His voice caught and that forced a huge change in him, because he surged to his feet. Stiff and jerky, as if every muscle and sinew was pulled taut.

Then he visibly went to war with himself, and Rose watched him fight all that raw emotion back inside. Within moments he was the no-nonsense physician again, completely in control.

'I trust that all I have shared with you will remain confidential, as I would prefer not to be the subject of gossip. At least more gossip than I fear we are both already about to be subjected to.'

'Of course.' She was touched and humbled that he had confided in her. 'Your past, like mine, is nobody else's business. But if you ever need to…talk… Sam…' They were so beyond mere acquaintances now that any formality seemed pathetic. 'Please know that you have a friend in me.'

He nodded, still awkward. 'Let us pray, for your sake, that your plan works, as I wouldn't wish what's left of me on anyone.'

Rose screwed up the note and tried not to feel upset by it. That was hard when it was the third such missive she had received in the last three days. Except this one had been poked into the thin gap under the front door by Mrs Spears, the Reverend's wife. A woman who was supposed to believe in the concept of forgiveness and of not casting the first stone! While that in itself was galling enough, and while the Reverend's wife had been the one to write it, it had actually come from the entire Friday Sewing Circle, who thought it best that she stayed away until the dust had settled.

Mrs Spears had penned the note in her small, neat handwriting.

> *Some of the ladies are worried about the message it sends to their own single daughters, to readily condone your regrettable lapse in judgement and decorum so soon without any apparent censure at all.*

As three-quarters of the sewing circle had made a point of crossing the road rather than speak to her since her 'regrettable lapse', she wasn't surprised her invitation had been rescinded, but it still stung.

Less than a week ago, and after six months of religiously attending the circle every single Friday since she had arrived in the village, she had counted most of those women as more than acquaintances. As such, she would have expected them to be on her side, or at the very least, as women, to have some sympathy for her unfortunate situation.

But no. She had been caught with a man between her legs, so obviously she was a harlot, just as it was somehow her fault that her former fiancé had replaced her. Women always held other women to a ridiculously higher standard than they did men. Probably because their reputations were so much more tenuous and easily destroyed. Women were also more spiteful than men, even if the initial censure had come from a man, which was why, every time one of those suddenly pious ladies crossed the road or cancelled her invitation to tea, they made an unsubtle point of muttering their abject disapproval to whoever they happened to pass. As if being a harlot were contagious, and any contact with her might label them fallen women too.

There were still those who were polite, but as those also scurried quickly by without meeting her eye they hardly counted as allies. Which left her with just Sophie, Isobel and Mrs Fitzherbert, who religiously took it in turns to call upon her and insisted on accompanying her into the square because they believed that her failure to hide would prove that she had nothing to hide.

Rose didn't hold out much hope that they were right, and feared that she would end up leaving here at Christmas as much a social pariah then as she was now.

She couldn't help wondering if Sam was suffering the same.

Or wondering about him in general and constantly since their *'incident'*.

People flung about the term 'a broken man', but it

was an apt description of him. Dr Samuel Able was a broken man, and she hated it that he seemed content to remain one. As if all his guilt and pain was his penance and that all he deserved to look forward to for the rest of his life was to work his fingers to the bone to heal the pain of others.

And work his fingers to the bone he did!

They might have been avoiding one another all week, while the dust apparently settled, but she had taken a keener interest in his punishing schedule now that she had had a window into his soul. It was easy to keep track of his comings and goings when his practice was a mere hundred yards across the square. Perfect for peeking at through the fussy lace curtains of her bed-chamber window. Sam certainly kept irregular hours. Even if he wasn't roused in the middle of the night for an emergency, he still visited his patients until late. Once his morning surgery finished at noon, he was off. Returning only to replenish his supplies once or twice over the course of the afternoon. He usually came home for an hour around six, where she presumed he ate what he needed to keep going, and then he was off again. As his practice covered not only Whittleston-on-the-Water but three of the much smaller outlying villages too, he did many miles in his curricle every day.

The mantel clock chimed noon and, without think-ing, Rose edged towards the parlour window. Clearly his morning surgery had ended on time, because she didn't have to linger for more than a few minutes before he emerged from his door, bound for who knew where. Looking all handsome and capable on the outside but so achingly vulnerable on the inside that it—

'Can I have a word, Rose?'

She had been so engrossed in her contemplation of the troubled doctor she hadn't heard anyone approach, and jumped with a guilty squeak. 'Uncle William! Shouldn't you be at the newspaper?'

A creature of habit, he usually returned for luncheon every day at one, so it was unusual that he was here an hour early.

'I'm afraid…' his expression was grave '…our worst fears to have come to pass.' He produced a folded newspaper. 'This arrived on the morning post. It is from Suffolk. I can only assume that news of your…um… misfortune has travelled back via the same method and your former fiancé's influential father has twisted it ruthlessly to his duplicitous son's advantage.'

The second she opened the paper her heart sank.

The *Suffolk Sentinel* was a tawdry rag that thrived on local gossip and frequently printed scurrilous stories for the titillation of the entire county. They had gone to town when the news of her jilting had reached their ears, painting her—in the guise of 'the unfortunate Miss H'—as a nice but dim woman who hadn't had the good sense to realise what everyone else already knew until her man and his lover had fled for Gretna. While there had undoubtedly been more than a grain of truth in that depiction, because only she had been blindsided by that betrayal, they had printed all manner of falsehoods since. Falsehoods which had obviously then been enshrined as fact. Especially once her former fiancé's father, who leased the *Sentinel* their building, applied some pressure on them.

The newspaper had led the charge to *'gently'* assassinate her character. In the immediate aftermath of the jilting they had printed several hurtful pieces to try to sway public opinion her former fiancé's way. One story had claimed he'd got cold feet because he had suspected that she was a fortune-hunter and actually had no real regard for him. Another that there was something 'not quite right' about her, although it was unsurprisingly vague about what that was. Whatever it was, her former fiancé was apparently 'too much of a gentleman' to embarrass her by voicing it—which was laughable when he hadn't so much embarrassed her as utterly humiliated her without saying a word! But this unspoken flaw was concerning enough that it had sent her beau running for the hills. And who could blame a man with such glittering prospects for not wanting to be saddled with that? The most hurtful story had implied that she was barren and had been concealing that from him. That one had come out to coincide with the announcement that the cheating wretch and his two-faced spouse were expecting their first child. It had been too coincidental not to have been intentional, and too cruel not to have had a profound effect on her, when he knew that she had been eager to become a mother.

Like a trickle of water over rock, each of those stories had gradually begun to wear away at their readers, and she had become more and more pitiable in the eyes of her neighbours and that had been truly soul-destroying. Just like the members of the sewing circle, acquaintances began to talk to her differently—or not talk to her at all—and she had frequently been the object of all those side-whispered conversations that were had when people suspected more was going on than met the eye.

Therefore, in many ways, the *Suffolk Sentinel* was as

much to blame for Rose's escape to Whittleston as the prospect of the impending birth had been.

She had hoped they would have forgotten 'the unfortunate Miss H' after six and half months of absence, but three pages in it became clear that she was wrong. The news of her ruination, even seventy miles away, was just too good not to use to over-embellish and further the ludicrous lies that had justified her former fiancé's betrayal.

The sleepy Essex village of Whittleston-on-the-Water is abuzz with scandal, thanks to a certain Suffolk native who is no stranger to these pages. After scaring off one eminent and monied gentleman almost a year to the day, the jilted Miss was obviously keen to secure herself another potential benefactor as soon as possible. When all conventional means failed to attract one, we now hear that, like Delilah did Samson, this forsaken spinster used her charms to lure a respected physician into her lacklustre web of seduction.

The full details of that seduction are too scandalous for us to print here, however, we have it on the highest authority that she spent a whole evening flirting with her latest target at a dance and then managed to entice the gentleman away for the entire night afterwards!

But that is not all the desperate Suffolk resident did to secure a betrothal, for she shamelessly importuned him again and on purpose in a public place the following dawn, ensuring they were caught in the midst of a tryst!

However, despite her determined efforts, her

wanton machinations have rather backfired as the gentleman concerned, while happy to sample her wares as any man served them on a platter would, has flatly refused to be honourable about it. And why should he when she went out of her way to entrap him? He has, rightly, called foul and has declared that he will not wed the pitiable wench for all the tea in China, no matter what the consequences!

We await, with bated breath, her family's reaction. Will there be pistols at dawn in Whittleston-on-the-Water followed by a reluctant groom at the altar? Or, as we suspect, will the unfortunate and unweddable Miss H remain discarded and ring-less for the second time in just twelve months?

'Oh, good grief!' Her head spinning and with bile rising in her throat, Rose groped for a chair. 'My mother and father will have read this!'

A quick glance at the newspaper's date confirmed they would have seen it two days ago—before her own letter of explanation had arrived in case word of her indiscretion made its way down the Colchester Turnpike. A letter she had foolishly dithered over writing because it had been difficult to explain to them how she and Sam had had their infamous dawn accident while still ensuring the quite damning series of events sounded completely innocent.

'I fear they have.'

'But how did all that rot reach Suffolk so fast?'

Her uncle laid a heavy hand on her shoulder. 'Nothing travels faster than bad news, and the post travels through here daily. All it takes is one careless word—'

'Whoever gave them this awful story said more than one careless word! They eviscerated me!'

Furious at that faceless, spiteful gossip, she abandoned her chair to pace. 'If it wasn't bad enough that I am seen as a fallen woman here, I am now Delilah in Suffolk!' And as she was not currently in Suffolk, to accuse the *Sentinel* of the most outrageous libel, the story would fester and grow like a malignant tumour.

'What am I going to do?'

'I think, in the first instance, we need to urgently summon your parents, and in the second...' Uncle William had the good grace to blanch before he said it. 'We need, with all haste, to revisit the prospect of you and Dr Able tying the knot.'

Chapter Ten

'You are going to have to take my word for it that my daughter's cough is better, sir, as I cannot, in all good conscience, have a scoundrel like *you* examine her ever again!'

With that, the farmer's wife slammed the door in Sam's face.

It was undoubtedly the most insulting rejection he'd had in the last week, but it wasn't the only one. Sadly, he had been refused admittance to see at least twenty similarly young female patients since he had apparently ruined Rose, and his usually packed morning surgery had been whittled down to just two patients this morning. And both of them had come more in search of gossip than healing.

Thanks to one ill-considered midnight quest to save a foal, he had become *persona non grata*. More worryingly, instead of things getting better as time went on and they brazened it out, they were getting worse. Everywhere he went he felt the accusing eyes of every woman and every father, who all thought he should do the right thing and were thoroughly disgusted that he hadn't.

Meanwhile, the troublesome winter cough that was doing the rounds was clearly getting worse, because every other person who passed him by with downcast eyes was hacking into a handkerchief! It beggared belief that rather than see him they would prefer to suffer illness and, for some, risk it perilously corrupting their lungs simply because he hadn't done 'the done thing' and married the woman he had ruined despite not ruining her at all!

Whereas Ned, who still snarled at him whenever they collided, had flagrantly ruined Isobel mere months ago but was treated like a hero for saving her from her hideous father and any mention of her ruination was forbidden! All forgiven because right was on their side. Yet right was on his and Rose's side too, because they had saved two horses and a struggling farmer. But nobody mentioned that while they criticised.

The double standard was staggering. But also worrying. He sincerely hoped that Rose was right and this would all die down once she left. He had put down roots in Whittleston-on-the-Water and did not want to sell his practice and start from scratch again elsewhere. Not when it had taken three years to build it into enough that it kept him occupied from dawn to dusk.

Or at least it had until last week.

Dusk was a long way off and, seeing the door slam on this, the last of the calls he could make, he was at an uncharacteristic loose end.

He consulted his pocket watch and groaned before hauling himself back into his curricle. It was barely three in the afternoon and at least another seven empty hours now loomed ahead of him before bedtime. That was more than he was prepared to endure, because he knew that idle hands were the devil's workshop—or in his case idle minds.

He supposed he could always go and check on Mrs Outhwaite…

Under the circumstances that would be an unconventional move while all the gossip was still so rife, but it might go some way towards convincing people that as far as he and his innocence was concerned it was business as usual. One of his patients had had a nasty fall and he would be doing his duty as her physician to see to her ongoing care. It wasn't as if he wouldn't have visited her by now anyway, if the incident in the field hadn't happened, so he should brazenly head there now with his head held high. So high he'd even force a cheery hello on every villager he passed and slow his curricle to wait for them to say hello back.

No! That was a very bad idea! Primarily because all the gossips would start speculating on whether or not he had finally agreed to do the right thing and secondly, more worryingly, he knew, deep down, that it wasn't actually Mrs Outhwaite he wanted to check on. It was Rose. He had, much to his consternation, worried about her all week. Far more than he was comfortable with.

Ergo it was best left.

But Mr Outhwaite had done a very good job of putting the whole truth out there for scrutiny. He had put the entire story on the second page of his weekly paper and sent it out two days ago as news under the headline *Foal and Mare saved from Certain Death during Whittleston's Worst Blizzard*.

Everything from the fake flirting to the reason why her stays had been swinging from the buttons of his greatcoat had been peppered through the narrative.

Alongside were robust quotes from both the Dewhursts and the constable who had placed the bet for Sam, which corroborated their story. The piece had been finished with a comment from the oldest living resident of the village—Mrs Fitzherbert—who claimed the snowstorm had been worse than the Great Blizzard of 1736, in which three villagers had frozen to death. She was, she concluded, supremely grateful that, unlike then, nobody had perished. Not even the Dewhursts' foal.

All Sam had to do now was wait for those truths to permeate the thick skulls of the stubborn and judgemental locals and that would be that. No more empty surgeries and no more slammed doors in his face. For his own sake, Sam gave himself a decisive nod as the spire of St Hildreth's loomed. Rose was right. They had done nothing to be ashamed of and all they needed to do was hold their nerve.

In which case, why shouldn't he just check on Mrs Outhwaite now and be done with it? Show all those gossips that he felt no compunction to give Rose a wide berth because they had done nothing to be ashamed of? Checking on her was hardly crossing the line between caring and *caring.* Together they had been accused of a crime neither had committed and were both suffering as a result. Common decency demanded that he show his face to see if things were bearable for her, and what better way to do that than visiting her convalescing aunt? Two birds with one stone and one less troublesome thing to have to worry about. He would not be cowed or bullied by a bunch of contrary villagers with the worst double standards he had ever seen!

That decision made, he nudged his horse to a trot and went at some lick through the melted snow, enjoying the sunshine until it was time to turn into the village square. Like the innocent man he was, he slowed and tipped his hat to the gaggle of ladies gossiping at the corner.

'Good afternoon, all. How are we on this fine day?'

The reactions were every bit as awkward as he had expected, with several of the group acknowledging him with nothing but pursed lips. The rest still refused to look at him.

'Isn't it lovely, after so many weeks of gloom, to finally see the sun again?' He was going to squeeze some blood out of this stone if it killed him. 'It does wonders for the mood.'

To prove that, he smiled at them. It felt unfamiliar, because he had resurrected one of his old smiles. The sort he had deployed back when he'd used to be charming and fun and the sort, he had often been told, which always had a particularly pleasing effect on the opposite sex.

Except this time it was met with outraged eyes and turned heads. As if suddenly commenting upon the weather was one of the cardinal sins.

Only Mrs Spears, the Reverend's wife, dared to look at him and it was a look that could have curdled milk. 'Have you no heart at all, sir?'

He didn't, but that was by the by. He still did not appreciate her tone. 'How does being buoyed by the better weather make me heartless, madam?'

'Do not waste your breath on him.' Mrs Denby, the fishmonger's wife, dragged her friend away by the arm. 'If he has the gall to behave indifferently after today's developments, he is more of a cad than we suspected and clearly content to remain so.'

With that, the entire gaggle moved away as one, all

effectively giving him the cut directly in the middle of the street.

Sam sat on his perch for several moments affronted, sorely tempted to shout after them and call them all two-faced idiots, when a fragment of that insult permeated his outrage.

Today's developments?

What the blazes had happened between now and noon to suddenly make his perceived crimes worse?

With a sense of foreboding, he glanced towards the Outhwaites' house. There was a smart carriage outside it which he did not recognise, but something told him it had brought trouble.

He hastily parked his own conveyance behind it. Then, with all the traders and pedestrians in the square staring at him, he grabbed his medical bag in the vain hope that it might convince them that this was an official physician's visit before he rapped on the door.

A wide-eyed young maid immediately ushered him into the parlour, where a sombre crowd was gathered. Mrs Outhwaite was sitting in the sturdiest chair by the fire. Her husband was balanced on the arm next to her and there were two complete strangers he had never seen before. He presumed they were husband and wife, as they were both of similar middling years. The woman was on the sofa, cradling a teacup, looking as though the world had just ended. The man stood to attention at the mantel. The only one of the five of those present who did not appear relieved to see him was Rose.

'What's happened?'

Because something had. By the looks of her pale, stunned face, it was very bad indeed.

'Is this him?' The older gentleman with Rose's green eyes jabbed a finger in Sam's direction.

'Yes, Papa.'

Her voice was small and, as that was so unlike her it unsettled Sam more than anything else.

'This is Dr Samuel Able. Sam, this is my father, Mr Bernard Healy.' The older man offered him a curt nod rather than a hearty handshake, which boded well. 'And my mother, Mrs Anne Healy.'

'Mr Healy... Mrs Healy.' As solemnity seemed to be the order of the day, he kept his own expression suitably taut as he inclined his head to both. Then, because there was such a fraught atmosphere in the room, he spoke directly to Rose. 'What on earth has happened?'

'This.'

She passed him a crumpled newspaper and sighed as he quickly scanned it. When Sam's jaw hung slack in outraged panic, she used sarcasm to minimise it all, as was her way.

'It arrived on my uncle's desk with the morning post. Fearing Armageddon, Uncle William thought it prudent to urgently summon my parents, although that turned out to be quite unnecessary as my parents had already summoned themselves. And now we are all here, and in view of this latest scurrilous nonsense, while I would much prefer we all have a nice tea party, I suppose we must discuss our options instead.'

'There is only one option, daughter!' Mr Healy's head looked ready to explode. 'The pair of you must announce your immediate engagement!'

'Why?' Anger swirled hot in her lovely eyes. 'Because the *Suffolk Sentinel* has printed more lies about me? Let's face it—it isn't the first time and I sincerely doubt that it will be the last. I shudder to think what they'll print if Dr Able and I cave under their pressure and marry.' She swept her arm in an arc in the air. *'The unfortunate and unweddable Miss H has finally entrapped a more unfortunate man into marriage. He doesn't love her, of course, because frankly who would? But at least the pitiable halfwit now has a ring on her finger, so nothing else really matters. Most especially what she wants!'*

'Your father only wants our good family name protected.' That tone deaf comment came from Mrs Outhwaite. 'It is the right thing to do, Rose.'

'For who? You?' Rose pointed at her aunt. 'Or you? Or you?' Her finger jabbed at her father, then her mother. 'Because, if I might be selfish for a moment, it is certainly not what is best for me!'

Mr Healy's eyes bulged. 'Something you should have thought of before you spent the night unchaperoned with a man!'

'Nothing happened!' Rose shot out of her chair like a firework, obviously at her wits' end with her father.

'She's right, sir.' As tempers were clearly seriously frayed, Sam tried to pour oil on troubled waters. Hoping some calm diplomacy would show them a way forward. 'Nothing happened. Beyond Rose saving a valued working animal's life because I did not know how to.'

As all he knew about this man was that he was a farmer, he decided to appeal to his farmer's sensibilities.

A decision which immediately proved to be the wrong one.

'I beg to differ, *sir.*' Mr Healy's bulging eyes fixed on him. 'The moment you allowed my headstrong daughter to leave the village with you at midnight, you had already compromised her good reputation! At the very least, knowing my stubborn daughter's tendency to ride roughshod over others when she thinks she knows best, you should have insisted her uncle or a maid or some other respectable adult accompany you both. But you didn't, and that is on you!'

The finger of accusation pointed, unflinching, and Sam supposed the man made a valid point.

'Thanks to your initial lack of forethought, my daughter is not only ruined here in Essex, she is now thoroughly ruined in Suffolk too! How are we supposed to take her home unless she is made an honest woman?'

'Then this *dishonest* and *disgraced* woman shall move to Cheshire or Gloucestershire or Argyllshire! She will become a governess or join a troupe of travelling players.' Rose was ranting now, unhelpfully. 'And she will never darken Suffolk's judgemental door again.'

'Don't be ridiculous, Rose!'

'Which part do you find the most ridiculous, Papa? That I would consider moving or that I might actually be able to earn my own living?'

'And how, pray tell, daughter, do you hope to earn your living in a blasted troupe of travelling players!'

'In case it has escaped your notice, I have passed the age of majority, Papa, and can technically do as I please! And being forced down the aisle does not please me in the slightest! I would sooner walk a fiery tightrope while juggling plates!'

'You cannot juggle! In case it has escaped *your* notice, you can barely even catch!'

As they parried, and while Mrs Healy put her head in her hands and Sam felt the walls close in around him afresh, it occurred to him that Mr Healy and his daughter had identical tempers. An odd thought when your entire world was about to implode in the worst possible way—perhaps even a hysterical thought—but it was the only one he currently had.

Rose had only ever talked about her father fondly up until now, and by the looks of her mother, who had clearly witnessed many a similar altercation between her two equally headstrong kin, there was a chance that father and daughter were two peas in a pod. In which case, it boded well that, if nothing else, he would like his new father-in-law a great deal if he had no choice but to marry his daughter—once the man was done with the urge to wring his neck, of course.

'I'd learn to juggle swords if it saved Sam from having to pay for my stupid mistake!'

And there it was. The line that shouldn't be crossed. He couldn't and wouldn't allow her to wilfully ruin her own life simply to save his. Especially when his wasn't worth saving.

'Rose…' He exhaled slowly to quieten some of the roar of his blood in his ears. 'Could I have a private word?'

'If you've got something to say, young man, you'll say it out here—not skulk off and feed my daughter more excuses like a coward!'

Before Mr Healy boxed his ears with his meaty farmer's hands, Sam raised his own hands in surrender. 'Actually, sir, I want to propose, and fear that I will need several minutes of privacy to convince your daughter to accept.'

'Oh,' said Mr Healy, the wind knocked out of his sails.

'No!' exclaimed Rose, looking ready to punch Sam in his stead. 'This isn't right or fair!'

'Hear me out.'

He caught her by the elbow and, without breaking his stride, in case she dug in her stubborn heels, whisked her down the hall to the Outhwaites' small but typically ostentatious dining room.

'None of this is right or fair. I think we can both agree on that. However, it was a *mutual* stupid mistake that led us to this point, and we will pay for it together.'

As he closed the door she folded her arms. 'I do not wish to be trapped in a loveless marriage.'

'Neither do I. But in the short term I fear that we must both accept that that is what needs to happen.'

'And in the long term? Or are you about to propose that we might grow to love one another—given time?'

She was being direct, as usual and she was right to do so because there was no point in lying.

'I gave all my love to Catherine. I am incapable of doing that again.'

'I thought you were supposed to be convincing me to accept you, not reinforcing all my reasons for turning you down?'

'I might not be able to give you my love, but I can save you from a life of fiery tightrope plate-juggling.' He shrugged, resigned and oddly calm in view of what was about to happen. 'In giving you my name, I will restore your respectability and mine, and in a few months, when this scandal has run its course, I can give you your freedom.'

Sam was making this up as he went along. Trying to find a reasonably palatable compromise in this wholly unpalatable situation which suited them both.

'What? By granting me a divorce?'

'If that is what you want.'

'Thereby creating yet another enormous scandal? Because that will not delight the *Suffolk Sentinel* at all, will it?' She painted another scurrilous headline in the ether with her palm, making him wonder exactly what this newspaper had said about her in the past to make her so concerned about them. '*Jilted Delilah Discarded Again Via an Actual Act of Parliament Because She is So Unappealing.*' Her arms began to wave. 'And on what grounds, Sam? My barrenness? My supposed unfaithfulness? Or perhaps my declining mental state? Because we both know that since Henry VIII brought in divorce it is always the woman who is to bl—'

He placed his finger over her lips to silence her and regretted it instantly, because they were every bit as warm and soft as they looked.

'Couples separate all the time, Rose, and do not have to divorce. We wouldn't have to unless you wanted to, and I would only envisage you wanting to because you'd found someone worthier to marry than the dried-up, dead inside husk that has been foisted upon you. Nobody will judge you for leaving me once they see how unhappy being stuck with me has made you. You already know that I am doomed to be a distant and unaffectionate husband, so I would not correct you when you told everyone that. Tell everyone in Suffolk that I beat you, if you think it would help soften the blow. I will not deny it. Even though I obviously never would. And if you do not have any desire to return to Suffolk, I am not without means. Every penny I inherited from the sale of my father's house is still untouched in the bank, along with a tidy sum left to me by my grandfather.'

All the money he had squirrelled away, along with most of his army salary, to buy Catherine their dream house to raise a family in. It was doomed now to sit there for ever, so it might as well make someone happy.

'I will buy you a cottage in Cheshire or Gloucestershire or Argyllshire, if that pleases you more, and keep you comfortably for as long as you need me to provide for you. This doesn't have to be hard, Rose. If we stick together for a few months, my home is big enough for us to easily avoid one another within it and then you would be free by spring.'

Her outraged expression softened into one of confusion. 'You propose that I marry you, then immediately leave you?'

'I do.' And as that parody of a wedding vow felt fitting, he found himself chuckling at the unintentional irony of it. 'Let us do what needs to be done for only as long as it needs to be done, and then part exactly as we are now. Not quite friends, but not quite acquaintances either.'

She sank onto a dining chair. 'I'm not sure what to say.'

'Say yes, Rose. It's not as if either of us really has any other option at this stage.'

Chapter Eleven

Regardless of the noticeable subduedness of the bride and groom, the packed congregation of St Hildreth's were in a celebratory mood. Not only were they all attending a wedding, they were attending a Christmas Eve wedding, and those were rare and special beasts indeed. Whittleston had certainly not seen one in many years.

The irony of the atrocious timing was, however, not lost on Rose. It had been on this day precisely one year ago that she was first supposed to be a bride, and she had anticipated that day with such optimistic excitement.

Conversely, and for obvious reasons, she had dreaded walking up the aisle today. Her voice trembled as she made vows she did not mean, and beside her, her press-ganged groom did the same. Then they were spirited out onto a carpet of fresh snow and showered in dried rose petals, before she and Sam ate an equally subdued wedding breakfast at Hockley Hall with her family and their few closest friends.

But thanks to it being Christmas Eve the day improved, and she was swept up in the yuletide merry-making irrespective of her melancholy mood.

As it was it was Sophie's first Christmas as the mistress of Hockley Hall, and because all the village remembered the previous lord of the manor as an unapproachable, tight old skinflint, she and Rafe had thrown open their doors at sunset to welcome everyone from the village in for a feast. Therefore it was easy for Rose and Sam to avoid one another while they were coerced into party games and dances, and to her great surprise, after the interminable day, the evening passed swiftly.

As the festivities wound down in time for Midnight Mass she was dancing a jig with Archie while her new husband—how peculiar it was to call a man husband!—was reviving the baker's daughter. The poor girl had fainted because she had tied her stays too tight, to try and catch the eye of the innkeeper's son. A cocky lad, far too handsome for his good, who was blissfully unaware that the unconscious even girl existed as he flirted shamelessly with someone else.

'Could I borrow you for a minute?' Her mother touched her arm, her expression furtive and her body twitchy.

'Of course, Mama.' As soon as she had disentangled herself from Archie and caught up with her scurrying mother, she whispered, 'Are you all right?'

'Of course, dear.' That was said with little conviction. 'I simply wanted us to have a little chat before you go home with your husband for the first time.'

Her mother's cheeks blushed crimson and that sent alarm bells ringing, as it rather than suggested that the 'little chat' was doomed instead to be *the* chat. The one her mother had been so reluctant to have last year in the lead-up to her first wedding.

She found an empty room well away from the party

and gestured Rose inside with such pained awkwardness that she knew this was clearly going to be every bit the cringing experience they both feared.

'As this is your wedding night…' Her mama cleared her throat and tried to appear serene and matter-of-fact—and failed, because her entire head and neck were beetroot-red. 'You need to be prepared for what is to come.'

Oh, good heavens above, this was awful! For two reasons. The first being her mother's inability to meet her eye, and the second Rose's uncertainty that she was even going to have a wedding night.

It had not been discussed in any way, shape or form, which she supposed spoke volumes, when in the last three weeks, since the first of the banns had been read, on the few occasions when they had conversed, she and Sam had discussed a great many things about their marriage. Pretty much everything, in fact, had been laid out in stark black and white, like a map.

By mutual agreement, she knew already that it would technically end on the first of April. April Fools' Day—an irony that was not lost on either of them, but a date which made sense. That would give them three excruciating months to be seen to give the marriage a go before Rose went to Suffolk to visit her parents for Easter.

She would extend her stay into May, and then some time around Whitsun would write him a letter informing him that she had decided to stay for the entire summer too. By autumn, when she failed to return, gossip would be rife, and everyone in Whittleston would realise that she had left him for good. Whether or not she wanted to remain in Suffolk or find a new home elsewhere was, to Sam's mind, a decision for her. But, despite all her protestations to the contrary, about her father being a wealthy man so Sam did not need to feel obligated to support her, he'd refused to have that. He would see her right—on that he was adamant—and she would leave the marriage with enough to purchase a new home and a generous annual allowance to support her.

While she was grateful for his generosity, Rose still had to find a way to properly refuse it. She was to blame for their predicament, and she certainly did not expect him to pay any more for it! However, as they had reached an impasse on that particular discussion, she had put it to one side for now. She had three months, after all, to figure it out.

Until her departure.

They had also had plenty of discussion about all the other provisions he wanted to make for her. She had had to put her foot down and insist that the ridiculous amount of pin money he intended to give her would also be used as housekeeping money too, because to begin with everyone would expect them to at least try to settle into wedded bliss. She would, therefore, take charge of the running of his house for the three months she was 'stuck in purgatory' with him—his words, not hers.

It was hardly an onerous task, when he would hardly ever be at home and a maid came in three times a week to clean everything. If he *was* home, he had said, he would likely be in his surgery downstairs, so her evenings would be her own to do with as she pleased— which sounded dismal and lonely. Daytimes would be her own too, as he did not need any help with the running of his practice, nor with anything in his busy, ordered life, really, so goodness knew what she was supposed to do with so many empty hours in the day.

But she was at peace with it. She would find something she could do for him. Whether he liked it or not.

Obviously, for appearances' sake, they had decided it made sense to attend all social occasions as a couple, and they had mutually agreed that the only people who needed to know that their marriage was a temporary affair was them. Therefore, as much as she wanted to tell her mother it was all a sham, to spare them both the horror of *the chat* now, she couldn't. Especially as a part of her still hoped that the wedding night would happen.

Not because she harboured any silly romantic notions about the pair of them. He had been completely honest about that, and even if he hadn't been a blithering idiot could see that he wasn't ready to move on from his dead wife. But if she and Sam did end up shackled together for all eternity, albeit living in different counties, she at the very least wanted to appease the curiosity she had always had about such things.

Her fiancé had absconded before their wedding night, and she wasn't brave enough to consider taking a lover, like her friends had suggested, so this might well be her only chance to finally discover what that side of things between a man and a woman was all about. Especially since she had found out at the last Friday Sewing Circle, to which she had immediately been reinstated the moment she had become respectably engaged, that Sam had bought a new bed from Hornchurch.

Rose had, scandalously, once or twice—or perhaps nearer twenty times—indulged in picturing them both in that bed.

'A bed big enough for two,' one of the sewers had said, with suggestively wiggling eyebrows, 'with the best feather mattress money could buy.'

'Oak too,' Mrs Fitzherbert had added with a wink. 'So the pair of you are unlikely to break it.'

And with that several of the married ladies had given each other knowing looks as they had giggled—including Isobel and Sophie—as if beds broke all the time when passion was involved.

Rose would have much preferred having this awkward conversation with them, and had almost asked Sophie twice. But she had stopped herself because her friends' marriages were based on love and hers wasn't ever going to have that. As she assumed that making love involved *love* in some fundamental way, whatever happened or did not happen between her and Sam in the bedchamber tonight would be a very different experience. Probably more perfunctory than passionate—at least on his part.

She wasn't going to waste time trying to delude herself that she didn't feel desire for him, however. It had been growing and bubbling for weeks now, along with her futile affections for him. The only thing that hadn't been growing was any hope that he might miraculously feel the same. For him, there had only ever been one fish.

She had wanted to confide in Sophie and Isobel about that too, because it hurt. But, as her friends knew she was as reluctant a bride as Sam was a groom, she had shied away from discussing such personal things with them because she could not bear to witness any more pity in their eyes.

'The marital bed is not a place to be feared.'

Her poor mama was now staring at a spot on the carpet as if her life depended on it.

'And, contrary to what you may have heard from embittered wives, it doesn't have to be a chore.'

Suddenly Rose was staring at a separate spot on the floor, willing it to open up and swallow her.

'In fact...with a generous and tender man...it can be...um...quite pleasurable.'

Unwanted images of her parents intimately entwined swam before her eyes and her toes curled in revolt.

'After you are undressed, the man will...um...'

Dear Lord, please take me now!

'You do not need to explain any more, Mama. I am a farmer's daughter and know the mechanics.'

'In sheep, cows and horses, dear.' Her mother was squirming in her seat, clearly determined to carry on, despite looking ready to bolt. 'But it works differently in people.'

She made an odd gesture with her hands that made absolutely no sense to Rose.

'Of course you can do it in the same hasty manner as animals if the mood calls for it, but...um...usually people face one another...take their time and...er...kiss and...do *other* things.'

Her mother attempted a smile as she stressed the word 'other', then caught her daughter's eye and almost spontaneously combusted. In case she caught it again, she twisted in her seat and found another spot on the intricately woven Persian carpet to scrutinise.

'Like I said, those things aren't unpleasant. Although...um...it might smart a little the first time. But after that it will all be plain sailing.'

With that, her mother stood, signalling that this torture was finally over, and forced another smile. 'I hope that answers all your questions.'

It didn't, because Rose had no idea what the '*other* things' were, or what 'plain sailing' was supposed to resemble, but she nodded dutifully for the sake of them both.

Her mother's entire posture collapsed with relief. 'Splendid. That wasn't half as bad as I thought it was going to be.'

Which was hilarious, because it had been twice as bad as Rose's worst nightmare, but she smiled too, and thanked her mother, before they both gratefully fled the privacy of the room.

By the time they returned to the ballroom most of the revellers were gone to mass. Only a few strays who were keen to imbibe as much of Lord Hockley's free ale as possible hung around, alongside their hosts, her parents, her uncle and her aunt—whose back had healed enough to finally be relieved of bedrest…and Sam.

Her handsome new husband looked as uncomfortable as she felt. 'Are we ready to go to church?'

He asked that with an overbright smile which told her that he too would much rather stay here until the first of April rather than face what came next. But, as that wasn't viable, she nodded.

'Your curricle is waiting for you out front,' said Rafe, and gave them both a look. One that warned them that the horror of today wasn't fully over, as if he understood that this wasn't the cheery day of celebration almost everyone else was determined to pretend it was. Then in an aside he whispered, 'Gird your loins.'

Only because it was expected, Sam offered his arm and she took it. Then they both did their best to look both delighted and surprised when they saw the entire village was awaiting them outside. His curricle had been festooned in flowers and ribbons, and as he helped her into it they were again showered in rose petals and rice as the crowd cheered. Then it parted like the Red Sea, to allow Reverend Spears to pass, dressed in his most extravagant cassock and already clutching his prayer book, ready to perform the Christmas Eve service.

'My most hearty congratulations, Dr and Mrs Able.'

It was the first time she had heard her new name and it felt odd. Ill-fitting. But not completely wrong.

'You will be delighted to learn that, in honour of your nuptials, you are both excused church this evening.' That elicited a bawdy cheer from the crowd. 'Have a very *Merry* Christmas.'

At that unsubtle euphemism the crowd cheered again and they were forced to set off for home.

A good hour before Rose had steeled herself for it.

They rode in stiff silence up the lane. It was only when they were well out of sight of Hockley Hall that Sam broke it.

'Well, that was…'

'Mortifying? Interminable? Excruciating?'

He chuckled. 'All of the above. But at least the worst is over.'

'Is it? We've still got the awkward crossing the threshold nonsense to manoeuvre, and our first official night alone, then a horrendous day of unsubtle nudges and winks to endure tomorrow, followed by three long months of a sham marriage to navigate.'

He chuckled again. 'You do like to tackle things head-on, don't you, Rose? Get it all out in the open… upfront.'

'Being jilted and the last to know about it does that. It also prevents any nasty surprises and sets expectations.'

'I suppose it does.'

'Especially when we are, again, partners in crime. Trying to perpetrate another fraud upon this village and mine. That's going to be tricky enough without having to tiptoe around one another. Therefore, I think, between us, honesty has to be the best policy. No matter how uncomfortable the topic might be.'

'Agreed. It has certainly worked up to now.'

She waited for him to execute the tricky turn from the lane at Hockley Hall to the road, and then decided to properly practise what she preached. 'I hope you have no intentions of carrying me over the threshold.'

He stared straight ahead but his smile was wry. 'I was only intending to do it if anyone was watching. As we've left everybody back there…' He jerked his head backwards. 'I'll spare us both that chore.'

As the word 'chore' echoed a portion of her mother's painful *chat*, she took a deep breath. 'And our wedding night? How do you envisage that to look?'

He stiffened, but tried to hide it, and that said it all. He didn't want one.

'With you retiring to your room and me retiring to mine.' Then he attempted to smooth over the jagged shards of that damning statement with a smile. 'I've bought you a lovely new bed. New sheets and pillows. I've even bought you a very feminine washstand too, with a bowl made from a local pottery that I found on my travels. I hope you approve of it.'

'I am sure I will.'

Clearly, for all their frank and open discussions, and all the mutually agreed decisions they had made together since this debacle had begun, he had decided she had no say in his decision to deny her a wedding night. Which was just dandy for him, as he had already had one!

For a moment she resented him for that—until she remembered she had no right to resent that or him. Or even his dead wife, to whom he was clearly intent on remaining faithful, because he hadn't lied about any of those things. In fact, he had been nothing but honest, exactly as she had asked. Perhaps more so than she had been. Catherine had been his everything and still was, and Rose could accept that or send herself mad railing against it. Either way, it wouldn't change things.

'But you really didn't need to waste money on furniture that is only going to be used for three months.'

'It can follow you to wherever you end up. Save you the effort of buying two things for your new house.' He slanted her smile. 'Unless you secretly hate them, of course, in which case feel free to give them away or burn them on a bonfire. It's not as if I'll know their fate.'

In case she was in any doubt as to his feelings, that was another innocent but depressing window into his perception of their future.

Once she was gone, as far as he was concerned, she would be gone.

Done and dusted.

Out of sight and out of mind.

Was a wedding night ever as lacklustre and disappointing as this one?

He pulled into the silent market square and solicitously helped her down, briskly severing the contact as they walked together towards her new but temporary home.

'I'll give you a quick tour before you retire, and I see to the horse. I keep the key here.' He pointed to a hook hidden beneath the eaves of the small gabled porch. 'It saves me having to remember it if I have to rush out on a call. Not that I remember to lock the door most of the time, as Whittleston-on-the-Water is perfectly safe.' He pushed it open. 'But you might want to.'

She was already familiar with the hall, as his surgery was the first door on the left and she visited it with Mrs Fitzherbert whenever her gout flared up.

Mrs Fitzherbert had, on every single one of those occasions, joked to him that Rose was her chaperon, because she didn't trust him not to become overcome by the alluring sight of her wizened old legs, and he had always taken it in the same spirit. Replying, 'Very wise' or 'Quite right' or 'It's always better to be safe than sorry where men are concerned.'

He lit a candle and sailed straight past that first door to open the next door on the right. 'This is my office.'

It was, unsurprisingly for such an ordered and organised man, as neat as a pin, but the décor did not suit him at all. It was all dark upholstery, darker wood and old-fashioned furniture. Dour and staid—which he wasn't, despite his traumatic past.

'Did you inherit this from the previous incumbent?'

'Most of it.' He frowned at the room, as if seeing it with fresh eyes, then shrugged. 'I bought the entire practice lock, stock and barrel, and I did mean to change it, but time flies and the practice is busy. It's all serviceable enough, so hasn't been a priority.'

He took her further down the hall to show her the kitchen. That, at least, looked less bleak, and would doubtless be quite light and bright when the sun shone through the large currently moonlit windows. There was a decent range, which radiated enough heat to ward off the December chill, and a door which led on to the yard beyond.

He noticed her looking at it. 'There's actually a little cottage garden out there. It's stuffed to the gills with flowers by May, which last all the way through to September.'

'It's too bad I shan't be here to see it as I've always loved a garden.'

'You'll see the early blossom and the buds, at least.'

He pivoted back the way they'd come and lit a lamp at the foot of the stairs. Just as they did in her aunt's house, a few yards away, the narrow stairs turned twice before they reached the upper floor. Then all similarities with her relative's home, disappeared because the bottom of this one was mostly used for business and the entire top was where living happened.

Except not much living seemed to occur in the parlour. It was a spartan space that smelled of beeswax. Neat and tidy, exactly like downstairs, but somehow even less like the man who owned it. All the requisite furniture for a parlour was there and, unlike downstairs, most of it was no more than a few years old. One wingback chair sat beside the fireplace, flanked by a small table. A short settee devoid of any scatter cushions seemed to have been purchased to fill the space, but it was too plump and rigid to have ever been sat on. There was an empty sideboard and an empty dresser, and a cold and empty grate which, judging by the frigid temperature which hit her in the face the second the door opened, clearly hadn't seen any sign of a fire in a long time.

She'd wager he didn't use this room and it showed, for there wasn't a single picture on the pale green walls nor a knick-knack in sight. It was an abandoned, forgotten, but telling space.

'Obviously I never have time to use this room,' he said, as if he could read her mind, 'so do not hesitate to make it yours for the duration.'

It was another window into his work-orientated existence and yet another unconscious reminder that their time together was finite, in case—what? She forgot he was only with her under duress and got ideas? That grated, but she bit back any comment and nodded. He was making her an honest woman after all, and that was her fault.

'The bedchambers are just along the landing.' Which was where he marched her next. 'There is a small attic room too, that is completely empty bar a table and a chair, which obviously you can use—or not use—whatever you wish, and this is your room.'

He paused between two opposite doors, the other clearly being his, and that brought her up short. She hadn't envisaged that they would be sleeping mere feet apart.

Would she hear him?

Sense him?

Probably. Every time he was within ten feet of her, her skin prickled with awareness, and it was always disconcerting.

He flung the door open and ushered her inside. The brand-new bed dominated the room and was indeed big enough for two. But it was the rest of the room which surprised her, because he had obviously gone to some effort for her in the last three weeks. Certainly more effort than he had put to his own comfort in the last three years. His considerations touched her and, oddly, felt significant.

The bedding was a crisp, plain white, lacy and feminine, although not in a fussy way. Four fat pillows stood to attention at the headboard. Each with a cluster of tiny red silk ribbon roses adorning one corner, while a thick, clearly expensive rose-printed eiderdown was folded across the foot. There was a small vase of fresh flowers on her nightstand—roses again, although heaven knew where he had found them this far from the city in wintertime—alongside a pretty beaded lamp.

The rose motif was echoed on the bowl of the pine washstand, which had been matched with the full-length pine looking glass, taking up one corner, and a wicker chair draped in a thick crimson blanket sat in another. It was the same crimson as the roses, and he had found a rug that matched. Beside a tall wardrobe were piled her two trunks. Atop them were all the books she had bought since she'd arrived at Whittleston.

'I arranged with your aunt to have everything delivered earlier. I thought you'd settle in easier with all your things close to hand.'

'That was very thoughtful of you.'

Rose had only packed a bag, and even that had been a last-minute thing this morning. Maybe because even until the absolute last minute she hadn't been entirely sure she could go through with this sham of a wedding. She had, of course, because there really hadn't been any alternative. Not only was it what everyone expected, her father had gone to great expense and trouble to engage a solicitor to force the dratted *Suffolk Sentinel* to print both a complete retraction and a correction. One which stuck closer to the real version of events, exactly like her uncle's article in the *South Essex Gazette*, but with the added embellishment that Dr Able had already pro-

posed to her before they had inadvertently got trapped
by the blizzard for the night in his curricle.

'Please tell me you didn't buy all this just for me?'

He waved the unnecessary and extravagant expense
away as if it was nothing. 'I couldn't have you sleeping
on bare boards, now, could I? Because that was all that
was in here before.'

'You matched all the colours and the roses?'

'A rose for a *Rose* and I know you like red.'

He ran an idle hand over one of her pillows, smiling
at his purchase, then froze as he realised what he had
just said. He yanked his fingers away from her bedding
as if he had been caught doing something wrong, and
just like that the atmosphere in the room shifted. Became somehow more intimate.

Her flesh heated with awareness.

He swallowed.

Hard.

Perhaps because suddenly he, like her, was reminded
that they were all alone in the candlelight with a bed big
enough for two. On their wedding night! And everyone
outside of this house—her own friends included—were
currently in church and expecting them to be having one!

'Anyway...' He used his candle to light her lamp
and strode to the door so fast it was a wonder he didn't
break into a run. 'Buying all this gave me something
to do while I was *persona non grata* and at a loose end,
so I hardly went to too much trouble. Hardly any at all,
really, as most of it came from the same shop and the
shopkeeper suggested most of the choices.'

Was he blushing? He was definitely babbling. Shuffling from foot to foot, looking boyish, self-conscious
and...and so appealing her pulse quickened.

'Obviously, if you hate it, you can replace everything.'

'I love it all.'

A rose for a Rose.

Heaven help her, but that had sounded so romantic. As romantic as this overtly feminine bedchamber was.

'Thank you.'

'Excellent…' He shuffled from foot to foot some more, winced, and then tried his best to pretend he hadn't. 'Then I'll leave you to get settled…um… Goodnight… Rose.'

'Goodnight, Sam.'

The door closed with a soft click, then she heard his boots hurry down the stairs. Leaving her staring at her pretty new surroundings, feeling off-kilter and wondering how a man who believed he had no heart left to give could be so utterly, charmingly, whimsically thoughtful.

Chapter Twelve

Bloody hell!

A rose for a blasted Rose!

What the blazes had he been thinking?

It was midnight on Christmas Day, snow was again coming down so thick and fast he could barely see the road ahead, and instead of concentrating on it as the weather demanded, Sam was still kicking himself for those wholly inappropriate and flowery words.

Who did he think he was?

Wordsworth?

Blasted Shakespeare?

Or, God help him, Romeo? Besotted and ready to woo!

And he had been so keen to show it all off too, and had basked in her approval. Patting himself on the back for getting things just right when in fact she was right! It was a ludicrous amount of effort for just three months. And, despite his hasty denial, sourcing all those things *had* been an effort.

He hadn't lied when he'd claimed to have been at a loose end, because he had been. During those first few days after their engagement, when the news of it hadn't spread the length and breadth of his practice and he had still been considered a libertine, a scoundrel and a cad, he had had too many empty hours to fill. He hadn't lied when he'd said that he had just been passing the pottery, because stopping to purchase the rose-covered wash-bowl and jug had been more by whim than design. But once he'd had it he had become a man on a mission to find the perfect things to go with it.

At the time, he had thought that he was being decent, because he genuinely did not want to make her short stay at his house any more awkward than it needed to be. However, with hindsight, he had been so obsessed with getting it right for her that he hadn't given much thought as to how that would look. He had lied about the shopkeeper choosing it all too, because not one of the dozen specialised merchants he had visited had suggested anything remotely suitable.

Everything had been too fussy, too frothy and too frilly for Rose's bold but understated elegance. So it had been he who had chosen the linens and the furniture. He who had matched the blanket and had the rug made to match the dark crimson of the lovely evening gown she had worn while they had waltzed on the infamous night of the blizzard, when he had been the envy of the room.

What the blazes had he been thinking, to treasure that memory enough that he'd instantly been able to pick the precise shade? He was supposed to be dead inside—had worked damn hard to be dead inside—and wasn't supposed to care about anyone like that. Yet he had cared then that she would like it, and to his horror he still cared now that she did.

He had tossed and turned all night, imagining her dark hair fanned out on those snow-white pillows, and she had invaded his dreams with a vengeance.

Worse than she ever had before.

He'd blamed the fact that she was sleeping directly across the hall, which was disconcerting enough for one used to being alone. He'd been convinced he could smell her perfume—blasted roses again—from his bed. The sultry, seductive scent had been a constant reminder that he was sharing his house with a woman, and his body hadn't enjoyed the touch of a woman in four long years. It hadn't helped that it was technically their wedding night, and wedding nights elicited certain carnal connotations that even a man who was dead inside could not fail to contemplate. Nor had it helped that their wedding wasn't a real wedding. Not when she had been mere feet away, lying warm and soft beneath the rose-covered eiderdown he had bought her, and each time his eyes had closed he'd wondered what it would be like to snuggle beneath it with her.

Then, as he'd slept, his imagination had run riot.

So much so he had awoken hot and hard. The hated nightshirt he had donned because he had a 'visitor' had been discarded in a fit of nocturnal pique, so he'd met the day naked, atop his tangled covers. His fist had conveniently already been wrapped around his painful, rigid cock so he could relieve himself. Which he'd figured he had to do to banish the hold the Rose of his dreams had over his body before he dared face her.

Then, to rattle him further, he'd had to face her almost immediately, because no sooner had he washed and dressed his less rampant body he'd opened his door the second she'd opened hers.

They had simultaneously muttered awkward greetings, with him hoping against hope that she hadn't heard the guttural grunt of his explosive release and her barely meeting his eye which rather suggested she might have. Then she had insisted on making his coffee while he finished getting ready for the obligatory Christmas Day church service, which they hadn't been excused from despite being newlyweds.

Newlyweds who hadn't spent the night honouring each other's bodies as their vows allowed—but only they knew that, and likely only he was suffering as a result.

The service at St Hildreth's had been every bit as cringeworthy as she had predicted, with everyone nudging and winking and slapping him on the back because they'd assumed he had had a good night. That had been followed by an interminable Christmas luncheon at the Outhwaites, with her visiting family, during which none of them had known quite what to say. Thankfully, a child with a fever in Ockendon had spared him the interminable evening of cold cuts and cards, and hot on the heels of that had come a youth who had broken his wrist after doing something idiotic with his friends in Great Ramstead.

Now Sam turned into the square, hopeful that his tempting new wife was already sleeping in her bed and he wouldn't have to relive that stupid, sentimental *a rose for a Rose* comment in front of her again until tomorrow.

The porch light glowed in an uncharacteristic welcome home. He'd certainly never had the forethought to light it before he dashed out to the next emergency in the dark, so she must have. Even so, he took his horse to its tiny stable first, rubbed him down, fed him, and put him to bed before he ventured inside. He wanted to prove to himself that he wasn't eager to return home, even though a part of him was.

That was a new and worrying development too, as this place was a means to an end more than a home. A place to conduct his business and rest his weary head. And it had been so until last night, when she had joined him here. But today he had thought of it as home for the first time, when that glowing porch light had felt like a beacon, beckoning him inside and away from it all.

She hadn't locked the door, and he toed off his snowy boots so as not to disturb her upstairs before he trudged towards the kitchen. Sam hadn't eaten since that fraught Christmas luncheon, and he was frozen stiff from the weather. In his mind there was a mountain of hot, thick buttered toast with his name on it, and by Jove he was going to devour it while he warmed his bones by the fire!

Rose had obviously tossed a fresh log on that fire before she had retired, because the kitchen was deliciously warm when he entered it. He retrieved a semi-stale loaf from the pantry, and was in the midst of sawing it to pieces when the hairs on his neck began to dance.

'You're home late.'

She was dressed for bed. Beneath her knotted robe the sensible high neck of her winter nightgown was visible. Her chestnut hair had been bound in a thick plait that hung over one shoulder and practically to her waist. Sam had no clue why the long length of her hair affected him so—but it did.

'What are you making?'

'Toast,' he said, his mouth suddenly dry. 'It's one of the few things in my culinary repertoire.'

'Toast isn't a proper supper, Sam, and I'm guessing you haven't had a proper supper.' She whooshed past him on a distracting floral wave to poke around the pantry. 'I'll make you something more substantial.'

'There's honestly no need.' He wasn't comfortable with her caring for him like this. It felt too wifely. Too personal. 'I am content with toast. I like toast. In fact, I practically live on the stuff.'

She emerged from the pantry empty-handed, with a furrowed brow. 'Well, that's just as well, as there is nothing in the pantry to make anything beyond toast. Please tell me that you don't really live off toast.'

'It's quick and easy for a man who keeps such odd hours. I do eat at the inn every so often, though, and the maid always makes a half-decent stew once a week, and that lasts a couple of days, so…'

She pushed past him to squeeze the bread and her dark brows kissed each other in consternation. 'Precisely how old is this loaf?'

'Er…no more than three days. The baker delivers it twice a week, along with a few pies and—' He stopped because her hands had gone to her hips and he knew he shouldn't be defending his poor diet when she was right. He was a physician, after all, and he'd have plenty to say if he discovered one of his patients ate like him. 'Stale bread always makes the best toast. Everybody knows that, and I'm quite capable of making it, so go back to bed.' He was too aware of her and it unsettled him. 'There is no point us both being up.'

She shot him a look of chastisement before she completely ignored him. 'Give that to me and go and dry your hair before you catch your death of cold.'

She snatched the knife from his hand and flapped him towards the table, tossing him a towel as he sat down. A towel which he was fairly certain hadn't lived in his kitchen before she had moved in, not twenty-four hours before.

With efficient economy of motion, several slices of bread were speared on a toasting fork and rested before the fire, before she returned to the pantry to fetch some milk, sniffing it gingerly and then pouring it into a pan once she had ascertained it wasn't on the turn.

'I see the snow has returned,' she said.

'It has, and I fear it's back for the foreseeable.'

'Well, I hope it pauses long enough for my parents to return home. I'd rather they left tomorrow as planned. My mother keeps trying to pull me aside to have chats about how to be a *good wife*.' She pulled a face full of distaste that said that Mrs Healy's advice strayed into areas that weren't quite as impersonal as making toast. 'And my father keeps interrogating me about your character and your prospects and asking if you are treating me as you should. My brother, obviously, still wants to kill you, but he won't—unless you give him due course.'

'And who can blame him?' Sam smiled at both her dry delivery and her uncanny knack of banishing awkwardness by tackling it head-on. Clearly she had come to the realisation much quicker than he that they were stuck with one another so they might as well find a way of existing that wasn't quite so painful as last night and this morning had been. 'Had I a sister, I'd probably want to murder the scoundrel who had compromised her.'

'I was so envious of you being able to escape today.' She slanted him an amused glance. 'Because the awkwardness didn't improve after you left. I almost stabbed myself in the forehead with a fork during supper, to end it all, it was such unmitigated torture. I do not blame you, either, for not coming back.'

'I couldn't come back.' He finished towelling his hair and found himself watching her as she made swift work of turning the toast. 'Lucas Midhurst, for reasons best known to himself, decided to ride his sled down the roof of his skinflint father's old barn. Suffice to say that the skinflint's roof hadn't been maintained, and the sled went halfway down before plummeting through it. Fortunately, he landed in the hay store, and that broke his fall, else I'd have had to set more than his wrist this evening.'

'Why on earth would he do a stupid thing like that?' She had found some forgotten chocolate, spices and sugar in his pantry, and was whisking it vigorously into the steaming milk. 'When sledding down a roof of any sort is never going to end well.'

'Because boys will be boys, I'm afraid, and do not have the sense of girls.' Much to his surprise Sam was enjoying this impromptu bit of domesticity. 'Honestly, of all the injured patients I have to attend as a result of stupid accidents that never should have happened, nine-tenths of them are males. The age of the male is no gauge of their stupidity either. Just last week the butcher, who must be at least fifty if he is a day, balanced a rickety three-legged milking stool on his countertop so that he could whitewash his ceiling, rather than fetch the ladder which was propped up against the wall of his yard not five steps away.'

'Is that how he lost both his front teeth?' She giggled, the sound so joyous it made him laugh too. 'He told my uncle that he was kicked in the face by a rampaging bullock at the slaughterhouse!'

'Yes, I heard that too.' Sam was transfixed as she slathered butter on the now perfectly golden toast, while simultaneously pouring two mugs of the frothiest hot chocolate he had ever seen. 'I always makes me laugh when I hear the outrageous stories men make up to cover for their stupidity. But sadly, if I'm involved, and it didn't happen in public, alongside other witnesses, I obviously cannot call them out on it, no matter how much I am tempted.'

'Why not?'

She deposited the toast and one of the steaming mugs on the table before sinking into the chair opposite, where she hugged her own mug in her hands. Clearly it wasn't enough that she had prepared his supper—she was going to keep him company while he ate it too. More peculiar was that he didn't actually mind. It was…*nice* to have some company for a change. To not come back to a cold, dark and empty house.

He decided not to worry about that. It was Christmas, after all, a time to make merry, and it was going to be impossible to keep her completely at arm's length when they were both living under the same roof—it wasn't a particularly big roof at that. They were doomed to bump into one another all the time, and the next three months didn't have to be awkward. Surely it wouldn't hurt if they were more friends than polite acquaintances for just twelve weeks?

'As a physician, I am bound by certain rules and regulations and one of those is the confidentiality of the patient. Their ailments are private unless they give me permission to say otherwise. Which means that I am privileged to know all manner of salacious things which I cannot technically tell another living soul, so kindly keep the truth about Jenkins' missing teeth under your hat.'

'My lips are sealed.'

She pretended to button them, drawing his eyes there.

Then those plump lips curved into a conspiratorial and very naughty smile.

'What sort of other salacious things can you technically not tell me?' She leaned her chin on her wrist and wiggled her dark brows, expectant.

'Nothing because I shouldn't have even told you that!'

'Of course you should have. I am your wife, after all. At least temporarily.' She batted her lashes. 'A good husband, even a transient one, should never keep secrets from his wife.'

'I really shouldn't...'

'But you are sorely tempted, aren't you?'

He was, because it would be fun to share some of the more ludicrous things he had squirreled away and, as she had so aptly said once, there really was no reason why two irrevocably damaged souls shouldn't take whatever amusement they could if the opportunity presented itself.

Chuckling, he took a sip of his chocolate and his eyes widened. 'This is delicious.' Ridiculously delicious. So delicious he would even go as far as saying it was the best cup of chocolate he had ever had in his life. 'How on earth did you make this with so few stale ingredients?'

She preened with mock arrogance. 'I have *the gift*. You have married an excellent cook, Dr Able. A truly *excellent* cook, if I do say so myself. And I'll be prepared to prove that every day for the duration of our temporary marriage, to spare you the next three months of toast, if I'm paid for my talents in scurrilous gossip that I swear I will never tell another living soul.' She batted her lashes again. 'You also have my solemn pledge that my stews aren't *half decent* like your maid's. They are legendary.' She kissed her fingers as she briefly closed her eyes. 'And the things I can do with pastry are *so* sublime they should be illegal.'

'All bold claims, madam…'

'Not claims, sir. The truth.' She leaned closer, elbows on the table and her pretty face resting in the cradle of both palms. 'So what do you say, transient husband? Bearing in mind that you did agree that for the duration of our sham marriage honesty was the best policy.'

He took a bite out of his toast and pretended to give it some thought, and when she huffed, he grinned. 'Do you remember, in August, Mrs Sheldon claimed to have been knocked out cold when she came home from even-song, after a gust of wind dislodged a roof tile which fell and hit her on the head?'

She leaned forward, her green eyes shimmering with mirth. 'Don't tell me she hadn't been hit by falling masonry, because I saw the huge bump on her forehead and it was so magnificent it could only have come from something very hard.'

'Of course it wasn't a roof tile. There wasn't a breath of wind all August, for goodness' sake… She carries a flask of gin everywhere, and had drunk so much that night that she tripped over her own doorstep and head-butted the doorknob.'

She threw her head back and laughed. It was an out-rageously earthy and slightly dirty laugh. 'Mrs Fitzherbert has always said that mother's ruin will be the ruin of Mrs Sheldon…'

Before either of them knew it half an hour had passed and all of it filled with laughter. It was only when they both started yawning that it became apparent that it was time to call it a night. Yet it was Rose who was the one to bring their evening to an end, and not him, which was probably also something he should worry about.

'I have to wave my parents and brother off at six. If they aren't snowed in.' She rolled her eyes. 'Perish the thought.'

While she moved the crockery to the sink, he glanced outside to assess the weather. 'Well, it's stopped for now. Three inches of fresh snow aren't enough to stop a big carriage like your father's.'

'From your lips to God's ears, Sam.'

She led the way out of the kitchen and up the stairs, forcing him to behold the intriguing way her hips undulated as she did so. They didn't stop until she reached her bedchamber.

'Goodnight, transient husband.'

'Goodnight, temporary wife.'

His last image was her sleepy smile before she closed her door. It was an image that tortured his dreams for the rest of the night.

Chapter Thirteen

'I'm sorry, Mr Purdue, but it is still a no.' Rose pointed to the engraved plaque by the front door. 'Surgery hours are from eight o'clock to noon, Monday to Friday, and today is Saturday. Unless it's an emergency—and by emergency I mean that the threat of your departure from this earthly realm is imminent—you can come back then to collect your stomach powders on Monday.'

'But I have run out!' He was incensed at being thwarted. 'I get gaseous if I do not have them because I cannot digest my meat properly!'

'Then I suggest you eat only vegetables until then and, going forward, come to see my husband during surgery hours well before you run out again.'

'Dr Able has never once turned me away on a Saturday. Or a Sunday, for that matter, so—'

Rose stayed him with her palm. 'That was before he was married, Mr Purdue. Now that he is, he will be spending his Saturdays and his Sundays with me.' As the ruddy-faced merchant huffed, she offered him a cheery smile. 'Have a good Saturday yourself, Mr Purdue.'

Then she promptly closed the door and went back

to her pastry, hoping that the exchange hadn't awoken Sam upstairs.

Thanks to a difficult delivery of twins in Little Ramstead, and the worsening snowy roads, he hadn't got home till four in the morning and desperately needed some sleep. He wouldn't agree with her assessment, and would have roused himself to assist Mr Purdue without a moment's thought. But then he seemed to think that he could exist in perpetuity on three hours of sleep a night and only toast for supper. So, despite his medical degree, Rose had decided to take certain matters into her own hands. Like his diet, the number of hours he spent working needed to be balanced with a suitable amount of rest and relaxation or he would run himself into the ground. If that meant she had to run interference between him and the many patients who had no respect at all for boundaries, then so be it. Sam was their physician, not their servant.

She had barely rolled the next ball of dough out when the door was knocked upon again. This time it was Mr Bunion, the odious apprentice of the local solicitor, who had the most apt name in the world because, despite his dandified clothes and over-pomaded hair, he smelled like feet.

'Good morning.' He tipped his hat, grinning like an idiot and looking like one too, in the most intricately tied cascading cravat Rose had ever seen. 'I wonder if I could steal a moment of your husband's time.'

As he presumptuously stepped forward, she folded her arms and planted her feet. 'Why do you need to see him?'

'Well…obviously I have an ailment which I would like treated.' His smile this time was so oily it might have been made of lard. 'Surely you do not wish me to discuss the intimate details of it on your doorstep?'

'On Saturdays my husband only sees emergencies, Mr Bunion. If you do not mind me saying, you look much too hale and hearty today for me to believe that you are one.'

'If you must know, I have a boil.' He leaned closer to whisper this, and singed her face with his rancid breath. 'In a most unfortunate place. I am in discomfort, Mrs Able, so surely that is enough?'

'I am afraid discomfort can wait until Monday, Mr Bunion, because a boil, even a big one, can just as easily be treated at home. Apply a hot cloth to it for at least ten minutes, to draw it out, and then pop the poison out with a needle.'

He puffed up like an affronted peacock. 'I am a single gentleman, madam, and so do not have any reason to possess a needle!'

Affronted herself by the inanity she was hearing, she pointed across the square to Isobel's new haberdashery. 'Then I suggest you go, forthwith, to Mrs Parker's, to purchase yourself one, because it is my husband's well-earned day off and he won't be lancing it for you today!'

'This is outrageous!'

'Isn't it just? The general surgery will open Monday at eight o'clock sharp, should you still require it. Until then, good day to you, Mr Bunion.'

The door was halfway closed when he had the gall to start again. 'Oh, I shall be here at eight sharp, madam, be in no doubt! When I fully intend to apprise your affable husband of the fact that his wife is a rude shrew who has quite forgotten her place!'

'You do that, sir. And while you are about it inform

him that his rude shrew of a wife also suggested that you should go and buy some soap and some tooth powders because you smell, Mr Bunion! Very badly indeed!'

She slammed the door, so infuriated by him, and every other who had encroached upon her Saturday morning, that she marched into Sam's office rather than back to the kitchen.

She found a plain sheet of foolscap and on it, in big, capitalised letters, wrote a new sign for the door. Then she stomped to the kitchen to get some string, and used it to tie the terse message to the knocker, in case anyone else with precious little wrong with them thought it appropriate to ignore the general surgery hours etched on the brass plaque. Because she would genuinely strangle the next timewaster who interrupted her baking and Sam's well-earned day off.

Miraculously, it did the trick, and her second batch of pies was about to come out of the oven an hour and half later when a rather dishevelled and disorientated Sam finally made an appearance. He blinked at her, shocked, as if he had literally just fallen out of bed.

'Is everything all right?'

She glanced around, mimicking him exactly, minus the adorable tuft of hair that was standing up at a right angle to his head. 'Everything seems to be. What were you expecting?'

'Well, it's almost noon,' he said, as if she had lost track of time. 'Doesn't anyone need me?'

'I would have awoken you if they did.'

'I never sleep this late.'

'You must have needed it, then, don't you think?'

He pondered that briefly, then nodded. 'I suppose I must have.'

'Do you feel better for it?'

He gave that a moment's thought too, as if he rarely contemplated his own physical health. 'I suppose I do. I feel guilty, though. For not being here for my patients.'

Rose made a great show of looking around again. 'What patients? Clearly the whole of Whittleston is in fine fettle today. Including you, now that you are properly rested. For once.'

If he registered her dig, he chose to ignore it. 'Hmm... odd. Saturday mornings are usually fairly busy, as that's when all the people who forget to come in during the week come to see me.'

Which just said it all. He was condoning their lack of organisation without any censure at all and running himself ragged in the process.

'They shouldn't be.' She pushed him towards the table, trying not to notice the intriguing dusting of dark hair visible in the deep V of his open shirt, which he had obviously donned in a hurry. 'When, according to your sign outside, there isn't supposed to be a surgery at all on Saturdays.'

'I inherited that sign from the previous physician. I've never really abided by those hours, though.'

'Then perhaps you should make the most of today's reprieve, don't you think?'

There was no point getting into a fight about it as he would dig his heels in. They had only been married a week, and already she knew him well enough to know that he had no boundaries where work was concerned. He toiled from the moment he got up until he went to bed. The only respite he gave himself was mealtimes, and she put that concession wholly down to her superior skills in the kitchen, because he claimed to be too busy to stop working otherwise and, worse, she suspected he believed that lie too.

Yes, this was a large and busy practice, but on top of his daily surgeries, endless home visits—which couldn't all be necessary—and the steady stream of emergencies that he had no choice but to rush to, he also spent every other spare hour in his office, meticulously rewriting his patient notes, filing them away himself rather than paying someone to do it for him and reading medical journals. If he wasn't doing that he was mixing potions and powders in his surgery, labelling them and storing them on the shelves like soldiers on parade. Not once, in the seven days since they had taken their faux vows, had he set a single foot in the parlour, let alone sat down in it to relax.

Rather than nag him about that, it was better to distract him from his unnecessary labours with food.

'What would you like for breakfast?'

His nostrils twitched as he sniffed the sideboard. 'Those pies look and smell delicious. What are they—apple?'

'You cannot have apple pie for breakfast.'

'Spoilsport. Can I have it for luncheon, then? It's practically luncheon anyway, so...' He reached for one of the smaller ones and she slapped his hand away.

'I've got sausages, bacon, eggs...or some toast.'

'Yes, to all, please. I'm starving.'

'As you wish.' Rose smiled as she retrieved the loaded plate of all those things, already warming on the range, and placed it before him. Then slid a freshly fried egg onto it with a thick slice of toast. 'And before you ask, yes, I am a mind-reader.'

'I sincerely hope you are not.' He pretended to look worried and she shrugged.

'I heard you stirring through the floorboards. The ones beneath your bed creak and you are clearly a fidgeter while you wake.'

'I'm sorry,' he said, looking oddly guilty as he picked up his cutlery, as if his morning fidgeting was somehow something to be ashamed of. 'Thank you for this.'

Rose busied herself while he ate rather than sit with him, because she was enjoying these mealtime interactions a little too much since their wedding and didn't want him to know. She was no stranger to love, and knew the early warning signs too well not to realise that she was futilely suffering from them. Tiny butterflies had begun to flap in her tummy each time she heard his footsteps or his curricle. She smiled more. Laughed more. Made more of an effort each morning with her hair and her clothes. Today's choice of gown was no exception. This warm green wool ensemble was too warm for inside and was intended for outside pursuits, as it had been made with a matching pelisse with fur at the neck and cuffs. But this fitted dress did pleasing things to her figure, especially around the bust, and had always garnered compliments.

Did she want one from him?

Probably.

Hopelessly romantic masochist that she was!

She certainly basked in the glow of every compliment he gave her cooking, and against her better judgement Rose seemed to be on a mission to please him. This might well be a short, sham marriage, but she was settling into it rather well and was already protective and possessive of her transient husband's welfare. Even so, she had no intentions of getting her poor heart broken again, and she harboured no lofty belief that she could make him feel the same way. The strange stirring in her chest was all her problem. Sam was eternally bound to Catherine, would probably never let her go, and had been nothing but honest about that.

Therefore, some prudent distance and boundaries would not go amiss, and she would limit herself to one cosy meal with him a day. She would not overthink why she would prefer that meal to be dinner, when it was dark outside, they had more time and seemed to have the world all to themselves. Nor would she give much consideration to the desire she felt for him after those dinners, preferring to see that as part of her healing process and part of being a woman in her prime, and therefore not really anything to do with him.

No indeed. As all the signs were definitely there, prudent distance was the order of the day. Now that she had saved him from himself, and all the non-urgent patients who wanted to sabotage his day off, and had finally finished her batch baking, she would take herself out. Give her smart green frock and matching pelisse an airing by calling on some friends and putting the handsome but tortured man who was calling to her out of her mind until she fed him again tonight.

He savoured the last mouthful of his food, then washed it down with the hot coffee she had placed before him. 'Seeing as today is a quiet day, I might as well visit the big apothecary in Romford. I'm running low on a few staples, and the snow outside isn't too bad, by the looks of it today. A bracing run in the curricle is always good for blowing the cobwebs out of the mind.'

'It has melted quite a bit. Thank goodness.'

And a bracing run in his curricle did sound like the perfect activity for a lazier Saturday. It would also be the perfect airing for her smart green wool ensemble.

'If you fancy some company, I'd love to do some shopping in Romford myself.' That had popped out before she could stop it. So much for some prudent distance! 'Do not feel obliged to say yes, by the way, if you would prefer your own space.'

'I wouldn't mind some company.'

His answer came with no hesitation or pauses, and it came along with a devasting smile, so the dratted butterflies flapped some more.

'Give me ten minutes to look more presentable and we'll get going.'

Just shy of ten minutes later he bounded down the stairs with a fresh spring in his step. The lack of shadows under his hazel eyes reassured her that she had done exactly the right thing in letting him sleep.

'That's a pretty coat, Rose. Green suits you.'

She practically melted at the compliment, and the accompanying smile which he bestowed with it, but sincerely hoped she hid it well. In case her quickened pulse showed on her face, she turned slightly to pull on her gloves. 'Thank you. It's one of my favourites.'

He opened the door for her solicitously, and without touching she sailed through it. It was only when he closed it behind them that she remembered that she had forgotten to remove her sign.

Of course it was too big for him not to notice, and he paused to read it, his eyes scanning every word with increasing incredulity.

ONLY KNOCK ON THIS DOOR TODAY IF:

1. *You fear someone is about to die or*
2. *They have a severe fever or*
3. *Are delirious or*
4. *Are bleeding profusely or*
5. *Vomiting extensively or*
6. *They have a pox of some sort or*
7. *Are oozing noxious things that they shouldn't or*
8. *They are unconscious or*
9. *A bone is broken or*
10. *They are in labour or*
11. *You are delivering something or*
12. *You are a friend paying us a social call and require no medical assistance whatsoever or*
13. *The world is about to end*

In all other cases, please behave like a decent person and return during the surgery hours or the physician's new and furious wife will not be responsible for her actions that you interrupted his well-earned day off!

The words were etched in half-inch letters on the one-foot by two-foot plaque screwed to the wall.

'Well, I suppose that explains my unusually quiet morning.' His flicked her a glance that was more amused than annoyed. 'Dare I ask what prompted it?'

'Mr Bunion's boil was the final straw.' As Sam instantly pulled a face of disgust, at the mention of the man more than his ailment, she couldn't resist a grin. 'In the spirit of our brutally honest relationship, I should probably warn you that he took such umbrage at not being granted admittance he claimed he is going to give you a piece of his mind on Monday, over me and my poor attitude.'

'Well, that should be interesting,' he said, heading around the back to fetch his horse and leaving the sign in situ. 'I'll look forward to putting uppity Mr Bunion in his place.' And if his amused smile was any gauge, he really was.

As Saturday was market day in Whittleston, Rose passed the next few minutes chatting to some of the locals while he attached the horse to the conveyance.

Once he was done, he held out his hand to help her up, then snatched it back before she could take it. 'Do you know how to drive a curricle?'

'Of course I do! I'm a farmer's daughter, aren't I? Why?'

'Well, as it's apparently my day off, I figure I might as well enjoy the pleasure of being a passenger for once.' He gently led her by the elbow to the other side. 'Let's see if you have as deft a touch with the reins as you do with pastry.'

Chapter Fourteen

Rose liked to drive fast. Of course she did. Because she was a fearless minx who loved to milk the fun out of every situation. Not even the dark fazed her, and that didn't surprise him. There was an intrepid, devil-may-care streak in her that reminded him of Catherine. His first wife had been a force of nature too, and had never missed an opportunity to push a boundary or find the joy or the excitement in a situation.

She had crashed her father's phaeton once because of her love of speed. She had taken it out without his knowledge, taken a bend too fast and the whole thing had tipped over. Not before she'd flung herself into a haystack—thank goodness—and fortunately the horses had been unscathed too, so no living thing had been hurt in the incident. The damage to the poor phaeton, however, had been extensive, and had cost her father an arm and a leg to fix. As a punishment, Catherine had been consigned to barracks, or at least the civilian equivalent, and had been banned from leaving her father's house unchaperoned for three months. She had hated that.

'What are you grinning at?'

Rose's question interrupted his reverie and brought him up short—because he had been grinning. Over Catherine. Which was odd when normally all memories of her were tinged with such sadness it brought a lump to his throat and such bitterness that acid burned it afterwards. But that had been a fond recollection and, to his great surprise, not only had it not hurt but it had been a pleasant thought. One that did nothing to spoil his buoyant mood at all.

'Nothing. I am simply in a good humour.' And had been all day.

From the moment he had sat at the kitchen table to eat his breakfast, his impromptu day off had been a balm to his soul. The hour-long drive to Romford had been delightful. With Rose at the helm, and thanks to the freshly cleared roads, he had been able to watch the snow-covered winter scenery whip past. To take it all in and appreciate what a pretty part of the world he lived in.

While she had explored the busy market—the oldest and biggest in the South East of England—he'd then spent another hour browsing the apothecary's. Now he was confident that, stored safely in the back of his curricle, was all the stock he needed for the next month, because he had taken his time selecting it rather than rushing the job, like he usually did, and consequently missing something.

Once he had finished his shopping he had found her browsing a stall which sold carpets, where he'd discovered that she had purchased him one for the parlour, so it had become his task to heave the thing back to his conveyance, where some other purchases had also found their way. Some cushions and some tablecloths were wrapped in brown paper. There was a basket of

eggs too, a wheel of cheese, a pile of second-hand novels and an enormous leg of lamb, which he was very
much looking forward to eating.

Because Rose hadn't lied when she had said she was
an excellent cook. She was better than excellent. She
was sublime. He had never eaten so well in his life as
he had this last week.

Despite knowing her food could not be topped, Sam
hadn't taken much convincing to partake in a late lunch
with her at the Golden Lion pub. Hence they were here
now, the sun already set and the first flakes of fresh
snow falling for the last mile of their ride home.

'If one day off puts you in such a good humour, Sam,
maybe you should do it more often? Grant yourself
maybe two or three of them a year?'

She had a particular expression when she wielded
sarcasm. Her dark brows quirked, her plump lips pouted
and her green eyes sparkled.

'Build yourself up gradually to perhaps even one
each season?'

'Is that a subtle nag, temporary wife?'

'Oh, it wasn't subtle at all, transient husband. When
one only has three months to try to make some meaningful improvements to a man in dire need of some im-
proving, one cannot waste time on subtlety. You work
too hard, do not look after yourself, and if you are not
careful you will send yourself to an early grave.'

He almost said, *Perhaps that's what I want*, except,
bizarrely, it wasn't any more.

When had that happened?

'Save your efforts, Rose, as I cannot be improved.'
To further surprise him, he found he was in the mood to
banter. 'How on earth does one improve on perfection?'

'Ha!' She never wasted an opportunity to skewer him. 'And you just inadvertently proved my point with that stupid response, as you are clearly so tired and addled you have become deranged and deluded. For there is a great deal of you that falls well shy of perfect.'

'Such as?' He folded his arms and pretended to be peeved. 'I am solvent and run my own business. I am well educated and well respected and certainly cure more than I kill. I have all my teeth and my hair, and even fancy myself not bad looking in certain lights. I'd wager any sensible woman would tell you that you have hooked yourself a catch, madam, so I have no idea what you are complaining about.'

'Stop!' She raised an imperious palm. 'That is almost too much humbleness to bear.' Then she snorted. 'Handsome you may be...'

The compliment heated his blood, because he liked the idea that she found him attractive. He shouldn't, but did.

'But you err too much on the side of seriousness and dourness to be considered a true catch. You are just four and thirty in years, but you seem to have forgotten that you are a youngish man in his prime and behave more like one three decades older sometimes. When was the last time you had some proper fun?'

Today—thanks to her. And yesterday and the day before. Mealtimes had become the highlight of his day—and not because she fed him like a king, but because she ate with him. Made him laugh. Made him feel lighter. Made him feel alive. At least in those moments they spent together at his kitchen table. He would miss all that when she was gone. Undoubtedly more than he'd intended and far more than was wise.

Rather than tell her that, which really wouldn't be wise, he rolled his eyes. 'That would be a month ago, when you enticed me into a foolish wager and, when it all backfired and we became social pariahs, I ended up shackled to you in a loveless, enforced sham marriage that neither of us wanted. *Such. Fun.*'

She threw back her head and laughed, and Sam experienced the most satisfying sense of achievement to have been the cause of it.

'You never resist an opportunity to remind me of my failings, do you, Dr Able? And with such pithy and precise sarcasm too!'

'You are not the only one fluent in it, you know.'

'What I do know already is that you will be *very* easy to leave and I sincerely doubt anyone will be surprised when I do.'

She twisted to look down her nose at him, but her smile spoiled the effect and that smile said it all. Said that she rather liked his company too, and that perhaps if fate had had them meet in a different life, where her heart not been irrevocably broken and his hadn't died and shrivelled to a husk, they might have gone together well. But…

As if she'd read his mind, she shrugged at the same time as he did, and the humour in her gaze morphed into bittersweet acceptance of their sad situations.

'Have you given any thought to what you might do and where you might go when this is over?' He didn't want to care what happened to her when she left, but he had a burning need to know she would be all right. 'Will it be Suffolk or the Outer Hebrides?'

She sighed and focussed on the road as she turned into the square. 'It will be Suffolk to begin with, but I think I should find myself a new place to live once the dust has settled. Close enough to my parents, so that I can easily visit them, but far enough away that I can spare myself all the inevitable gossip and start afresh. Reinvent myself somewhere I am not the unfortunate, unwanted and unweddable Miss Healy.'

Was that really what she thought of herself? Or was it what the local gossips and that rag of a newspaper had made her and others believe. Either way it was a ridiculous injustice. There was nothing unfortunate or unweddable about her, and as he swept his gaze down her jaunty green pelisse he couldn't imagine that any man with blood in his veins didn't want her. She was too alluring. Too attractive. Too effervescent not to want in all the improper and impertinent ways it was possible to want a woman. His heart might be cold but she certainly fired his blood.

'Norfolk is within a stone's throw, and there are some pretty villages in that neck of the woods.'

Her voice dragged him back from his lingering contemplation of her womanly figure.

'Or maybe I'll head to a town. Ipswich or Norwich, perhaps, where it's easier to live a life not scrutinised by all and sundry. Then I might set myself up in trade, like Isobel has. I quite fancy the idea of owning a shop and earning my own keep.' Before he could offer, she shot him a defiant stare. 'I do not need your money, Sam, and I do not want to spend the rest of my life doing nothing of any consequence. You, of all people, should understand how important having a purpose is. I'll go mad if I don't have one.'

He did understand. Only too well. If he hadn't been a doctor, with essential skills in constant demand, he dreaded to think where he would be now—or how he would be, for that matter. Drunk in a gutter somewhere, probably. Or still in uniform, chasing bullets. Or in the ground because one had finally found him and put him out of his misery.

A thought which suddenly left him cold rather than regretful. Which was…sobering. And…new.

'Then might I suggest you open a bakery, Rose? As the things you can do with pastry really should be illegal. You'd make an absolute fortune in a village or a town. Your cakes are pretty spectacular too.'

'Do you really think I could?' For moment she forgot to be bold and blasé, and he saw how much being jilted had knocked her confidence.

'Enough that I would happily invest in it.'

He wanted to reach for her hand. Squeeze it in reassurance. But of course he didn't, because that wouldn't be appropriate. Or wise. They might be temporary partners in crime, but he didn't need to muddy the waters by adding any unessential physical contact to their arrangement. Especially when he increasingly wanted to touch her, and most especially when he touched her with too much impertinence already, nightly in his dreams. Which reminded him… Now that he knew that the floorboards creaked beneath his bed, he would have to find a quieter place in his bedchamber to relieve himself of the torture of those dreams every morning.

His growing sexual attraction to her did bother him, but only in so much as it was dashed inconvenient to be so riddled with lust at the start of each day that he had to expel it immediately. He might not want to feel that way, but it was a normal bodily function. One that was universally acknowledged in academic circles to be intertwined with life. In all the creatures of the earth, the urge to mate was much like the urge to eat or breathe or sleep. It lived inside the blood. It was imprinted somehow into the muscles and the sinews in a way human science was still too primitive to understand. An intrinsic part of the laws of nature and not any sort of reliable sign that he wasn't still dead instead.

Ergo, his voracious morning lust for her meant nothing—just as Rose meant nothing and would remain meaning nothing to him beyond what they had now: a situational friendship borne out of unusual circumstances. Accepting that and enjoying it for what it was did not make him in any way disloyal to Catherine's memory. He hadn't broken any vows. He had simply said a second set, which he had no intentions of honouring. Enjoying a few months of Rose's company did not miraculously make him mended in any way. The status quo was unchanged.

Thank goodness.

'Will you stay here in Whittleston, Sam, or will you move somewhere your slate is clean too?'

It wasn't a question he had expected, or even considered until she had mentioned it, but seeing as she had, he shrugged. It made sense, he supposed, to seek a fresh start. Rose's aunt and uncle lived here, after all, so he would by default hear about her. It would be a darned sight easier forgetting about her if there wasn't that constant reminder—

'Dr Able! Thank God!'

Out of the snow, Bill Anderson the miller emerged, arms waving. By the looks of the twin icy quilted epaulets settled on his shoulders, and the amount of snowflakes covering his horse's mane and saddle, he had been waiting outside Sam's house for quite some time.

'My mother needs you! Her face has dropped.' He pulled down his cheek to illustrate. 'And she cannot move a muscle apart for the littlest finger of her right hand.'

'We'll meet you there!'

Rose didn't wait to be told to turn the curricle, and with a decisive crack of the reins they were flying back down out of the village within seconds.

Rose had never experienced death at close quarters before. Her only family members who had passed had been both sets of her grandparents and, while she had known many Suffolk acquaintances die, their connection had been distant enough that it hadn't touched her. Therefore, to be a quarter of a century old and first witness the exact moment of death was as unsettling as it was humbling.

One moment Mrs Anderson had been staring up at Sam, scared, petrified and frozen by the massive stroke she had suffered, her breathing so ragged and erratic it was haunting. The next the fear in her eyes had been replaced by an odd serenity and she'd sighed and that had been that. She was gone.

To a detached onlooker it seemed peaceful. It was also, strangely, a privilege to see, because something otherworldly had happened to the old lady in her final seconds. Whether that had been resignation or acceptance or, as Rose had decided to hope, the fact she had caught a glimpse of what lay beyond this realm and whatever it was it had given her enough comfort to stop fighting to stay in it.

Odder still was the shroud of death which fell over the room as Sam released Mrs Anderson's wrist, gently closed her eyes and confirmed that she was gone. By then, those gathered around her bedside had already begun to weep. Her son, her two grown grandsons and all their wives had felt her passing in the same visceral way Rose had, and had, within moments, passed from extreme worry to grief.

Mr Anderson Senior, however, was not ready to accept what everyone else had and still clung to his wife's hand, begging her to wake up.

In silent, tacit agreement, she and Sam both rose and left. Staying simply to watch his realisation dawn felt unnecessary and voyeuristic.

'I'm so sorry, Bill.' Sam rubbed the miller's shoulder as he followed them to the door. 'It's no consolation, but with a stroke that severe there was no chance of any recovery. Take comfort in the knowledge that she is free of any pain now.'

'Thank you for trying, though, Doctor.'

'Would you like me to notify the undertaker tonight?'

Bill shook his head. 'They'll be time enough for all that in the morning. Tonight we'd prefer to say our final goodbyes in private as a family.'

As there was nothing else to be said, they left on leaden feet, and a very ashen and subdued Sam was in the process of helping Rose up into the curricle when Mr Anderson Senior suddenly dashed out of the house, tears streaming down his wizened old face as he cried noisily, 'Dr Able, please!'

He grabbed Sam's sleeve and wouldn't let go, even when his son reappeared and tried to call him back.

'You need to give me something. Something strong that will take me to where my Eliza has gone.'

'I'm s-sorry, Mr Anderson.' Raw emotion choked her transient husband's throat. 'I cannot do that.'

'Yes, you can!' The old man dropped to his knees in the snow. 'Please! I don't want to be here if she isn't! I want to go with her! We've been together fifty-seven years! I'm no use to anyone anyway nowadays, and I don't want to spend another minute knowing she's dead and I'm not. You can fix that for me. Nobody needs to know...'

It was pitiable to watch.

'I'm sorry, Mr Anderson.' To his credit, Sam did not try to pull away from the man's iron grip, and left that to his son to do. 'My job is to save lives, not end them.'

'Even if mine just ended anyway?'

As Bill tried his best to gently extricate his aged father and drag him back inside, the old man lunged again and caught Sam's hand this time.

'You have to understand...she was my everything, Doctor. My everything!'

Words that made poor Sam's face blanch and rooted him to the spot.

Even when the bereaved father and son had disappeared indoors, he still stood on the same spot, shoulders slumped, as if reliving his own tragic past. Entirely lost in his own living hell.

Rose slid down from the curricle's perch and slipped her hand in his, tugging him gently. 'Come. Let's get you home.'

She practically had to push all six feet plus and goodness knew how many stones of him into the carriage, where he sat shocked and stunned while she hauled herself in beside him and then drove all the way home.

The snow was coming down thick and fast by the time they returned to his house and Sam's teeth were chattering. She suspected that had more to do with what had just happened than the cold, but despite her insistence of seeing to his horse, so that he could go inside and warm his chilled bones by the fire, he would have none of it. While she unpacked the curricle and took all their Romford purchases inside, so they didn't get ruined by the weather, he took the animal to the little shed it lived in around the back and spent so long rubbing it down and feeding it that the pot of tea she had made them both was cooling on the kitchen table.

He wasn't shivering when he returned, but he was still ashen and looked in dire need of some proper comfort.

'You did all you could have, Sam.' She reached for his hand but he snatched it away, as if angry all of a sudden at his own perceived incompetence.

'Did I? She'd been suffering there an hour before I got to her!' Guilt etched deep lines in his handsome face and his eyes were so stark they frightened her. 'Perhaps if I had got there sooner—'

She wasn't going to let him do that to himself and grabbed him by the shoulders and forced him to face her.

'She had a massive stroke, Sam. Massive. One that left her completely paralysed. That was your initial diagnosis. Before she died, you even told Bill on the quiet that you didn't expect her to survive the night. She was eighty. Very frail already. And hadn't been well for months. I heard you tell Bill that, too, just as I heard you explain to him that there are no effective treatments for stroke victims. That in time, if the patient is lucky, they might regain some of what it has stolen from them, but even if they survive they will not emerge from it unscathed. That in severe cases, such as his mother's, the immediate risk of a second stroke is very high and that would likely be fatal.'

As he tried to dismiss his own words, she shook his shoulders.

'Tell me, what else could you have done beyond giving her the pain relief that you did? You are a physician, Sam, not a miracle-worker.'

She thought she had snapped him out of it, because he blew out a calming breath and nodded.

'Sit down. Have some tea. It will not make you feel any better, I know, but the knowledge that a miracle from above was the only hope she had left should. People die, Sam. With the best will in the world, even you cannot save them all.'

She pulled out a chair for him and he eyed it with distaste before he spun on his heel.

'I'm going to bed.'

'To what? To stew? To second-guess yourself? To punish yourself with guilt?' But his long legs had already taken him to the foot of the stairs, so she caught his hand again. 'Sit with me. Talk to me. Rant at me. Let it all out and don't let this fester!'

He yanked his hand away and stomped up the stairs. 'I want to be alone, Rose!'

She raced up behind him. 'If you think I am leaving you alone like this, you have another think coming! You couldn't have done a thing more than you did!'

He stopped dead on the landing and she crashed into the solid wall of his back. 'Of course I could have! I could have done the decent thing and put that poor bastard out of his misery, like he begged me to!'

'You couldn't have done that!'

When he refused to turn around at her insistence, she pushed her way past him so that she could look into his eyes. They were lost in the hideous memories of Catherine's passing that tonight's parallels had clearly conjured and her heart bled for him.

She gripped his lapel with one hand and smoothed the other over his cheek tenderly. 'You knew that and he never should have asked—but he had just been plunged into the abyss of grief and didn't know what he was asking.'

'He knew what he was asking.' His voice was desolate. 'She was his everything.'

'And that will be reflected in the level of his grief. And, while unbearably tragic to witness, I know that if you asked him now if he would spare himself all of the pain he's in in return for not enjoying every single minute of their fifty-seven years together, he wouldn't. There is only one certainty in life, Sam.' She used both hands to cup his cheeks now, to ensure he listened to her every word. 'That is that each and every one of us must die. We walk blindly into love knowing that ultimately that must happen and accepting it as a fair price for all the joy it brings. The Andersons had fifty-seven years before one of them had to pay that price. He loved her so completely that if she hadn't died tonight he'd be willing her death by the morning, as watching her in pain would have broken him too. Don't make what happened about you and Catherine. No good can come of that.'

'I know... I know...' He nodded, swallowing. 'Usually I can keep it all locked within, but...'

'Tonight felt too akin to your own experience, and that's all right in the moment, but you are not being fair to yourself by torturing yourself with similarities when every death is a tragedy for someone and not every death needs to be a tragedy to you.'

He nodded again and allowed her to pull him into her embrace. 'I'm so tired of feeling broken, Rose…so tired of all the pain and hurt and bitterness that festers within me breaking free and overwhelming me.'

She stroked his hair, grateful that she could be his pillar of strength when he needed one. 'Perhaps it has to for you to finally let it go?'

He pulled away far enough to frown at her. 'I hate what it does to me. How helpless and hopeless it makes me feel.' He pressed his fist to his abdomen. 'How it overtakes all reason and renders me…useless.'

'All the more reason why you shouldn't be alone and why you need company. What can I do tonight to distract you?'

'Don't ask that.'

He huffed and shook his head, as if he had had an idea but quickly discarded it. Then his indecisive gaze locked with hers for the longest time, while he was clearly at war with himself, before it dropped to her mouth. She knew the moment he lost the battle, because he swiftly closed the distance between them and pressed his lips to hers.

Chapter Fifteen

It was a gentle but urgent kiss. Both an exploration and a surrender and potent as a result.

Rose melted against him, winding her arms around his neck in blatant invitation so that he was left in no doubt that she wanted this too. If this was the distraction he wanted then she was all for it. She deepened the kiss and Sam sighed against her mouth. Beneath her fingers, the knotted muscles in his shoulders and back softened as he let go of all the pain that had gripped him mere moments ago and lost himself in her.

He snaked an arm around her waist to tug her closer while his tongue tangled languidly with hers, pulling her hips flush with his so that she could feel the hard length of his desire. Had they not been married, it would have been an outrageous, improper gesture during a first kiss, but because they were—at least temporarily—it was oddly appropriate. Brutally honest from the outset.

He wanted more than a kiss, so she did something she had never done. Never dared to do. And pushed her hand between their bodies to stroke that impertinent bulge so that he knew he could have whatever he wanted.

He half moaned, half growled at her touch and walked her backwards, still kissing her, until her back touched a bedchamber door. She had no clue whose it was until he groped behind her to open it and they stumbled into his.

With no fire in the grate, and no moonlight or stars to illuminate the uncovered windows, it was pitch-black inside and somehow that was fitting. It suited the situation and it empowered her to be bolder than she would have ever thought possible, because she made short work of the buttons of her pelisse so that he could strip her out of it, then helped him untie the laces of her gown.

His hungry mouth never left hers as he smoothed the garment from her shoulders. Then the weight of the heavy green wool worked with gravity to puddle on the floor around her feet. It was immediately joined by his greatcoat, coat, and then his cravat. Her fingers fumbled with the small buttons on his waistcoat. It was impossible to concentrate on the task while he unlaced her stays and tossed them to one side.

They used each other for balance as boots were toed off. Rose tugged his shirt from his waistband, and he broke contact only long enough to strip it from his with one hand.

She was a wanton, breathless creature by the time it came to unbuttoning his falls, in a hurry to move on from kissing to more, and so was he. His breathing was ragged and erratic as he stepped out of his breeches. The meagre light was robbing her of the pleasure of seeing his nakedness in more than shadows—but, oh, my goodness, those shadows were filled with sinful promise. Broad, square shoulders that were almost twice the width of his hips. His erection standing rigid and proud and desperate for her.

Impatient, she ran her palms over his skin. The dusting of hair on his chest was an intriguing contrast to the satin-smooth skin stretched taut over the muscles in his arms and across his belly that she did not possess. Sam wrapped his arms around her waist loosely, nuzzling her neck as he manoeuvred them both to the bed, then lowered himself to sit on it so that he could peel her out of her chemise.

He removed that last barrier between them reverently, and with torturous slowness, trailing his lips over every inch of skin he revealed. The fabric caught on her breasts, which seemed fuller and heavier than usual, so he used his hands to free them, sliding his fingers beneath the tight neckline to cup one, then lifting it out so that he could kiss the upper swell of it, before repeating the task with the other.

Her puckered nipples tightened some more in the chilled air of the room, brazenly poking towards him and begging to be touched. As if he knew that was what her body craved, he kissed around them to torment her, smiling against her skin as she arched her breasts shamelessly towards his mouth.

His hands spanned her ribcage beneath them and fanned down over her fevered skin her to hips. The chemise whispered along her legs on its journey to the floor. He kissed her belly, her navel. Caressed her buttocks. Then, to her surprise, pressed a kiss at the exact spot where her womanhood met her thighs, his hot breath gently ruffling the soft curls between them.

He stood then, opened his arms, and without hesitation she stepped into his embrace, looping her arms around his neck as his tightened around her and their bodies touched everywhere. Her needy breasts found some satisfaction as they flattened against the hard plane of his chest and she marvelled at the insistent throb of his cock against her pelvis. Odd things happened between her legs as warmth and moisture seemed to pool there, but although they were both obviously now ready for more, they simply kissed instead. Thorough, lazy, but intensely intimate kisses that acknowledged there was so much more to come but they both wanted to squeeze every drop of pleasure from the experience by denying themselves the carnal release they craved.

Then, out of nowhere, they simultaneously concluded that the moment had arrived, because he edged her back towards the mattress as she pulled him down on her. They landed together, as they had on that fateful dawn in the snow, with his hips cradled between her legs, perfectly positioned to do what nature had intended those intensely personal and private parts of them to do. Even so, of their own accord her legs fell further apart and her hips tilted, to give him unfettered access, and his hardness dipped to sit in the crease—almost there but nowhere near enough.

She did not recognise the woman who gave the needy moan, begging for more, but as he denied her that his lips finally worshipped her nipples, and the pleasure was so intense, so unexpected, that she cried out into the silent night. Then she writhed beneath him, grinding her hips against his in utter desperation as he tortured each puckered tip with his lips, tongue and teeth. All the while his hardness seemed to grow and pulse against her sensitive flesh, and beneath her palms his body trembled from the force of his own need that he was now fighting to hold back.

'Please, Sam—have me.' She genuinely did not think she could last another second without feeling him inside her. 'I want you so much.'

'You cannot possibly want me more than I want you.'

He stared down into her eyes and she believed him. Because saw it all there. Lust. Desire. And once again surrender. And she rejoiced in all three.

'Every morning I wake up hard for you because you haunt my dreams. I crave you, Rose. Yearn for you. It's like a sickness and nothing cures it.'

'This will.' She tilted her hips enough that the hot tip of his manhood kissed her opening. Then, in case that wasn't a blatant enough invitation, she repeated herself. 'Have me…before I combust from wanting you.'

In one swift, fluid movement he pushed inside her, filling her completely but instinctively pausing at her maidenhead. That seemed to momentarily bother him, because clearly he did not want to hurt her, so Rose gripped his hips and jerked hers up to dispense with it herself, gasping at the slight discomfort while he held himself still above her.

He kissed her tenderly, waiting for her body to relax as it familiarised itself with the intrusion, before inching inside her a little more. He rolled his hips slightly, and that caressed the inner walls of her body so perfectly she sighed, and he smiled against her mouth as he did it some more. It did not take her long to learn the dance, and once she had she embraced it. Revelled in it. Her body blossomed and bloomed beneath his, every nerve-ending she possessed gloriously alive and tingling with each increasingly fervent but exquisite thrust.

She was almost there, although she had no clue where 'there' was, and knew that he was holding himself back, waiting for her to get there. Her hips bucked almost violently as she tried to find a way to get there for him and, as if sensing her frustration, he kissed her.

'It's all right, love.'

And suddenly it was as if the tenderness in his eyes made the universe tilt, and she realised that this—him—was exactly why fate had sabotaged her first wedding. Because she was destined for this. Heaven help her, but he was the one, and her damaged, foolish heart rejoiced at the realisation.

She smiled up and him, and he smiled back, and she decided not to fight it. Instead, she kissed him tenderly back. Infusing it with all of those wonderful, precious feelings that she hadn't intended to feel but that now swamped her.

He slipped his hand between their bodies to dip his thumb between her damp curls, where it found a knot of nerves she had not known existed and gently circled it. Once. Twice. The third was all she needed, and the intimate walls of her body began to pulse around his hardness as stars shimmered behind her eyes and her heart burst with joy inside her chest. And then she was falling. Falling mindless and boneless into an oasis of pure pleasure as she called his name until his release exploded on a cry and he joined her there. Holding her hand. Her name a benediction on his lips and his body pulsing within her in euphoric rhythm with the glorious fading ripples of her own.

Sam awoke feeling lighter and more at ease with himself than he had in years. Every muscle was loose. He was cosy and toasty, rather than hot and sweating as he was often prone to be when bad dreams plagued him or, as recently, when his dreams had been so vivid and carnal they left him wanting. This morning, however, his old chap wasn't standing painfully upright like a flagpole. At best, it was semi-erect, and as sleepy as he was, and that felt good. In fact, apart from the glaring daylight that permeated his eyelids, everything felt good.

He scrunched his eyes tighter and twisted his face further into his pillow to block out the sun—and then froze when hair tickled his nostrils. Because it wasn't his hair. His hair wasn't that luxuriant, and nor was it scented with a delicate hint of floral perfume. Just as the soft surface beneath his hand wasn't his mattress. It was skin. Silken, warm, caressible, feminine skin.

Rose's skin.

He cracked open one eye and indeed there she was. Lost in sleep. Her long lashes were sooty crescents against her alabaster cheeks. Her tousled chestnut hair fanned out over his pillow exactly as he had imagined in all his wild nocturnal fantasies—only better. One bare arm was thrown carelessly above her head, exposing the swell of a plump breast above the edge of his eiderdown.

She was utterly breathtaking in her beauty.

Enough that something unsettling and…scary stirred in his chest.

He retracted his hand gently, because he wasn't ready to face her or this right now, and it roused her. Not enough to wake her, but enough to make her stretch. The half-exposed breast instantly became a fully exposed breast, the dark nipple cresting and hardening in front of his eyes as the chill of the room hit it. Forcing him to watch, transfixed, as her hand appeared from under the blankets to unconsciously caress it until she sighed with sleepy contentment, as if it were a lover's fingers instead of her own.

It was the single most erotic thing he had ever seen.

Until the whole night before assaulted his memory with a whoosh and he was forced to recall that this wasn't the first time he had watched her caress her own nipple. Because sometime around dawn, he now remembered, he had witnessed it from another angle. From below. With her lovely long legs resting on his shoulders while he lapped at her core like a cat that had got the cream as she came to shuddering climax against his mouth.

That had undoubtedly been the single most erotic thing he had ever seen.

At least in this lifetime…post-Catherine.

His first wife had enjoyed that too, and he winced at the memory, feeling disloyal somehow for pleasuring another woman with such single-minded and selfish determination.

And everything he had done to Rose last night had been entirely selfish. In his addled, vulnerable state, after the sad events at the Andersons', he had forgotten to be dead inside and had been so desperate to stop the horrific pain and celebrate feeling alive he had used her outrageously. Taken her virginity without a second thought and then had her twice—no, thrice—over the course of the night, because after witnessing her shuddering climax at dawn he'd had to have her again.

Had to watch her come again while he was buried to the hilt inside her.

It had been, if he said so himself, quite a night, and one that in another life he might have been proud of, because he had always been a very attentive and thorough lover. But it had been the stupidest and most ill-considered thing in the world a man who was gratefully dead inside could have possibly done, when she had to leave and he had to let her, because he couldn't—wouldn't—allow himself to care for anyone like that again.

Bloody hell! What the blazes had he done!

He had just complicated the one thing he had needed to keep as uncomplicated as possible, and all because he hadn't been able to resist hauling the woman he needed to keep at arm's length into his arms!

They were hardly acquaintances now!

Not when his hands and lips had explored every single inch of her lush body and hers had done the same to his. Hardly friends either, seeing as she had kissed him down there too. Nor simply temporary, transient, situational partners in crime either.

They were lovers now!

Possibly even potential parents, as he had been so caught up in her he hadn't had the wherewithal to withdraw at the optimum moment.

Correction—optimum moments!

Because, heaven help him, there had been three of them!

Bloody, bloody hell! What had he been thinking?

Sam gazed at Rose again and his old chap instantly hardened, thanks to that one gorgeous and highly sensitive breast still on show. He groaned aloud. Then wished he could claw it back when she stirred and stretched again, rubbed her eyes with both hands, flung both arms above her head and, to torture him further, dislodged the other breast from beneath the covers. Then, after

another undulating, wholly feminine stretch of her spine
and wiggle of her hips, slowly her lids fluttered open.

She took one look at him and didn't balk or panic,
like he was doing. There was not an ounce of regret on
her stunning face as she smiled.

'Hello, you.' Her voice was deep and husky as she
woke, so seductive he felt it everywhere. 'Did you sleep
well?'

'Like a log,' he said, wondering how the hell he was
going to fix this now that the cork was literally and figuratively out of the bottle and couldn't ever be put back
in. How the blazes did you *un*make love to a woman?

It was a fairly momentous thing to make love to one,
after all. Especially one who had never lain with another man before. He was always going to be her first.
And the first time was significant. So significant, good
manners dictated that he had to mention it.

'I hope I didn't…er…hurt you too much last night?'

She shook her head, shy all of a sudden at the mention
of her 'downstairs', despite being apparently unasham-
edly bare-breasted upstairs. 'Some mild discomfort that
didn't last long.'

'And now…?' *After I rutted inside you repeatedly
like a randy, foaming bull in a field of cows in season!*
'Are you sore at all?'

The physician in him had to ask, but the guilt-ridden
man dreaded the answer.

'I'm aware that you've visited, Sam, if that is what you
are asking.' A bubble of embarrassed laughter popped
out of her mouth and she blushed a little. 'But I rather
like the feeling, so please don't offer me any poultices
or potions, *Dr Able*. I am not in need of your medical
services today.'

'All right, then…'

Was now the right time to bolt? To run screaming for the hills while he figured out what the hell to do next? Probably not, despite the internal chaotic whirling of every emotion he possessed. She didn't deserve that when she had bent over backwards to please him, both literally and figuratively. He suddenly recalled that the second time he'd joined with her, when she had briefly left the bed in the small hours to do…whatever she had needed to do…he'd met her in the middle of the bed-chamber on her way back, moved her hair to kiss her shoulders and her back, and then had her hard and fast over the bedstead.

Bloody hell!

He glanced at her with remorse, and then, like the randy beast he had been, felt his eyes drift to her breasts. She noticed. But instead of covering them, like most for-mer blushing virgins would have on the glaring dawn of their deflowering, Rose, of course, met him head-on. Fearless to the last and determined not to let him faze her. With the covers still bunched around her waist she rolled onto her side, propping herself up on her elbow while her hair cascaded over one shoulder in a riot of satin brown curls, and traced a seductive finger over his chest.

'But while I do not need your medical services, and we are already too late for the Sunday service at St Hil-dreth's, I am not so sore that I would say no to some of your other unique services, though.'

And just like that he was as hard as granite and des-perate for her again.

Would it really matter if he had her for the fifth time?

The unholy mess was already made…

Her finger began to trail downwards, then disappeared beneath the covers, and her touch felt so good he was sorely tempted to ignore the screaming voice in his head to get the hell out of there. He would have too if he hadn't stared deep into her eyes, seen her smiling in anticipation of the mindless fulfilment to come, and that unsettling, scary thing stirred in his chest again. Jolted, actually. So dangerously close to his shrivelled husk of a heart that it had him sitting bolt upright.

'Sorry. Can't.'

Won't!

'I've got calls to make…' Which was a pathetic excuse for a Sunday, when everyone was likely currently sitting in St Hildreth's listening to the Sunday sermon. 'The Andersons…' He grappled for something—anything—vaguely plausible. 'I need to check on Mr Anderson Senior. I'm worried about him.'

'Oh…'

Her lovely face fell and he hated himself for hurting her, then hated himself more for making her feel ashamed of her desire as she gathered the blankets up to cover herself, as if she had somehow done something wrong.

'Of course…the poor man.'

She knew he was lying through his teeth. Knew he was trying to soften the blow of rejecting her—all of her—with nonsense, because he was too cowardly to tell her the truth.

'It's really not you, Rose…it's me.' Which was true. She was perfect and he was…nauseous. Suffocating.

Petrified.

'I need some time and space to think about…' He flapped his hand between them. 'This.'

'I understand.'

She nodded again, making him feel wretched, because he really didn't deserve her understanding after what he had done. Or what he was doing. How was this any better than jilting her? Rejection was rejection, and she was again bearing the brunt of one. But, typically, she was stoic about it.

Hiding her hurt behind an uncertain smile, she sat up in the bed and hugged her knees to her chest beneath the covers. 'I suppose this is…unexpected. But not so awful, I hope?'

'No,' he lied slipping gratefully off the mattress and groping around for his clothes. 'Not awful at all. Just… big.'

Huge. Monumental.

Unsurmountable!

'I need some time alone to square it in my mind, Rose.'

Had he broken his vows to Catherine? Were they even still valid now that she was gone? Did it matter when he wasn't capable of honouring them anyway? To love, honour and cherish involved caring, and he no longer had the capacity of will to care. Lust was lust, but Rose deserved so much more than that, and he…couldn't.

Wouldn't.

'Will you be back in time for the whist game later? Sophie and Rafe did invite us to luncheon too… But if you'd rather I cancelled and we talked about this instead…once you've squared it in your mind?'

And already *'this'* had become more complicated than he could bear, because he knew there was nothing really to square. The die had been cast, he had nothing tangible to offer, and he was going to have to hurt her some more however he tried to deliver that news.

'I'll be back in time for that, I promise.'

As he backed out of the room, clutching a bundle of clothes, he desperately wanted to kiss her goodbye and reassure her that he would try to work through the blind panic that had gripped him by the balls and made him sick to his stomach.

But he couldn't risk it and he couldn't lie to her. So instead he said the only thing that he could under the circumstances before he closed the door. 'This really isn't about you, because you are…perfect. But…'

'But Catherine was your everything and you cannot let her go.' She tackled the great unsaid head-on once again. 'I know that, Sam, so don't feel wretched about it.'

'Wretched' didn't even begin to cover what he was currently feeling. His insides were contorted with wretched guilt. Wretched pain. Wretched desire and wretched regret.

'I really am sorry, Rose.'

Chapter Sixteen

Rose had hated every minute of the weekly whist tournament so far. It might have been more bearable and less tortuous if Sam hadn't come, but he had kept his promise to be there, albeit arriving late with a profusion of fake apologies to their hosts, and somehow that made it all worse.

With some concerted effort, they both behaved as if nothing was wrong, still played as partners and still managed to win their first game, but to her it was obvious that the parameters of their relationship had shifted. And once again she hadn't seen it coming. Hadn't realised that she had stupidly opened her heart to a man incapable of loving her as she loved him.

And Lord help her, but she loved Sam. She wasn't sure how she had allowed that to happen, despite the manifestation of all the worrying signs beforehand, but she knew that it had as she'd floated back to earth after the first time they had made love. Knew it without a shadow of a doubt. Because she absolutely wouldn't have been able to have made love quite so freely and whole-heartedly, and with such blind trust otherwise.

Thankfully, she hadn't blurted out as much in the

throes of passion, so he was none the wiser. However, she did not fool herself that if she had his reaction this morning would have been any different. For him, it had been an unexpected and now regrettable night of passion, and not a celebration of overwhelming feelings that he did not possess. He had wanted her last night but did not want her now. He certainly did not want her for ever, and at some point today he was going to try to explain that to her as gently as he could. Because he wasn't a cruel man. Just another one whose heart belonged to another.

'What say you we swap the pairings up a bit for the second round?' Mrs Fitzherbert didn't like to lose, and was still smarting at the loss of her shilling in the last game. 'It might be fun if all the gentlemen move one seat to the left?'

Which would put Rose, who was considered by all present to be the best whist player, with Archie, who was undeniably the worst. It would also give her wily nonagenarian friend Sam, who was the second-best player, so nobody was fooled by the ploy.

Their host, Rafe, glanced at Isobel, who would become his de facto partner and shrugged. 'I'm game.'

Of course he was. Because Isobel could hold her own. But Sophie, who would be paired with Ned, was less keen, because Ned didn't really see the point of whist and only ever came for the food.

'Two chairs to the left,' said Sophie in challenge. 'Otherwise I say we keep things as they are. What do you say, Rose?' Her friend shot her a pointed look, searching for an ally, and it was then that Rose realised she couldn't bear it any longer. If an awkward conversation needed to be had, and she was going to get her heart broken again anyway, she might as well get it over with.

'I apologise—but I need to go home. I'm not feeling particularly well.'

Which wasn't a lie. She had been feeling wretched and humiliated—again—since Sam had bolted from the bed this morning. The look of complete abhorrence on his face was now carved into her bludgeoned heart, right beside the awful letter she had received from her former fiancé, in which he had said he was relieved to be shot of her. One look at Sam, however, confirmed that he wasn't anywhere near ready for the conversation, as all the colour had drained from his face.

'You can stay if you want to, Sam. I'm not that ill. I just need some fresh air and some quiet.'

And a private place to curl up into a ball, cry her eyes out and castigate herself for being such a bloody fool all over again.

He stood, looking concerned, and headed her way, every inch the concerned and caring husband despite his lack of any real care for her at all. 'Of course I am coming with you.'

'Indeed,' said Mrs Fitzherbert with a thud of her cane. 'What sort of a husband would he be if he didn't rush to your ailing side? We would all judge him—and very ill too. Of course, we shall all judge the pair of you once you leave, Rose, as we are not fooled in the slightest by your swift decline into a malaise that will doubtless necessitate, by doctor's orders, an entire afternoon in bed. But newlyweds will be newlyweds.'

She winked and everyone except Archie, who was oblivious to such blatant innuendo, sniggered.

Rose smiled tightly at her friend, wishing she was

brave enough to air the sham she was living so that she didn't have to pretend any more. 'You can think what you want, and doubtless will anyway, so I wish you all a pleasant afternoon. Please don't get up.' She gestured to Rafe and Sophie, who were now also standing. 'We can see ourselves out.'

Fortunately, that assurance was respected, and they were left alone to wait for Sam's curricle to be brought out front. He clearly sensed the real reason for their departure, as he stood beside her stiffly for all that time and didn't say a word. It was just as well, because Rose wasn't anywhere near ready to have a civil conversation with him. Not when she was so furious with the pair of them she wanted to lash out, with her fists as well as her tongue.

And she still had her pride.

He might not want her, and she might be both humiliated and devastated by that fact, but by Jove she still had her pride!

As their conveyance rattled into the courtyard of Hockley Hall she decided she would not be the wounded victim this time. At least not openly.

'Can I drive?' Being in control of the curricle would give her the upper hand and, if she needed it, the whip.

He nodded, his expression wary. 'If you want to.'

She did not wait for him to help her up, because the last thing she wanted to endure was his touch, and that left him severely on the wrong foot too as he had to traipse all the way around to the other side. By the time he climbed in next to her she was settled, and she purposely set off before he was ready, taking some small pleasure in the way he lurched and then had to grope for the seat to regain his balance.

'I take it you aren't actually ill?' he said, trying to take control of the situation—or at least the conversation. 'And that we need to talk.'

'You know me. I hate the great unsaid. And after you hot-footed it out of bed this morning, as if your absent breeches were on fire, there definitely need to be some words said. And, if you don't mind, I would like to start.'

She could tell he did mind, because his dark brows kissed each other in consternation and his eyes were troubled. He was bothered and scared that she was about to beg him to love her back, or at least give them a chance, the blithering idiot! When she would rather walk on hot coals barefoot than let him see how much he had hurt her.

'Go ahead.'

He stiffened his spine and physically braced himself against the sides of the curricle, and it took all of her strength not to scream at him.

'Say what you need to say.'

Rose focussed on the road, rather than the ache in her chest, and forced a wry smile. 'Well, firstly, I wanted you to know that while last night was…um…nice enough…' It wouldn't hurt to knock him down a peg or two with such an insipid endorsement of his exceptional skills as a lover. 'I am not sure it is wise to repeat the experience.' In her peripheral vision she could see that had surprised him. 'I need to leave in a few months, and I fear that any repetition of the passion which exploded between us last night might lead to inconvenient and uncomfortable feelings that neither of us need.'

'I see…'

But judging by his rapid blinking he didn't. He had intended to make this speech, had expected her tears and tantrums, and he wasn't able to dissemble quickly enough to accommodate the fact that there weren't any.

'With hindsight, we probably shouldn't have done it, because now everything has become horribly awkward.' She shuddered and then shrugged. 'But I'll confess I've decided not to regret it, because after being denied the first one I am actually relieved to have had a wedding night, as it makes everything more believable going forward. I mean, once we are separated it would seem very odd that I am still intact down below when the time comes for me to take another lover, wouldn't it?'

That made him frown some more. 'I suppose it would.'

'And what we did doesn't have to be more complicated than it is if we can both be adults about it. You and I have always been brutally honest with one another, after all, and it's not as if there is any love lost between us to make last night anything more than the slaking of some mutual lust. I like you and you like me. But your heart remains with Catherine and mine, much to my chagrin, still remains with Justin, no matter how much I also loathe the scoundrel.'

What was sauce for the goose was sauce for the gander, after all, even if she had just uttered a complete pack of lies. Apart from the loathing bit, of course, because she meant that. Just saying Justin's name made her boil with fury.

'Was that his name? *Justin?*' He said that final word with some distaste.

'It *is* his name. Sadly, the duplicitous wretch is still around to taunt me, but I feel that I can properly move on from him now, thanks to our sham marriage. Now when I return to Suffolk I can do so with my head held high, because I shall return a married woman. And thanks to that, and to you for making me an honest woman at last, once our separation becomes official I won't have to worry about nonsense like propriety any more. I can do what I like—and I will.'

She made sure her smile looked mischievous.

'Especially now that I've discovered that I don't dislike bed sport. So thank you for opening my eyes to all those delightful possibilities.'

His eyes widened with shock at that statement and so, purely for a little petty revenge, she decided to embellish it.

'I've also been giving some thought to where I will live, and in view of all the new freedoms I can look forward to I've decided to move to a big town rather than a village. More people but, conversely, less prying eyes.' She wiggled her brows like Mrs Fitzherbert, to let him think that she would be naked and on her back while she enjoyed most of those freedoms. 'And before you offer again, I shall do it without your money. My father is a wealthy man who will happily gift me the money to buy my own business, and once we separate I'd prefer a clean break, Sam. Not one muddied with unnecessary financial ties that bind us together. I hope you don't mind, but I want to be free and not feel obligated to you in any way.'

'Of course I don't mind.'

He was, she could tell, completely flabbergasted by all that he had just heard, and did not approve of most of it, so she patted herself on the back for a job well done. He had no right to tell her how to live her life. Not when he still had no intentions of being any part of it.

'Good. I'm glad we have had this talk and cleared

the air, transient husband. I'd hate to think that one ill-considered night of passion would ruin everything we have done so far to make our temporary marriage bearable.'

He was quiet for the longest time, clearly stewing in his own juices and still put out by her lacklustre endorsement of his *'nice'* performance in bed.

She was turning the curricle into the square when he broke the silence. 'Obviously we will have to rethink all that if we accidentally made a child last night.'

A sobering statement that brought her up short. 'I didn't think a woman could conceive during her first time?'

'That is a stupid old wives' tale—much like all the nonsense that you hear about breastfeeding being a barrier to conception too. Because a woman very much can get pregnant during both of those things. However, even if it wasn't an old wives' tale, we did it more than once—didn't we, temporary wife?'

'I suppose we did.' Off-kilter, she pulled up outside his house. 'But I sincerely doubt we have anything to worry about.'

Without waiting for him again, she alighted and sailed inside leaving him to see to his horse, supremely worried despite all her bravado. She hadn't considered the possibility of them making a child. Not once during their three splendid couplings and certainly not at all today.

To vex her, Sam didn't see to his horse and instead followed her inside and up the stairs. 'When were your last courses? And when do you expect the next?'

'That's really none of your business!'

She stalked into the parlour and slammed the door

behind her. She probably should have wedged a chair under the handle as it flew open again.

'Oh, I think it is, if I'm going to be a father, don't you?'

He didn't sound so much angry as horrified by the prospect, and that wounded. It must have showed because he spread his palms and tempered his tone.

'In some scientific circles it is believed that the middle of a woman's cycle affords her the best opportunity to conceive, and we can only rule out that worry if we know the usual duration of your cycle, the date of your last one and, more importantly, when you anticipate the next. I'm not trying to pry, Rose, more to be pragmatic. Just in case.'

'Two weeks,' she blurted, horrified herself now at the potential implications of having a child with a man who didn't even want a wife, let alone a family. To corroborate that fact, his brows flew skyward before he dragged them back down and tried to appear calm. 'They always coincide with the new moon.'

'All right...' He exhaled as he nodded, all the colour draining from his cheeks. 'Then we won't have to wait too long for the answer and we shall cross that bridge only *if* we come to it.' He attempted a reassuring smile, but it was anything but. 'Until then, we keep calm and try to make the best of things.'

Chapter Seventeen

With the frigid late February wind whistling through the dark village square Sam should have been grateful to finally be home, but he wasn't. It hadn't felt like home much since he and Rose had spent that fateful night of unbridled passion together almost six weeks ago. They were still civil, and on the surface did their best to behave as if nothing was amiss, but it clearly was. Their intimacy had changed things irrevocably, and no amount of pretending otherwise was going to alter that.

They had made a stab at their short-lived version of normality in the immediate aftermath, and he was certainly still making the effort to regain some of the easy friendliness they had enjoyed in that first week of their marriage. That pleasant initial seven days when they had been making the best of things while sharing their meals and laughing about their days felt like a short and much too sweet honeymoon now, compared to the stilted collisions they had nowadays. With each passing day, things seemed to get worse, too, and he didn't really understand why as usually some distance from an event lessened its significance as the world moved on.

In public at least they were their usual selves, and he found himself wishing away the days between all the obligatory social events that he'd used to dread. Probably because around others Rose and he still shared witty repartee, while being unbeatable at whist, and they had even danced together twice at the last assembly. All for show, of course, to maintain the façade, but he wished it wasn't.

When they were alone it was a very different story, because it was obvious that she was making a concerted effort to avoid him. She now ate at different times from him and went out more, so that they were little better than ships passing in the night. When they did collide, irrespective of the inanity of their safe but forced attempts at a chat, he could tell by the way she looked at him that she hadn't been able to get past the morning he had bolted from the bed. Whereas he, no matter how hard he tried not to be bothered by it, couldn't move on from her matter-of-fact dismissal of what had happened in it.

He veered between wanting to find evidence that it meant more to her than she had claimed and trying to feel relieved that she had let him off the hook as far as any uncomfortable emotional attachments were concerned.

He wanted to say that it all suited him just fine, but it didn't. He missed their conversations and he missed her sunny company. He didn't want to miss either, but there it was. He also didn't want to keep wanting her—but every time he saw her it took all his willpower not to haul her into his arms and kiss her until they were both mindless and breathless and beyond the realms of the common sense which paralysed them.

Or at least until he was breathless.

Since she had dismissed his efforts that night in his bed as uninspiring and 'nice enough', which still smarted, he wasn't entirely sure that he had ever truly made her breathless at all. Thanks to the disastrous attempt to hoodwink the village gamblers that had led them to this point, he already knew she could be a good actress, and now he worried incessantly that she had pretended to come apart in his arms that night simply to make him feel better.

At the time, he had been convinced that she had been overcome with pleasure from his efforts, and constantly placated himself with the fact that a virgin who had believed that a woman couldn't conceive during her first time wouldn't have any notion of faking an orgasm. Especially when she had been so surprised to have one in the first place it had been spectacular to watch.

But what did he really know?

For all his detailed medical knowledge of human anatomy, the simple truth was that a woman's body worked very differently from a man's. There had been tangible proof left behind on the sheets from his own orgasms that night, but all he had as confirmation of hers was what he had seen in the moment.

Or thought he had seen in his emotionally charged and irrational state.

Because, as Rafe had quite rightly said, way back before Christmas and before this mockery of a marriage had even started, people might not always believe what they saw, but they always saw what they believed. And that night, after he had made mad, passionate love to a woman for the first time in four long years, he had wanted see Rose enjoying it as much as he had. The fact that she had been quick to state that she wanted no repetition of that night, with him at least, all rather suggested that she hadn't, and he very definitely wasn't at peace with that.

Any more than he was at peace with the idea of her taking a lover in the future, after she left him a free woman, despite them both being free to live the lives they wanted always being the original plan.

Nor, if he was honest, was he happy about her leaving at all. But, as she made a point of reminding him—regularly—that she was eager to 'move on' once their transient sham was over, he kept that to himself. She seemed to be filled with gushing plans in which he didn't feature—and who could blame her when all he could offer was more of what they already had? Which was basically them muddling along stoically, thanks to the dried-up husk in his chest.

Perhaps things would have been different if they had made a child together. But, alas, that complication had quickly evaporated into nothing. On the morning of the new moon she had been visibly relieved to tell him that they had avoided the dreadful possibility of parenthood. Announcing it as she served him a particularly sumptuous breakfast with such a beaming smile of joy that had proclaimed, for her at least, that the arrival of her courses was a cause for celebration, and that had smarted too. Not because he'd wanted there to be a child, of course, as that was a complication he did not need. But...

As he closed the stall gate on his horse, he huffed at the stupid lies he was telling himself over and over again, when he knew, deep down, a part of him *had* wanted the complication. A baby would have been such an insurmountable problem that the pair of them would have had to change tack and at least try to make a go of things. But fate had either decided to be kind to him or to be cruel—he still wasn't sure which—and that had been the end of that.

In a month she would leave, and his life would return to its previous even and comfortable keel. Devoid of all temptations and all the messy, unpalatable emotions that he did not want to have to contemplate.

Just him, all alone again, undistracted from his work. With his toast.

The latter depressed him. The former... Well, what he felt about that was probably best pushed into the back of his mind with all the rest of the things he didn't want to think about, because each time he did he felt queasy. At least in a month he wouldn't have to think about it— her—at all. Except he suspected he would. He might not be capable of loving Rose, but he liked her a great deal more than he had thought himself capable of doing, and had, foolishly, become...used to her being around.

Sam stamped the slush from his boots in the porch, trying not to acknowledge how much the thought of seeing her buoyed him, and the rich aromas of one of her legendary stews wafting from the kitchen was already making his mouth water. However, when he pushed open the front door he could tell straight away that she wasn't there, because his flesh didn't tingle with awareness as it always did when she was near, and that, in one fell swoop, royally spoiled his appetite too.

Drat her.

Even so, he still trudged to the kitchen to eat what she had left for him. He needed the sustenance, and a lifetime of toast stretched before him, so it made sense to make the most of Rose's delicious cooking while it lasted.

He was halfway through his miserable, solitary but delicious repast when there was a hammering on the front door.

'Sam!' It was Rafe's voice and it was panicked. 'Sam! Are you home?'

'Yes.' He flung open the door, took one look at Archie's limp and profusely bleeding arm, clutched tight to his chest, and knew that something very bad indeed had happened.

'Bloody poachers!'

Rafe had to help his brother into the hall, because he wasn't in a good way. A great deal of that was probably down to blood loss but, knowing Archie as well as he did, Sam knew that the lad's panic and fear were also playing their part. He'd been crying so much his breath now sawed in and out in ragged gulps and all the blood had clearly frightened him.

'They've been laying deer traps again on my land.'

Sam rushed to support Archie's other side and together he and Rafe half walked him, half dragged him into the surgery.

'Archie tried to move one out of the way of his dog, and before I could stop him it snapped shut.'

'How long ago did it happen?'

'No more than fifteen, maybe twenty minutes ago. I figured it made more sense to bring him straight here than send a messenger and then wait for you to come to us.'

As a former soldier, Rafe knew only too well how dangerous blood-loss could be, and had used his cravat to tie a tourniquet around his brother's upper arm and kept it elevated, but it hadn't stemmed all of the blood, which dripped off Archie's fingers to the floor.

Aware of that, he dropped his voice. 'I didn't want him to lose too much, but—'

'You did the right thing.'

He didn't want Rafe to feel unnecessarily worse when he must be feeling wretched enough already. The truth was, had Sam been there, it was exactly what he would have done too, until he could work on the wounds.

He kicked open the door to his surgery and gestured to the table. 'Help me lift him up there and keep him as calm as you can while I work.'

A task that was easier said than done when the swooning, scared Archie lolled like a dead weight in their arms.

'I'm going to need to examine the wound, Archie, all right? Try to hold still and I'll do my best not to hurt you more than it hurt already.'

The lad nodded, clearly terrified, while Sam did his best to swallow the rush of nausea which always accompanied treating someone he knew well. Unfortunately, Archie wasn't the sort to allow you to keep him at arm's length, and Sam liked this man-child far more than was useful for either of them in this precise moment. The best medicine was always best administered dispassionately, and with a clear head, and Sam's was currently spinning with all the potential complications and implications.

He sucked in a few subtle, calming breaths, then gave himself a stern talking-to as he fetched some scissors to cut away Archie's bloody clothes, some water, and enough linen towels to clean the area enough when he had an idea of how to proceed.

Pull yourself together, man!

Archie needed all Sam's wits and none of the unhelpful panic which had gripped him. Rafe, too, needed to see the confident, icy calm of a competent and well-trained physician. The sort who wouldn't make a mistake.

The sort who wouldn't let either of them down.

'Let's take a look at that arm, then, shall we?' He smiled a smile he didn't feel for both their sakes. 'I'm going to leave the tourniquet in place for a minute and cut your sleeve away. It might sting a bit, but I'll be as quick as I can, Archie, I promise.'

He was about to start cutting when Mr Outhwaite skidded through the open door, dressed in just his shirt and breeches and still in his slippers.

'I saw the commotion and have come to help!'

A timely offer, which Sam would have taken up if the older man hadn't balked the second he saw all the blood.

Recognising that Mr Outhwaite might be more of a hindrance than a help, Rafe was quick to divert him. 'Go and fetch my wife from St Hildreth's. Archie will need her.'

'Mine too,' added Sam, without a moment's hesitation, realising that he needed Rose here more than anything. Not only did she face everything head-on, and with no excuses, she was strong and tenacious and he needed both of those attributes now—in spades.

He also just needed her beside him, and right now, when Archie needed him so very much, Sam wasn't going to question why that was.

'You do know that if you made your stitches smaller, your fabric would sit flatter?'

Isobel reached for her stitch-ripper to unpick the haphazard patch that Mrs Fitzherbert had just added to the quilt they were making and the old lady bristled.

'I still do not see why I have to make quilts for the cold and needy of this parish and cannot simply purchase some for them instead.'

'Because this way is more thoughtful, and it is harder to refuse a gift that has been made than it is to turn down one that has been purchased.' Isobel made short work of removing the offending patch and tossing it back. 'The needy of the parish might well be cold and poor, but they still have their pride, and pride always comes before a fall—isn't that right, Rose?'

As the quilts were all Rose's idea, she nodded, a little ashamed that she had badgered the entire Sewing Circle into giving up three evenings this week to the endeavour when they could have just as easily raised some money and purchased them to give out with the food baskets they were also collecting. They had agreed because they were good people and it was a good cause. Only she knew that it was a convenient ploy to help her avoid Sam this week. Until she knew for sure whether she was with child or not, she could not trust herself to keep her anxiety about it to herself.

'It's been a long and bitter winter, and people's reserves are depleted, but most would rather freeze to death than admit it. Nobody likes to feel beholden or a burden to others.'

She certainly didn't. The last thing she wanted was to feel beholden to Sam, and she certainly did not want to become his burden. Not for any longer than they had mutually agreed at least—no matter what occurred or didn't in the next few days.

All her anxiety might well be for nought at this stage

anyway. Yes, her courses were six weeks late, but according to all Sam's medical books it was too early to say for sure that she was pregnant until she had missed two in a row—which wouldn't be for another few days yet. She would have a better idea of her predicament with the next moon. And perhaps it would take even longer than that to be sure, as his books all recommended that to be the time to have it confirmed with a physician's examination, and she certainly couldn't ask for one of those!

She had no clue what to do, and had no forward plan if she was pregnant, but she did know, with absolute certainty, that the last person she wanted to know of her potential predicament was him, when he had been nothing but honest about the depressing fact that he didn't want her in his life any longer than he had to. He didn't want a wife, let alone the additional inconvenience of a child.

Thankfully, after the shocking lie that she still felt so wretched about, he was blissfully ignorant of her turmoil and, rightly or wrongly, she wanted to keep it that way. If she wasn't pregnant, she would leave as planned on the first of April, and if she was, she would probably still leave as planned on that day anyway, leaving him none the wiser.

She already knew that Sam would insist on doing the honourable thing, but would then feel doubly entrapped, and she wouldn't be able to stand that. It was one thing to be unwanted and unloved in the short term, but another entirely to be so for all eternity! If it had been soul-destroying to be jilted by a man she had loved, and then have to watch him find happiness with another, she dreaded to think what living cheek by jowl with a man she loved but who felt nothing but resentment in return would do to her.

Neither of them deserved that misery—and, the honourable thing or not, it didn't strike her as the healthiest environment in which to bring up a child. In which case, the least said, the soonest mended, and she would cross that bridge if she came to it.

Rose did not need to have all the answers figured out yet. She just needed the one answer first—and that wouldn't come until this relentless February finally drew to a close.

Mrs Fitzherbert's bony elbow nudged her out of her reverie. 'You are quiet and contemplative this evening. Are things not going well between you and your handsome doctor? I know the old adage is "marry in haste and repent at leisure" but I have high hopes the pair of you will be the exception to the rule, despite your inauspicious start.'

'I wouldn't put a bet on that if I were you, Mrs Fitzherbert.' If she was leaving in a month regardless, she might as well sow the seeds of their very real discord with her closest friends here. 'Neither of us wanted the marriage, and two months on I am not sure that sentiment has changed. We are still more acquaintances than husband and wife.' Especially now that their friendship was well and truly dead. 'It isn't working and I hold out no hopes that it will.'

There, she'd said it.

'Give it time,' said Sophie as she reached out to squeeze Rose's hand. 'I am sure things will get better. You share a sense of humour, after all, and have always seemed to rub along together well. Perhaps you can build on that?'

Rose pulled a face of disbelief, because they didn't even share any laughter any more, thanks to *that night*. 'That is hardly the most secure of foundations—and how much time do you waste flogging a dead horse?'

Especially when theirs had been shot in the paddock, by mutual agreement, before the race had even started.

'If I were you, I'd give it a bit longer than a few months, because I've always sensed a promising frisson between you both.' A hopeless matchmaker to her core, Isobel wiggled her brows. 'And that will undoubtedly firm up those foundations swiftly if you act upon it.'

'I sincerely doubt that.' Rose couldn't help scoffing, when making love had done nothing but the opposite. Rather than pull them together, it had ripped an enormous chasm between them.

'I sense it too, and I think Isobel is right. Act on the frisson.' Sophie wiggled her own brows. 'Once Rafe and I did, it soon turned into love.'

'It was the frisson that sealed the deal for Ned and me too...' Isobel sighed, then chuckled as if she was remembering something wholly improper. 'A frisson that wouldn't be denied.'

'Not that she tried very hard to deny it.' Mrs Fitzherbert cackled, and then nudged Rose. 'I hope you haven't actually spent the last two months denying it? A decent frisson with a devilishly attractive man should always be acted upon. Especially when two people are married, irrespective of if they want to be, and can legitimately indulge the frisson whenever the urge strikes.'

She cackled some more, and nudged Rose so hard she almost knocked her off her chair.

'Which begs the second obvious question—has the

urge struck yet? Have you allowed your handsome doctor to thoroughly *examine* you?'

'Well... I...er...' Rose's face glowed as red as a beetroot, and then glowed some more when her friends, rather than telling Mrs Fitzherbert off for embarrassing her and asking grossly inappropriate and improper questions, all sat forward, grinning and expectant.

'Well? Has he?' Sophie had at least whispered that, whereas Isobel pointed and laughed.

'Of course he has! The blush never lies, and that one is a particularly guilty one.'

The pointed finger touched Rose's cheek and her outrageous friend made a sizzling sound.

'Our blushing Rose has finally been pricked!'

'Excellent!' Mrs Fitzherbert exclaimed this so loudly all the other sewers stopped to stare at their table. Including Rose's prudish Aunt Agatha. 'And about time too. Five and twenty years is too long to wait for a good pricking.'

'Could you *please* keep your voices down?' Rose hissed, while furiously pretending to the rest of the room that she was focussed on her sewing. She feared the blush on her cheeks, neck and ears had now reached such a level of incendiary ferociousness her hair might actually burst into flames if she touched it. 'Whether he has or he hasn't, it clearly isn't the magical solution you all seem to think, as we are still little better than strangers stuck under the same roof and are both thoroughly miserable to boot.'

Undeterred, and now thoroughly waylaid by thoughts of the actual deed rather than the unfortunate consequences of it, Mrs Fitzherbert spoke with an exaggerated whisper so loud that everyone must hear it.

'Well? Is he as good a lover as we all hoped a man with his medical knowledge would be?'

'Well? Is he?' asked Sophie and Isobel in grinning unison.

'Er...well...um... What difference does it make when we are both still miserable?'

'Sophie, Rose, come quick!' The Reverend Spears suddenly slammed into the village hall and dashed into the centre of the room, with her Uncle William out of breath behind him. 'There has been a dreadful accident—Archie is hurt and you need to go with all haste to the physician's!'

Chapter Eighteen

'I need you all to wait upstairs in the parlour!'

To Sam's relief, Rose shooed the sudden influx of well-meaning onlookers out of the surgery.

'Give poor Archie and my husband some space! And, yes, that does indeed mean you too, Mrs Fitzherbert! The only two people who can stay are Rafe and Sophie!'

She practically pushed the last of them out and went to follow.

'Could you stay too, please, Rose?' He flicked his gaze at their distraught friends, willing her to see that he was in dire need of another level head in this room which currently only possessed one. 'While Sophie and Rafe keep Archie calm, I am going to need an assistant.'

She took one look at Rafe, who was clearly riddled with guilt while he tried to keep his brother still on the examination table, and Sophie, who was cradling the inconsolable Archie to her bosom, and nodded.

'Of course.'

She held up her finger before poking her head back out through the door, where she spoke to someone in hushed tones—mostly likely Isobel—asking her to ensure someone stood guard outside in her stead, then returned, smiling to cover her own anxiety about the situation for their patient's benefit.

'What do you need me to do?'

As she was the second most medically qualified person in the room, albeit in horses rather than humans, and because he wasn't entirely sure himself what needed doing yet and he trusted her, he figured explaining the problem was the best place to start and they would go from there.

He gestured towards the wounded arm in his lap, choosing his words carefully so as not to alarm the others. 'The claws of the trap missed the bone, thank goodness, but they did catch the skin.'

Now that Archie's sleeve had been cut away, and the worst of the wounds cleaned, Sam knew he had a job on his hands.

'These three cuts will need stitching.' They were deep and jagged puncture marks, each about an inch wide and a good half an inch deep. 'This one...' he gently twisted the arm to show her the large chunk of missing flesh which he was most concerned about and her pretty eyes widened '...will need cauterising to stop the bleeding, and that will need to be done first.'

She nodded, grasping the scope of the problem immediately. 'Which cautery do you want me to prepare?'

He answered by widening his thumb and finger several inches. This was going to need one of his substantial old battlefield tools and not the daintier sort he frequently needed here.

'You will find it in the top cupboard to the left.'

Rose retrieved that, and several others, wrapped them in a cloth so Archie did not catch sight of them and hurried out through the door to heat them in the kitchen fire. He was pleased that she'd had the foresight to take them out of this room, as the sight of glowing red metal in here wasn't going to calm anyone.

'I think it's best if we give Archie a bit more laudanum now,' he whispered to Rafe in an aside. 'The less he is aware of what needs to happen next, the better. Once I start, I'm going to need you and Sophie to hold him down.'

Rafe nodded, blanching, because as a former soldier he'd likely seen similar procedures hundreds of times before—but never on his beloved brother. 'Archie's strong, so it might be prudent to tie him down too, once the medicine kicks in.'

'There's some strapping in that drawer over there.'

Good grief, but his profession was brutal sometimes! The fact that Sam was going to have to hurt poor, sweet, gentle Archie to try to heal him made him sick to his stomach, but he had no choice. If he didn't seal that big wound the young man might bleed to death, and even if he did there were no guarantees that he would have done enough.

Once the laudanum was administered, between the three of them they lay Archie flat on the table and prepared both him and themselves for the ordeal to come. By the time Rose slipped back in to check on them, several minutes after leaving, Sam and his patient were as ready as they were going to be. All he had to do was nod his head for Rose to go and fetch the red-hot cautery.

While he composed himself, by getting used to the weight of the iron in his hand, she did something that hadn't ever occurred to him before. She held up a sheet between the business side of the wound and Rafe, Sophie and Archie, and fastened it in place.

'It will be awful enough without having to see it.'

She squeezed her friend's hand and Rafe's shoulder, then came around the other side to rub Sam's back. As if she read his mind, she said exactly what he needed to hear.

'It's what needs to be done, Sam, so don't second guess yourself.'

When he nodded, grateful for the reassurance, she offered him one of her wry, make-the-best-of-it smiles.

'And if it gets too much, or you faint, know that I've branded many a cow and can take over.'

It was almost one in the morning by the time the Hockley carriage left, and everyone was shattered. The sealing of Archie's wounds hadn't taken more than forty minutes, but Sam hadn't allowed Rafe and Sophie to take him home until he was certain that his patient was in a fit enough state to travel. That had meant waiting for the heavy dose of laudanum he had given him to wear off enough that poor Archie was lucid—which had also meant that he was in pain. Pain that was unavoidable under the circumstances, but managed to an extent by the much weaker tincture of laudanum that he had been sent home with. It was still more than Sam was comfortable with.

He was greatly troubled as Rose closed the front door and, as they had on the night when Mrs Anderson had passed, his broad shoulders seemed to bear the entire weight of the world.

'You did an excellent job, Sam. You stopped the bleeding and repaired all the damage.'

She wanted to touch him, to hug him, but couldn't. For a month and a half she had done the best she could not to allow her unreciprocated and unwelcome feelings for him to show, and now that they only had a month together left prudence dictated that she kept it that way.

While she harboured an irrational anger with him for not being able to love her, she also knew that her anger wasn't fair. She had entered this marriage with her eyes wide open, fully aware of the fact that it wasn't a permanent arrangement and that he wasn't capable of ever loving another again. He was too good a man—too good a human being—to be burdened with her predicament. He might not be able to love any more, but he certainly felt a huge responsibility for the people under his care, which she supposed was the category she now sat in, and he was plagued by guilt. Especially for his own perceived limitations and failings.

Rose wasn't going to add to that. She loved him too much to hurt him.

'Once those wounds heal, all Archie will have is a few more scars.'

'*If* those wounds heal.' His entire body sagged as he sighed. 'Unfortunately, we still have a mountain to climb.' At her frown, he sighed again. It was a resigned but frustrated exhalation. 'Infection is the enemy now—just as it always is. It is the curse of medicine. We have learned how to stop bleeding, to an extent, and can to a lesser extent manage pain, but there is nothing in the arsenal to battle infection—and it will be a battle if it sets in.'

'Do you think it will?'

He threw up his palms, his expression fearful. 'That is in the lap of the gods. Archie might be one of the lucky ones who avoids it, but we all need to prepare ourselves that he might not. Like so many things in medicine, there is no rhyme or reason to it. Infection is one of those things that our science is still too primitive to understand, and nobody really knows what causes it. It is arbitrary and ruthless in its selection of victims, and once it's taken hold, it festers quickly. With wounds as large as Archie's, the arm could be gangrenous within days.'

'And if it is?' Rose asked, even though she suspected she knew the answer.

'A swift amputation might stop it.'

Sam's complexion was as green as she felt, and it was obvious it was not something he would find easy to do. Especially to such a gentle, innocent soul as Archie.

'But if the blood is poisoned by it, then…' His voice trailed off and he ran an agitated hand through his hair, looking suddenly so much older than his thirty-four years. 'Let me just say that during the war we lost more men to infections than to bullets. The tiniest injury could be fatal.'

When he had laid it out in such stark terms, she knew that he wouldn't take any comfort from empty platitudes. 'When will we know?'

'The next five days, while the bulk of the healing takes place, will be critical.'

'And the odds?' She had to ask it, even though she dreaded the answer.

'At best, it's evens. In reality, knowing what I know about the unpredictable nature of the beast, Archie has a one in three chance of avoiding it. News I shall have to break to Rafe and Sophie in the morning, when I go and check on him.' He leaned his back against the wall, as if he needed it to support himself. 'I suppose I should have told them tonight, but…'

'Tonight was difficult enough for all concerned, and they didn't need more torment to add to their worries. Do not castigate yourself for sparing them that for a few hours more, Sam.'

'Sophie's expecting again.' He blurted that out as if he needed to purge himself of it. 'Early days, barely eight weeks, so she wants to keep it a secret because she's miscarried before. In truth, I resisted telling them because the stress of something like this so early in her pregnancy might well cause her to miscarry again. The first twelve weeks are always the most precarious while the foetus develops. That is when, metaphorically, it would be the ideal time to wrap the prospective mother in cotton wool.'

Rose suppressed the urge to stroke her own tummy and reassure herself that the child that might be growing in her womb was safe, despite all her fears for Archie. Instead, she gestured for him to follow her to the kitchen and casually asked, 'Does trauma always end in a miscarriage?'

'Not always, but the risks are definitely increased. If she was further along—say four or five months—I would be less worried about the impact of this, but...'

'Then maybe just tell Rafe about the infection risks for now. Sophie doesn't need to know unless the worst happens.'

'I suppose you are right.' He sat at the kitchen table and stared at its surface, lost in thought while she gathered what she needed from the pantry to make them both some hot chocolate. 'Of all the people fate decided to do this to, why Archie? He's never hurt a soul in his life and the scamp does nothing but spread joy.'

'There is no rhyme or reason to it, as you said. Sometimes bad things happen, and often to good people. Life is never plain sailing. Mrs Fitzherbert claims that we need the awful to remind us to celebrate the good.'

'And again I say, why Archie? Why is fate that cruel?'

As his question clearly wasn't just about Archie, Rose couldn't stop herself from reaching out and rubbing his shoulder. 'The only guarantee any of us have in life is that one day it will end. For some, much too soon, and for others too late. All the pondering and philosophising in the world isn't going to make any sense of the reasons why, and perhaps they are not meant to be understood. They just are.'

'To a man of science, that is a very unsatisfactory answer,' he said. He reached up to squeeze her fingers, unaware of the havoc such a simple touch created within her. 'But I suppose the crux of what you are saying has merit, and I suppose I need to learn to accept what nobody yet understands.'

'Or you could continue punishing yourself for things decreed by the cosmos and out of the sphere of your influence so that you will never experience a moment's happiness ever again.'

She hadn't meant that to sound like an accusation, but it had. As he stiffened, she tugged her hand away to pour his drink. 'Here—this will help you sleep.'

'Thank you.' He took the drink with knitted brows. 'But I sincerely doubt an entire vat of this will help me sleep tonight.' He stood. 'I'm going to work through the night instead. Use the insomnia productively and see if I can't find something in my medical journals that will improve Archie's chances.'

He went off at speed, clutching the cup, forcing her to jog to keep up with him.

Rose darted in front of him before he reached the office and blocked the door. 'Oh, no, you are not! You are a brilliant physician, Sam. There is nothing in those books that you do not already know, and probably nowhere near enough in them to encompass all that you do!' She prodded his chest. '*You* are Archie's best chance and he needs you to be at the top of your game tomorrow—not a frazzled, exhausted wreck! So you are going to bed right this minute, even if I have to drag you up those stairs! If sleep eludes you, a few hours of rest will still be more restorative and of more use to Archie than you tormenting yourself trying to find answers that we both already know do not exist!'

For a moment she thought he would argue, but instead he huffed. 'Has anyone ever told you that you are a very bossy woman, Mrs Able?'

'Somebody needs to take care of your physical health, seeing as that is never you.' While she seemed to be winning, she pointed an imperious finger to the stairs. 'Go to bed, Sam—now. Or I will drag you up there by the hair.'

Miraculously, he did as he was told, and within moments they were both on the narrow landing above. Him outside his bedchamber door and her outside hers, directly opposite. Yet instead of heading into the room she had banished him to he lingered, staring at her oddly.

'Thank you,' he said.

'For what?'

'For the chocolate. For nagging me just now. For looking out for me.' He glanced down at the mug in his hands, fingering the handle. 'For all your help tonight with Archie. You were my rock tonight, Rose, when I needed one and...' He winced and stared into the dark depths of his chocolate rather than look at her. 'I don't suppose… No…that's a bad idea. Hugely inappropriate.'

Her pulse quickened. 'You don't suppose what?'

'That you would keep me company.'

His eyes lifted. Locked with hers. They were filled with something akin to yearning. Tortured yearning. As if he was at odds with himself and really didn't want to be feeling any of it.

'I'm not suggesting that we…you know…unless…' His gaze dipped to her lips momentarily, making her want him. 'I'd just like us to talk for a while and…' He blew out a tortured breath, reached out and traced a hesitant finger over her cheek before he twirled it in her hair. 'I've so missed talking to you.'

Rose wanted to lean into his hand. Wanted to touch him. Kiss him. Spend the night with him. Talking with him and making him feel better and making love— which she knew would be inevitable if she followed him through that door. But she also knew that she could only risk the avalanche of emotions that came with that if there was hope.

'Talking and then what?'

He swallowed, and the yearning in his eyes was shuttered. She supposed that said it all. He just wanted a night with her again. The temporary distraction of her body and not all the unpalatable complications that went hand in hand with that.

'Does there have to be a *then*? Can't *now* be good enough for the time being?' he asked.

'For me there does.' She stepped away from his touch. 'I have to leave in a month, and I need to be able to do that knowing exactly where I stand.'

'You don't have to leave in a month.' He closed the

distance again, suddenly too close, but not close enough as he searched her gaze. 'We could extend the deadline and see if…perhaps we can find a way to muddle along together.'

It was the 'if' that did it first. The 'muddle along' was merely the icing on the inedible cake.

'To what point or purpose, Sam? To prolong the agony? To add more layers of complexity to an already untenable situation? You were right the first time—that is a bad idea.'

'Perhaps… But doesn't the fact that I still don't want to let you go count for something? Can't that be enough?'

'No—because you don't want to let Catherine go either, and that's the heart of the problem.'

He jerked back as if she had slapped him, and that was the final nail in their coffin.

'I'm so sick and tired of being the woman a man makes do with, Sam. You are effectively expecting me to agree to always being second-best.'

'You know that I cannot make any sort of—'

She pressed a finger to his lips rather than hear his truth. 'I *do* know, and I'm not asking you to. It wouldn't be fair to you when you have never been anything but brutally honest with me about that. So please do not ask me not to leave next month, as that wouldn't be fair to me. I have to be brutally honest with you too, Sam, as well as with myself. I don't want to "muddle along", or wait and see, or waste my life hoping for more that likely won't come. I deserve to be someone's *everything*, and if the last year has taught me anything, it is that I am not prepared to accept less than everything going forward. No matter what the expectations of others are or the direness of the circumstances. I'd honestly rather spend eternity alone than settle for half-measures ever again.'

It was her truth, and her right, whether she was with child or not. That was a depressing, frightening but still empowering realisation, which made her resolute now.

'I'm sorry, Sam, but there it is, and you need to respect that.'

He nodded, still frowning. 'I shouldn't have asked… I'm sorry.'

Doubtless he wasn't as sorry as she was—but then why would he be when he wouldn't allow his heart to be engaged? And she was in no doubt any more that he still had one. He cared too much about too many things for it to be a dried-up husk in his chest, no matter what he chose to believe to the contrary.

'I just wish that—'

'Don't.' Rose shrugged as she opened her door—because what else was there to say? 'Goodnight, transient husband.'

'Goodnight, temporary wife.'

His answering smile was wry but his eyes…

His haunted, hazel, part-warring, part-molten eyes were suddenly anything but.

Chapter Nineteen

Rose eyed the quarter to noon post to Colchester and wondered for perhaps the fifth time in less than a minute if she shouldn't simply climb on it and go. Call it quits now and escape Whittleston and her temporary marriage a few weeks earlier than planned and just be done with the misery of it all.

Especially as the second new moon had come and gone and there was still no sign of her dratted courses.

Not that she needed the continued absence of them to confirm the worst when her body suddenly wasn't behaving the way it always had for the last quarter-century of her existence. Her breasts were fuller and more tender, her belly was firmer, but rounder, and her skin was positively glowing. And, as bizarre as it sounded, she could feel the life inside her getting stronger by the day.

Therefore, Rose had to immediately face two hard but undeniable facts. Firstly, she needed to accept that she was definitely having Sam's baby, and secondly, for the sake of her own sanity, she needed to have it alone. Preferably without him ever knowing, as the only way her poor, aching heart was going to survive this second bittersweet heartbreak was to never have to see him ever again.

It was a week since he had offered her the lacklustre proposition of muddling through, and each time she saw him she experienced the overwhelming urge to weep. She also felt the overwhelming urge to weep when she didn't see him, because she thought about him constantly, so it was clear that something drastic needed to be done before she did the unthinkable and broke down and wept before him.

She glanced at the quarter to noon post again, as the driver called a warning to the last of the passengers still lingering in the inn that he was off, and almost hurried across the square to join them. And perhaps she would have too, but Mrs Fitzherbert's antiquated barouche box suddenly rattled alongside.

The faded velvet curtains snapped open, closely followed by the door. 'Get in, girl, before you catch a chill!'

'There really is no need when my house is there.' She pointed to the surgery door, feeling slightly pathetic to have been seen avoiding it until Sam's surgery finished and he left for all his afternoon calls. Which was likely imminent. 'Also, I have a few more errands to run.'

She didn't want them to collide in the street. Didn't want to witness that sad but accepting smile which he had developed in the last week. The smile that told her he really didn't want her to leave, but he really couldn't offer more than half-measures and so would respect her decision.

In her current melancholy state, that smile might just be her undoing.

'Urgent errands, are they?' Mrs Fitzherbert's lips flattened. 'Because if they are that begs the question as to why you have been stood on this corner staring wistfully at nought for the last fifteen minutes. And do not dare deny it when I could see you as plain as day from my parlour window, young lady, looking all lost and lonely. So get in! You are clearly miserable and at a loose end—and actively avoiding going home—and I'd appreciate some company.'

As Sam was likely about to burst forth from the front door, Rose climbed in. In case Mrs Fitzherbert continued on her 'lost and lonely' vein, she changed the subject. 'Where are we going?'

'To Hockley Hall. To visit Sophie and Archie.'

'Are they up to visitors?'

'Who knows?' Mrs Fitzherbert threw up her palms. 'I suppose we'll find out once we call upon them.'

The barouche pulled away just as Sam appeared at the front door, but Rose pretended not to notice, pulling one of the many blankets folded on the seat beside her over her lap.

'Isn't it funny how sometimes you do not realise how cold you are until you step out of it?' she said.

'It doesn't help that it's been freezing since November and we've all forgotten what being warm feels like.' The old lady's wizened finger pointed out of the window to the eerie pink-and-grey-hued clouds with a quaking finger. 'Doesn't the Almighty realise that it is March and we are due spring, not more blasted snow? I am sick to the back teeth of all this cold weather.'

'So am I.' Rose relaxed against the seat.

'Marvellous—that's the weather thoroughly discussed, then. Now, let's move on to more pressing things. Like why you've gone shopping every morning this week at eight without fail, have hardly bought a thing, and don't return home until your handsome husband has left it?'

'Well... I...'

'Or, even better, explain why you look constantly sad, and he looks sadder, or why the middle buttons of that fine green pelisse that fitted you like a glove a fortnight ago are suddenly straining?' That wizened finger tapped one of them, while a wily white brow quirked. 'Does he know that he's planted a bun in your oven?'

A week's worth of weeping gathered behind Rose's eyes and then, without a moment's warning, suddenly burst out in a flood of biblical proportions. '*No!* And you c-c-can't tell him! He can n-n-never know!'

'Why ever not?'

'Because we agreed to end our sham marriage on April Fools' Day and s-s-separate. That was always the p-p-plan. We never intended to make a g-g-go of it!'

Then it all came spilling out. Everything from their pre-planned separation to his devotion to his dead wife, and then a painfully abridged retelling of *that night*, her own futile feelings and the chasm both had created, and his subsequent and confusing offer to 'muddle through' when he had needed another distraction. She finished with her current dilemma, confessing that she was sorely tempted to leave early in case Sam spotted the obvious changes happening to her body before March finished.

Throughout it all, Mrs Fitzherbert did not speak. At least not with words. Her expressive face, however, spoke volumes. It was only once Rose had finished the sorry tale and was a quivering, hiccoughing mess that she realised the barouche box had been doing laps up and down the lane to Hockley Hall for goodness knew how long.

'I just don't know what to do.'

'What an unholy mess.' Mrs Fitzherbert shook her head. 'No wonder you are both so miserable.'

The sympathy was all well and good, but what she needed now was the older woman's wisdom. 'If you were me, what would you do?'

'I haven't a clue, dear, but I'll certainly give it some thought.'

Not at all the advice Rose so desperately needed or had hoped for when the confession had been prised out of her.

'In the meantime, let's enjoy a nice cup of tea at Sophie's, shall we?' She rapped on the ceiling of the carriage and smiled. 'I've brought a lovely cake.'

More confused than she had been before she had poured out her heart, Rose had to hurry to repair her face and then paste on a smile in the scant few minutes that it took to pull up on Sophie's drive. Uncertain as to whether their friend would be up to visitors, she tried to hover in the hall while the butler enquired whether or not his mistress was receiving today, but Mrs Fitzherbert wasn't that subtle.

She had already removed her coat and hat and was already halfway to the drawing room when he returned. 'Lady Hockley will be with you presently.'

That was when Rose disrobed. She was barely out of her coat when Fred, Archie's giant dog, galloped down the stairs to greet her. Hot on his heels was the beaming young man himself, and to her untrained eye he appeared to be in the finest of fettles despite his bandaged arm.

'Hello, Rose! I've missed you!' Never one to hide his feelings, Archie was down the stairs like a shot, and flung himself at her and hugged her tight with his good arm. 'Thank you for visiting. I've been so *bored* stuck here indoors I thought I'd die of it!'

'We're in the challenging stage of his convalescence.' Sophie's voice came from the landing. Her friend looked tired, but otherwise well. 'This morning has been particularly trying, so your visit is a timely one as Archie and I are both desperate for diversion.'

'Archibald Peel, come and kiss me this second!'

As he dashed to respond to Mrs Fitzherbert's summons, Rose hugged Sophie. 'He looks well.'

'He *is* well, thank goodness.'

Close up, she could see the shadows around Sophie's eyes and how pale she was. 'And you? How are you bearing up?'

Instinctively, Sophie rubbed her tummy and smiled. 'Much better than I was this time last week. But life does like to toss us these reminders not to take things for granted, so I am grateful that all our worst fears weren't realised and also completely frazzled by Archie's rapid recovery.'

She shot Rose an unamused look.

'Your brilliant husband ordered bedrest, and I am sure you can imagine how well that went down with my exuberant brother-in-law. Rafe threatened to tie him to the bed yesterday. Today, we have both given up trying to keep him horizontal in favour of simply keeping him inside. Suffice to say, after battling him solo for the entire morning, poor Rafe has had to go and chop some wood as he feared he would murder him otherwise. I've managed an hour so far and already need a lie-down.'

'Then allow me and Mrs Fitzherbert to take up the slack while you put your feet up. She's brought a cake.'

They settled in the drawing room with tea and a large slab of fruitcake each. Archie demanded a double slice, because of his war wounds, while Fred gnawed on the enormous bone Mrs Fitzherbert had brought him.

'If you do not mind me saying, you look much too wan and haggard, Sophie.' Never one for tact, Mrs Fitzherbert said this with a scowl. 'Are you coming down with something?'

'I'm going to be an uncle again,' said Archie around a mouthful of cak—before he slapped his forehead. 'Whoops! That was supposed to be a secret, wasn't it?'

'You're pregnant?' The old lady raised her quizzing glass to study Sophie's tummy, then quirked a brow at Rose. 'There must be something in the water as there seems to be a lot of it going around. Congratulations.'

Fortunately, her friend missed that unsubtle hint, and rubbed her barely protruding belly again. 'Thank you—I am delighted, but the morning sickness has been dreadful this time around. It was bad with Lillibet, but nothing like this.'

'Then it's probably a boy,' said Mrs Fitzherbert, giving Rose the side-eye again, as if she should know. 'The male of the species is always the most troublesome, and morning sickness is the devil's work.'

It was a comment which made her question her own pregnancy as she hadn't felt sick once. Did that mean she might not be? And if she wasn't should she be glad rather than sad at the prospect?

'I wouldn't mind if it was confined to the mornings, but it's not. It waxes and wanes throughout the day,' said Sophie.

'It does that,' said Mrs Fitzherbert again, with another pointed glare at Rose. 'And it makes you weepy.'

At least that was reassuring, and probably explained why she felt so tearful. It wasn't all Sam's fault, drat him. Or maybe it was. If he hadn't been so...vigorous, she might not be in this predicament at all, and if he hadn't been so entrenched and devoted to the sainted Catherine maybe she wouldn't be suffering from a chronic case of unrequited love.

As if she'd read her mind, Mrs Fitzherbert dragged him into the conversation. 'What has our eminent local physician prescribed for the nausea?'

'Ginger—in tea or biscuits. Although sadly both make me retch. Along with some sympathy and some jolly good mollycoddling, which does help a bit.' Sophie smiled. 'Sam has been lovely.'

'Then perhaps there is hope for him yet—although I daresay his wife might contradict you, as he's still making her exceedingly miserable.'

Rose contemplated strangling Mrs Fitzherbert before her loose tongue caused irreversible damage, but was denied the chance when she heard Sam's voice out in the hall. In case either of her friends continued the awkward conversation, she placed a finger to her lips for Sophie and shot warning daggers at the nonagenarian to whom she had foolishly confessed all. It seemed to do the trick, and the three of them were all wearing fake smiles when he strode in with Rafe.

He beamed at Sophie—then his step faltered as he realised she was there. Instantly he was uncomfortable. His Adam's apple bobbed twice before he realised his smile had slipped.

'Hello, Archie...ladies.'

Their eyes locked briefly before he snapped his away to address Archie.

'Your brother tells me that you have been an unbearable patient.'

Archie shrugged, only a little contrite. 'I feel fine, so I don't see why I can't go out.' Then he pouted. 'It's been seven days, Sam. *Seven.* Whole. Days!'

'And if I am not happy, it might be seven more. Give me your arm.' He was about to unwrap it when he seemed to realise he was about to reveal a gory wound in polite company. 'Maybe we should adjourn to another room while the ladies take their tea?'

'Don't mind us,' said Mrs Fitzherbert, shuffling her chair closer to get a better view. 'You do what needs to done. None of us are squeamish.'

'Perhaps I will adjourn to the other room...' Sophie looked bilious. 'Not because of Archie's arm but—' She covered her mouth and bolted, with Rafe just a few steps behind her.

Sam glanced at Rose, a question in his eyes, but it was Mrs Fitzherbert who answered it. 'We all know that she's expecting now, so there's no need to pretend that you don't.'

In case he thought she had betrayed his confidence, Rose was quick to add, 'Archie let the cat out of the bag.'

'Oh.' He visibly relaxed. 'Then you won't mind if I go and see her next. But in the meantime...' He held out one hand and Archie dropped his arm into it in a manner which suggested the pair of them had done this many times in the last week.

Rose knew that he had checked on Archie daily, because it was one of the few essential conversations they had. Usually in the short window of time between him arriving home for his dinner and her leaving him with it. She wanted to know how the lad was faring and he needed to know if there had been any urgent messages for him while he had been out. It was a brief and concise exchange of words that rarely took more than five minutes—which was just as well because anything more than five minutes tended to become excruciating in its awkwardness.

Sam made short work of unravelling the dressing and tossing it in a heap on the side table before he checked on the jagged collection of injuries beneath.

'Everything seems to be healing nicely.' He gently probed the edges of the biggest, cauterised wound, which had now completely scabbed over. 'This one remains nice and dry.'

Which was music to Rose's ears because that was the one which had always been of the most concern.

'All the swelling has gone down.'

'It itches,' complained Archie, trying to scratch it, only to have his hand slapped away.

'Itching equals healing. Scratching leads to trouble, and at least another seven days cooped up inside.' He reached into his medical bag for a clean dressing and Archie groaned.

'The bandage *really* itches!'

'And what does itching equal?' Her transient husband had the patience of a saint with Archie.

'Healing.'

'Then you can suffer it until I take the stitches out in a few more days. Until then, young man, you need to keep these wounds covered and—'

'Urgh!' Archie rolled his eyes like a petulant child. 'Please don't say I need more bedrest, because I'm not doing that!'

'Actually...' Sam dabbed some salve on the stitches

and then briskly set about binding the arm in fresh linen. 'I was going to suggest you could take Fred outside once a day for some fresh air—but only if Rafe is with you and only if you refrain from scratching your arm. However, seeing as you are determined to be stubborn rather than sensible, I might change my mind. Perhaps you are not ready?'

'Oh, I am Sam, and I won't scratch, I promise.'

'Well, all right, then.' The bandage secured, he ruffled Archie's hair as he smiled knowingly at Rose. Mrs Fitzherbert caught her smiling back, and she was forced to take a sip of her tea to hide it.

'In my humble opinion, when the time comes you will make an excellent father, Dr Able.'

While Rose almost choked on her tea, and shot the old lady more daggers over the rim of her cup, Sam struggled to find a suitable response.

'I…um…' Panicked, he glanced to her and assumed—so she hoped—that her stunned reaction was down to the fact that she had no clue how to respond to this rather than suspect anything was amiss. 'Maybe…if we are blessed.'

'I am so glad to hear that you think children a blessing rather than a curse, because they are. In the main. I am sure yours will be delightful, like their affable parents, and far too clever for their own good.' Mrs Fitzherbert sipped her own tea as if butter wouldn't melt in her treacherous, indiscreet mouth. 'And what handsome children you will make too.' The wily old eyes wandered to Rose's belly before they arrowed on Sam. 'Would you prefer boys or girls?'

'Er…no preference. So long as they are healthy I have no preference either way.'

'The correct answer, Dr Able.' Then, as an aside to Rose, she said, 'You married a good one, so make sure you keep hold of him.'

'Well…um…' It was her turn to stutter now, because she had no idea if Mrs Fitzherbert was merely having some fun at their expense, or if she had just advised Rose not to leave.

'Are you able to drop your lovely wife back home? Only it's time for my afternoon nap.' Their aged torturer then stood, as if her work was done.

Hers might be, but Rose's very much wasn't, so she stood too. 'I shall leave with you, Mrs Fitzherbert, if you don't mind. Sam still needs to see Sophie, and then he has more rounds to finish, and I need to get back to the village straight away as I have a long list of things to do.'

Wringing this old lady's neck was at the top of it.

'Suit yourself.' Annoyed at being thwarted, Mrs Fitzherbert curled her lip. 'But you'll need to walk back from my house, as I am very, very tired.'

Rose didn't trust herself to speak until they were alone in the barouche box and cantering along the driveway. 'What do you think you were playing at back there? When I specifically told you that I do not want Sam to know that I am with child!'

'I was testing the ground and observing.'

'By stating aloud that I have found myself "a good one" and need to "keep hold of him"?'

'Oh, that was for his benefit, dear. A test. To see if he deserves you to stay or not. Which he failed.'

'He did?' Her anger giving way to disappointment, Rose slumped back into the seat. 'Then you do *not* think that I should keep hold of him?'

With Mrs Fitzherbert's tendency to talk in riddles, it would make sense to clarify.

'Absolutely not. You have to leave the wretch. In fact, I think your instincts this morning were right, Rose. If I were you, I wouldn't wait until April Fools' Day. I'd leave tomorrow. Nothing can come of you staying, apart from more misery. Not when it's as plain as the nose on your face that he doesn't love you even slightly and isn't ever likely to.'

Rose knew as much, because he had always been up front about it, but it still hurt to hear it. Until she had, she hadn't realised how much she'd harboured the hope that he might change his mind.

'How could you tell?'

'The eyes don't lie, dear, and his were…well…frankly horrified when I suggested that you keep hold of him. And he actually looked disgusted when I mentioned the prospect of children.'

'Disgusted?' All at once Rose wanted to weep again. 'That does not bode well.'

'It bodes awfully, dear. Especially when I get the impression he is as eager to get your sham over with as you are. He'd see the addition of a child to the mix much like the trap that caught Archie last week. He might accept that he has been caught for a short while, out of a misplaced sense of duty, but it won't take long for him to do what all beasts do when they want to be free and chew one of his limbs off to be rid of it.'

'Oh.' It was a blunt and depressing answer that was difficult to hear, but sadly accurate. 'So much for him wanting us to muddle through.'

Mrs Fitzherbert shook her head. 'Men will say anything when they're feeling as frisky as a horse, and you

know that deep down, don't you? Or you'd have gratefully spent the night with the wretch when he asked you
to. But you didn't. You turned him down flat and I am
proud of you for that. You deserve everything, Rose,
and his version of half-measures would ultimately suck
all the joy out of your soul.'

Because this brutal dousing with ice-cold water
hadn't already rendered her poor soul joyless?

'Then I should leave?'

Why did she keep asking for reassurance when she
knew Mrs Fitzherbert's customary bluntness was accurate?

'One cannot make a silk purse out of a sow's ear,
dear, and you'll get over him quicker if you accept that.'
She patted her arm. 'Now, speed is of the essence in
your delicate condition.' The old lady eyed her belly,
as if it had grown exponentially in the space of the last
few hours. 'You need to get away before more snow falls
and you are stuck here.' She patted her stomach. 'Another week and you'll show too much, and our clever
doctor is bound to put two and two together to make
four. Then his sense of duty will ensure that he never
lets you leave, and all three of you will then be doomed
to suffer the sow's ear for ever.'

She huffed, her white brows knitted together.

'But how to get you away as fast as possible without
putting the cat amongst the pigeons…?'

Chapter Twenty

It was late by the time Sam reached his front door. He was purposely late because he had taken an impromptu trip to Hornchurch to visit the apothecary when he'd run out of afternoon calls to make and hadn't been able to face going home. Or, more accurately, hadn't been able to trust himself to go home and not say something stupid and reckless that he would likely regret or that would make everything worse. Especially when she had, quite rightly, told him that he needed to respect her wishes.

It was constantly on the tip of his tongue to blurt out that she did deserve everything—and he wanted the chance to try and give her it.

It was probably a futile hope. He knew that too. The husk in his chest was too battle-scarred to ever be what she needed it to be, and he was too scared of a thorough resurrection to commit to the cause fully. However, the only thing he knew with any certainty was that, selfishly, he didn't want her to go. At least not on the first of April, as planned. Maybe another month or two might bring more hope, or confirm the futility of it, but he couldn't let her leave until they had both made some effort to fix things.

They had taken vows, after all. They might not have meant them at the time, but some of them definitely resonated with him now.

'To have and to hold', for example, was something he was all for. He also had no issues with 'for better or worse', 'for richer or poorer' and 'in sickness and in health'—that was no less than his duty as a husband and a decent human being. He could also certainly cherish, because he already did cherish Rose. He might have struggled to show her that, but he was thankful for every day they'd had together, and absolutely cherished all the wonderful, unique things that made Rose… Rose. From her sarcasm to her naughty sense of fun. From her lovely smile and lush body to the way she looked after him even though he didn't expect or need her to.

But could he love again? Fully and without reservation? Was he capable of it? Brave enough to risk all of himself again? Allow her to become his everything and then…?

From the reliable way his stomach lurched and he came out in a cold sweat every single time he dared to ponder it, that was probably a no.

So really, pragmatically, there was only one sticking point. Granted, it was the most important one as far as she was concerned, but if he genuinely meant all the rest, and did his best to prove them all to Rose from this day forward, maybe she wouldn't notice?

And maybe pigs might fly, because she had always read him like a book.

But he still had three weeks to ponder and consider, and maybe—if a miracle occurred—he would find a way to keep her with him? Finding better words than the unattractive 'muddling through' might be a good

start. He had once been charming, after all. And flirtatious and…fun. Some of that perhaps still existed. If
it did, he needed to haul it out of hiding, give it a bit of
an airing and then deploy it at the right moment.

But tonight wasn't it.

He wasn't ready, and felt ill-prepared after their
stilted encounter earlier at Hockley Hall, when she had
made it plain she could think of nothing worse than
sharing a curricle with him alone. The look of horror which had skittered across her pretty face had suggested that it might be appropriate for him to lay some
proper groundwork before he tried to broach the subject
of their future again. The last clumsy attempt had been
disastrous. Another might send her running to Suffolk
the moment he started speaking.

He pushed on the door and found it locked, which
was odd. But as it was past eleven, the porch lamp was
lit, and the key was where it always was, he brushed
that aside. The lock was stiff, and creaked slightly as it
turned, despite him trying to be as quiet as possible. He
was hoping she might, in the spirit of her determined
avoidance of him, have long gone to bed.

That hope was dashed the moment he stepped into
the hall and she appeared on the landing. She was
dressed for bed in her prim, knotted robe, and her posture was as stiff and awkward as it could possibly be.

'You're late. You missed dinner.' She fiddled with
the knot of her belt, chewing her bottom lip momentarily. 'I was worried.'

Worried was surely a promising sign?

'Can we talk about us, Rose?' The question tumbled
out before he could stop it. 'Only, I think—'

She stayed him with her palm, her jaw and spine instantly rigid. 'It's very late, Sam, and I am tired.'

'I know...' He raked a hand through his hair, then started up the stairs. Something within him was screaming at him that if they didn't talk now it would be too late. 'But I have things I need to say and we are running out of time.'

'I think we already have.' She folded her arms, defensive, as his boots hit the landing, and they remained folded when he attempted to reach for her hand. 'No amount of talking is going to change that.'

His hand dropped impotently to his side in defeat and he nodded—then immediately shook his head as his fingers fisted. A sharp pain ripped through his chest. 'But we've still got three weeks, damn it, and I want to at least try!'

'To "muddle through"?'

'To do right by you, Rose!' How to put into words the turmoil churning up his insides? 'I need to do right by you.'

'You have already done right by me, Sam. You married me out of your innate sense of nobility when you really didn't need to. We both know that you were well within your rights not to, when everything that happened was all my fault. From the bet to the flirting to the foal and the night we spent unchaperoned in that blizzard. I was to blame for all of that, and I refused to listen to your repeated cautions to the contrary. You have restored my good reputation and given me the ability to return home with my head held somewhat higher than it was when I left it. I shall be eternally grateful for all of that and require nothing else from you.'

'I want to try. I want to talk—'

Her finger pressed against his lips.

'Not tonight.'

'Tomorrow, then.' His hands found her hips as he stared deep into her eyes, willing her to see that all was not lost. 'Promise me that we can talk about us tomorrow?'

It seemed to take for ever for her to nod. 'Tomorrow.'

But she didn't look convinced that any talk would fix all that needing fixing.

'I want to do right by you, Rose—and that's the honest truth.'

'I know you do.' Then she traced the shape of his mouth and smiled the saddest smile he had ever seen. 'And I want to do right by you too.'

'Then that's a start, isn't it?'

Rather than answer, she pressed her mouth to his, and they both poured everything into a kiss so poignant and sublime that even the dried-up husk in his chest lurched with hope. Because a kiss was a very good start indeed...especially when she seemed to want to prolong it.

When it finally came to an end, neither pulled away and they simply stared deep in to each other's eyes. He wanted to lean in and do it again. Lose himself in her. But that wouldn't be fair when there was still the great unsaid to tackle.

So he smiled down at her and tried to be noble. 'It's very late and you are tired.'

'I am.' She chewed her lip and stared at his. 'But I still want you to make love to me, Sam.'

'Mr Bunion—how can I help?'

Normally the sight of the oily, obnoxious, fusty-smelling solicitor's apprentice in his waiting room would

royally spoil Sam's morning, but today he was so filled
with sunshine and light he even managed a smile for
the man.

His buoyant mood and cheery disposition was undoubtedly all the fault of Rose, who had kept him awake
for hours last night, doing all the things to his body that
he had yearned for since the first time they had made
love. This time he was in no doubt that she had thoroughly enjoyed it, because he had poured his husk of a
heart and his soul into showing her that he intended to
honour his vows to her.

She had shattered in his arms, or beneath his mouth,
four times between midnight and dawn. And as the
first rays of the morning had bathed them on his mattress they had made such slow and tender love that it
had felt like a rebirth. Without the disguise of darkness, there had also been an honesty to those proceed-
ings that added a new dimension to them. Enough that
he had begun to tell her what she meant to him before
she'd swallowed his words in a kiss and they had come
together.

It had been the fresh start that they had both needed,
and it certainly paved the way for some proper honesty when they talked. Which, he thought, with a quick
glance at his clock and a smile, he was looking forward
to doing in less than fifteen minutes.

He would have happily initiated the conversation
as soon as he had awoken again, as all the words had
seemed to be there in his head, eager to burst forth,
but Rose had already been downstairs and the enticing
aroma of bacon had been filling the house. Because
she had had to dash to the Friday Sewing Circle, to
do something important with quilts, there had been no

opportunity to tell her how he was feeling over breakfast. But she had kissed him goodbye as she'd placed his plate in front of him and she had promised that they would talk at luncheon.

'I'm afraid my problem is of a delicate nature,' said Mr Bunion, already unbuttoning his falls, but even that didn't spoil Sam's good mood too much. He'd even find some perverse enjoyment in lancing the enormous boil on the odious fellow's backside, because Mr Bunion had once had the audacity to be rude to his wife, and he figured that the man deserved it.

His wife.

As he washed his hands, Sam realised that it had to be a good sign that he could now think those words without wanting to vomit into a bowl.

There was a brisk rap on his surgery door and Mrs Fitzherbert strolled in, without waiting for him to invite her, and made herself comfortable in the chair. He glanced at the clock again, noted that it was already noon, and almost said something he had never said in all his years as Whittleston-on-the-Water's physician— *Surgery hours are over, so please come back on Monday.* But the woman was ninety-four, and if she was ailing from something she might not last till Monday.

So he swallowed his irritation and smiled. 'How are you, Mrs Fitzherbert?'

'In the finest of fettles, Dr Able, apart from the wicked ache in my bones caused by all this persistent cold. Can you believe that it might snow again?' She shook her head and thumped her cane on the floor. 'Snow! In late March! And all the puddles in the square are so icy it's a wonder nobody has broken their neck this morning. Anyone would think Essex had suddenly turned into Norway.'

'Are you taking the powders I gave you for your rheumatism?'

'Of course not!' She curled her lip in disgust. 'They taste like rotten cabbage! I have to water them down with brandy just to make them palatable.'

'How many times do I have to tell you that brandy isn't a medicine, Mrs Fitzherbert?' Sam knew it was a moot point, because this old lady had always been a law unto herself, but thanks to the Hippocratic Oath he was duty-bound to tell her anyway.

'Until you go blue in the face, Dr Able, as I've managed to get this close to a hundred on the stuff without any issue.'

She made a valid point, he supposed, as she was the oldest patient he had and nothing much ever ailed her. 'Then how about we try some willow bark tea?'

'For what?'

'For your rheumatism, Mrs Fitzherbert.' Sam jumped up to fetch the powders and couldn't resist riling her. 'Or has senility finally set in and you've forgotten what you came to my surgery for?'

'Oh, I didn't come here for my rheumatism, Doctor. I came merely to ask your permission for my man to go upstairs and retrieve Rose's things for her.'

Dread settled like a stone in his stomach. 'I'm sorry?'

'Well, she's gone, hasn't she? Back to Suffolk.'

'Has she?'

'Yes...permanently.' Mrs Fitzherbert pulled an awkward apologetic face. 'She was supposed to leave you a letter. I told her to tell you to your face, but she said she didn't like goodbyes and—'

Blood rushed in his ears as Sam surged to his feet and on unsteady legs dashed to the kitchen. There, in the centre of the table, was nothing but a plate of sandwiches.

A plate of sandwiches only big enough for one.

'Oh, silly me,' said Mrs Fitzherbert, limping in behind him. 'Perhaps I am going senile. She didn't leave the letter here because she didn't want you to find it before the post left. She gave it to me to give to you instead.'

She rummaged in her reticule and finally produced one, then seemed surprised when he snatched it out of her hand.

Chapter Twenty-One

Sam tore the missive open and scanned the contents, then sank into a chair because the ground had suddenly been ripped from beneath his feet.

She had indeed gone to Suffolk—and for good. She thought it was for the best, and she didn't want him to attempt to contact her there because she also thought a clean break was the healthiest thing for them.

A clean break!

After they had spent the night making love!

After she had promised that they would talk!

After the minx had kissed him goodbye this morning!

How dare she do that and give him false hope when she had known it was for the last time?

Mrs Fitzherbert gestured to the crumpled lump of paper in his fist with her cane. 'I hope she mentions in it that she wants me to arrange for her things to be sent on? We thought it most prudent that she travel light, as the quarter to noon post to Colchester is always full. Her decision was last-minute, and we didn't want to risk her not being able to travel today because she had too much baggage.'

'We!' He had the overwhelming urge to grab that cane she had made a point of whacking against the floor with every damned 'we' she uttered and snap it over his knee. 'You knew she was leaving at a bloody quarter to noon today? You knew it and didn't think to tell me so I could stop her?'

'It wasn't my place to tell you, young man, because she did not want to be stopped. And it's not as if your separation wasn't planned—and by both of you to boot, which I must say was very underhanded of the pair of you. All that has changed is the date, and you can hardly blame Rose for bringing that forward when she has been so miserable.'

She prodded him with her cane.

'I cannot imagine how hard it has been for the poor girl to have to live with a man she has fallen hopelessly in love with but who constantly tells her that he is incapable of loving her back! That must be soul-destroying.'

'What?' Now his head was spinning. 'She loves me?' The husk in his chest creaked as it leapt. *'She loves me!'*

And this was how she chose to show it? By abandoning him without a by-your-leave? Without a word? After he'd begged her to talk! To stay! To try! With no mention of that pertinent detail in her bloody awful letter!

'Then why the blazes has she gone?' He probably shouldn't be shouting at a woman in her nineties, no matter how exasperating she was. But with Rose already on the way to Colchester he had nobody else to shoot but the messenger.

The cane jabbed again. 'Because you are a coward, Samuel Able, that's why. A shocking coward and an outrageous liar! Incapable of love, my arse... I cannot think of a bigger-hearted man in the whole of Whittleston! You work all the hours God sends.' The tip of that damn cane found his ribs now. 'Care deeply about every single patient, including the unworthy ones, and punish yourself if you cannot save them! What is that if it is not caring?'

'My job. My duty. My blasted vocation.'

'Poppycock and hogwash. You love your job. Duty is love and so is vocation. A man truly incapable of caring would never have married her in the first place. You're just scared to commit to Rose as she deserves because your first love died. Because the grief was unbearable. Because it's easier to shy away from life than live it to the full, isn't it? Because lightning cannot possibly strike twice, and it cannot possibly be as deep and as meaningful as the first time? Well, shame on you for wasting the life that the good Lord gave you and which he expects you to live to the full! And congratulations for driving your second great love away with your downright insulting offer of "muddling through". Be still my beating heart!'

When her cane hit his breastbone he caught it in his fist to stop the pain—but it didn't stop her verbal assault.

'Did you hear that, coward? For my decrepit old heart still beats and leaps and loves with hope and abandon and I've put three husbands…three great loves…in the ground. And I'd bury another if I could experience the sheer joy of loving a man wholeheartedly again. Because the joy is worth the sacrifice! The pleasure is worth the pain! Because it truly is better to have experienced love and lost it than to have been denied that joy.'

For a moment he thought the old lady might spit in his face, but she spat more vitriol instead.

'It'll serve you right if she does what she intends, and what I have thoroughly encouraged her to do, and finds someone worthy enough to deserve her love back in Suffolk—because only a blithering idiot allows a woman that wonderful to get away!'

'We were supposed to be talking about all that today!'

What the blazes had Rose been thinking to just go?

'Before she ran off without giving me the chance to say my piece!'

'Good for her! You don't deserve the opportunity to say it!'

'Well, I am going to!' He pointed a quaking finger at Mrs Fitzherbert as he stalked to the door and grabbed his coat. 'And, as God is my witness—' his finger shook towards the heavens '—my lawful wife is going to bloody well listen!'

The door slammed behind him.

Which was why he didn't see Mrs Fitzherbert holding her sides as she threw her head back and cackled.

Rose watched the spire of St Hildreth's disappear on the murky grey horizon and fought back tears while she tried not to regret her decision. Yes, it was a tragedy, and her heart was breaking to be leaving him, but Mrs Fitzherbert was right. This *was* for the best. You couldn't make a silk purse out of a sow's ear and there really was no point in putting off the inevitable when the pair of them had reached such a momentous impasse.

She wanted everything and he could only give so much, which ultimately would result in them both being unhappy.

Besides, she couldn't risk staying, even though she had been sorely tempted to have the talk Sam had wanted to have, to see if there was any hope. Staying and slowly watching his innate sense of responsibility turning into resentment and then into loathing would be far worse. Therefore this was definitely the right decision.

She also had a child to think of, and while Sam might not be capable of loving it, she was. She already did. Their child would be the one glorious, precious positive she could take away from her short-lived, enforced sow's ear of a marriage.

'Are you all right, miss?' The woman directly opposite her in the cramped and swaying carriage smiled kindly. 'Only you look like you've found a penny but lost a pound.'

'Yes... I'm fine.' Rose forced herself to smile back. 'I'm just a bit sad to be leaving Whittleston after eight months, that's all. It is such a lovely village.'

All the passengers bounced as the carriage hit a bump in the road, then swayed as the driver swerved slightly without slowing at all, clearly determined to get to his next stop in record time.

The older man beside Rose, who was trying to read his newspaper, dropped it and frowned as they clonked through another pothole, and rapped the ceiling in complaint. 'I think they have given us the worst driver in the world,' he said, to nobody in particular, as he snapped his paper back.

'What kept you in Whittleston for eight months?' asked the lady.

'Family.' Old and, she supposed, new.

'Then doubtless they will drag you back there soon enough, so this is only a farewell and not a goodbye.'

Rose nodded, even though she knew that it was goodbye. She couldn't set foot in the place again while Sam

lived there. Even if he moved away she would still strug-
gle. Whittleston-on-the-Water held too many memories.

To that end, before she'd left she had spent the entire morning saying her farewells to all the friends she
had made. Ned and Isobel had been first, and both had
promised to visit her in Suffolk just as soon as she was
settled. Sophie, Rafe and Archie had been next, and
they had all promised to visit her too. And to write—
although letters would be poor second to their actual
company. Archie had cried, which of course had set her
off, and then that had set Sophie off, and poor Rafe had
been stuck in the middle of the three of them, beside
himself because he couldn't stop them crying.

Finally, she had gone to say goodbye to her dear
aunt and uncle, who had given her refuge at one of the
most difficult periods of her life and helped her find her
smile again. It might be lost again now, but for the sake
of the babe growing inside her she would find it again.
She had to search for a new home to raise it in, after
all, and then all the unpleasant ties to her past would be
cut and she truly could start afresh. It was scary, but it
was going to be an adventure, and she was determined
to grab it with both hands.

She deserved that. Almost as much as Sam's son or
daughter deserved it. It was a thought that warmed her
enough that her hand settled contentedly over her belly,
despite the film of unshed tears gathering in her eyes.

In a few hours, when this carriage made its first stop
in Chelmsford, Mrs Fitzherbert would deliver her letter to him and that would be that. Rose had kept it purposely short, as she had not trusted herself not to pour
some of her forlorn hope into it, which might, in turn,
force him to feel beholden to come after her. He'd be

angry initially, and maybe even a little upset, but once the news had settled he'd be relieved. Then he'd likely bury himself in work to distract himself, and after a respectable amount of time he'd be back to where he'd been before she had turned his ordered life upside down.

Back to working ridiculously long hours, not looking after himself and doubtless living on toast again.

By which time, hopefully, she'd have enough of her own distractions to be able to blot him out of her thoughts. At least for the bulk of her time. Until then he was destined to occupy them and she would mourn the loss of him.

A stray tear tumbled over her lashes, and to hide it from the other five people crowded into this juddering confined space with her she twisted towards the window. The bitter cold outside combined with the warm breath of six people inside had misted the glass with condensation, so she cleared a circle with her glove just in time to see the Dewhursts' farm fly by. Outside was the foal she and Sam had delivered on the fateful night she had been ruined. A few yards away was its mother. Both were covered in blankets and nibbling at the greenery in the meadow.

That was another positive of their sham marriage, and another fond memory she would take back with her to Suffolk to cherish.

They were all pushed sideways as the carriage turned at speed to climb the big hill into Little Ramstead, and the horses slowed briefly with the weight they had to pull. But thanks to their careless and impatient driver and his cracking whip they were soon running at a lick again. Straight through another pothole that had everyone reaching for something to hold on to.

Rose gripped the windowsill as the carriage lurched suddenly to the left with such force that it smashed her head against the window. Pain exploded behind her eyeballs at the impact and a strange mist seemed to engulf her.

She tasted blood in her mouth as she felt the carriage tilt.

Heard the screams of her fellow passengers as it began to roll.

She hit her head hard again, against something that made her see bright, unbearable white.

And then the world went black.

Chapter Twenty-Two

Sam was muttering to himself as he hauled himself into his curricle, so furious with Rose he could barely think straight. Across the square Mrs Outhwaite was eyeing him with blatant hostility, along with a gaggle of ladies who were all tutting in his direction. Clearly all of them had been aware that Rose had left him long before he had. He supposed they had all warranted proper goodbyes this morning. But not him!

No!

All he had been granted was a complete pack of lies and a final kiss that he hadn't realised was final! It was supposed to be men who used a woman in bed and then discarded her without a by-your-leave, but *he* felt used now, damn it! How dared she leave his bed and his life without any warning whatsoever, as if his feelings did not matter? Especially when she apparently loved him!

'Dr Able! Dr Able!'

A cart rattled into the square and on it was none other than Ted Dewhurst.

'You've got to come quick! It's an emergency!'

Sam decided to ignore the cry for help. Someone else would have to deliver the breach foal or calf or pig, or whatever the hell else it was the Dewhursts expected him to be a doctor to now. He was a man on a mission. And as the lad waved his arms, frantic, he snapped his reins and set off.

He was almost free of the square when Ted flung himself in front of his horse, and he had no choice but to come to an abrupt stop. 'Someone had better be about to die, Ted, or you will be!'

'I think someone is.' The lad looked ready to burst into tears. 'There's been an accident. A dreadful accident. The post hit some ice on Little Ramstead hill and overturned.'

'What post?' Ice filled his veins and somehow he knew before Ted confirmed it.

'The Colchester post—and there is blood everywhere!'

Sam had no memory of his journey to the scene, only of the overwhelming compunction to get to it as fast as he could. All the while panic consumed him like a maelstrom. Panic and fear and so much hope he could barely breathe, while over and over in his head he prayed that Rose would be spared.

Please don't take her! Please don't take her!

He had no idea he was repeating that mantra aloud until he saw the devastation on the side of the hill and had to choke the words out.

The carriage was on its side. One wheel was missing and there was baggage strewn everywhere. Clothing spewed from shattered trunks while locals tended to the wounded.

As he scrambled from his curricle he saw a prone body on the ground, surrounded by a crowd of grim faces. So many he could not tell if the ominous black toes of the boots pointing towards the sky belonged to a man or a woman.

The onlookers parted as he ran towards them, and Sam experienced a moment of elation when he realised that it was a man. He was alive, and groaning on the floor.

'Bloody idiot!' Mr Dewhurst was bent near the man's bleeding head, trying to stem the flow with a handkerchief. 'He was running those horses too fast and paying no attention to the ice! He stinks of gin too, the blighter!'

'Who else is hurt?' Sam scanned the scene, frantically looking for Rose. Emotion choked him. Fear mingled with a grief so intense it engulfed him. 'Have you seen my wife?'

'Aye.' Sensing Sam's panic, Mr Dewhurst pointed to his house. 'She's safely in the house with all the others. Thankfully nobody was seriously hurt by this bloody idiot's reckless stupidity.'

'Thank God.' The rush of relief came so fast and so thoroughly Sam struggled move as it flooded his body. Overwhelming tears fell unbidden as he thanked whoever had spared her and ran to the building.

'Rose!'

He flung the door open and burst into the kitchen, his eyes searching, not caring that he must look like a madman to all the blinking people seated around the Dewhursts' kitchen table, gratefully clutching steaming mugs of tea.

'Where is Rose?'

Because she wasn't one of them, and he needed to get to her. To see her. To reassure himself that the woman he had only just realised he loved with all his heart was all right.'

'She's in the parlour.'

He had no idea who said that but barrelled on, slumping in relief when he finally saw Rose, sitting wrapped in a blanket by the fire.

'Oh, my darling…thank God.' He collapsed at her feet to examine her. 'Are you injured anywhere?' He did not care that his profession dictated that he see to the most seriously hurt patients first. That idiot on the grass out there had almost stolen Rose from him, so he felt no guilt. 'Bleeding?'

Her face was as white as a sheet. Her expression stark and sad. 'I bumped my head and blacked out for a few seconds…'

Her fingers went to her hair, to show him the way, and he checked the bump. It was reassuringly hard and the bruise was already angry. He cupped her cheeks, stared deep into her eyes to see if she was concussed. Her pupils were as they should be, so he held up three fingers. 'How many?'

'Three,' she said, as her bottom lip trembled, and he hugged her tight.

'I thought I'd lost you.' He had so much to say. So much she needed to know. 'I thought you were dead… and it broke me, Rose. Shattered me completely. It was just like Lisbon, only worse, because I'd been there before and I couldn't believe that fate would do that to me again. Be so cruel and callous… I am so sorry, my love…because you *are* my love… I didn't realise that I could ever feel again what I felt for Catherine…but I do. I love you. It took almost losing you for me to realise that you are my new everything.'

Her sob exploded against his chest as she held him tight. 'I love you too, Sam, so very much.'

'Then all is good…' He sat back to stare into her soul.

'You'll come home and you'll never, ever think of leaving me again?'

She nodded, struggling to smile through her tears. But then the tears took over and she sobbed for all she was worth. 'I'm pregnant…for now at least…nine weeks.'

She hugged her belly and something else overwhelmed him. Something instinctive and proprietorial.

'But I'm terrified that I am going to miscarry.'

His palm flattened over her belly in wonder while he forced himself to think like a doctor. 'Any pain, cramps or bleeding?'

'Not yet.'

'Then let us hope it stays that way.'

'And if it doesn't?' She was already devastated by the prospect, and he knew he was too, but…

'We will cross that bridge when we come to it— together.' He took her hand, laced his fingers through hers and kissed the wedding ring that he had so reluctantly put on her finger, suddenly grateful that it was there. 'But I do know that this won't be your last pregnancy. If you are game, I think there might just be room in the shrivelled husk in my chest to love a houseful.'

She laughed through the tears and he kissed her.

'I love you, Rose.'

It was bizarre and strange and wonderful, but he was compelled to keep telling her. Not to convince her that he meant it, but to revel in the joy of it. For however long it lasted. Because Mrs Fitzherbert was right. Love was worth the pain of loss, and he was going to revel in every single moment he had been gifted with Rose.

'You are my everything.'

Epilogue

St Hildreth's was filled with flowers. In a testament to how much Mrs Fitzherbert was loved, the locals had stripped their quaint corner of Essex of all the last of the summer blooms for today, because Mrs Fitzherbert loved flowers. There were almost as many floral arrangements as there were people crammed into the pews.

Everyone from Whittleston-on-the-Water was there, which wasn't a surprise, but many of the friends she had made elsewhere in her long life had also come. Her three sons, all grey-haired old men themselves, were seated at the front with their wives and grown-up children. Dotted amongst them were grandchildren and great-grandchildren, and every single one of them had inherited that canny, wily, mischievous look from their matriarch. However, despite the enormous crowd, there was hardly any noise, as all of them were oddly quiet and bemused.

Rose was one of them—because all this still hadn't sunk in.

'Ninety-five—almost ninety-six. That's a good innings.' Ned Parker stared at the enormous floral arrangement bursting from behind the altar with a shake of his head. 'We should all be so lucky as to make such old bones.'

Beside him, where they all stood in the porch, his vivacious wife Isobel rubbed a thoughtful circle over her protruding belly. 'I intend to live to a hundred.'

After putting off starting a family for a year, while she established her haberdasher's shop in the village, she was now five months pregnant, and it suited her. It hadn't slowed her down in the slightest. Of all of them, she was probably the most likely to usurp Mrs Fitzherbert's record as the oldest ever person in the village.

'I am going to miss her,' said Sophie, while gently rocking her new born son.

The sleeping Lord Gabriel Peel was a chubby little angel, blessed with his mother's features and Rafe's sandy hair. Which was funny, because his toddling sister Lillibet, who was currently being supervised and entertained by a very frazzled-looking Archie, was the opposite. She was dark, like her mother, but the image of Rafe.

'It's time.' Reverend Spears appeared, clutching his Bible, and Sam nodded.

Reluctantly he passed their baby daughter back to Rose, as Mrs Fitzherbert had expressly stipulated that she wanted him to be part of the service.

'Wish me luck.'

He kissed Rose's cheek tenderly, then bent and did the same to their precious little Violet, whom he was absolutely besotted by. She had only been in the world ten days, and already he could not bear to leave her side.

It had been his idea to call her after another flower. He had said he liked the irony, and after red roses, violets were his favourite.

'Good luck.' Rose squeezed his hand, and he took a deep breath.

'Of all the things that I thought I'd being doing today, this wasn't it.'

She watched him disappear into the vestry and smiled at her remaining friends. 'It's the end of an era, isn't it? Whittleston-on the-Water won't be the same without Mrs Fitzherbert.'

'Oh, do stop talking about me as if I'm dead, girl!' The formidable old lady prodded her with her cane from behind. 'I'm merely moving two miles up the lane!'

'But we are used to you living within spitting distance of the square,' said Isobel.

'Interfering in everything,' muttered Ned under his breath.

'Which I can still do from my new home—and I will.' Then she cackled. 'I was due a new adventure, and living in a windmill will certainly be one. There's something so romantic about a windmill, don't you think?'

'There you are!' A frustrated Sam returned and offered her his arm. 'You were supposed to be waiting for me in the vestry and the Reverend wants to start.'

To prove that, with perfect timing, the organ began to play.

'Well, the Reverend can jolly well wait, can't he?'

She took Sam's arm and then passed her infamous cane to Rafe, who in turn passed her a vivid posy of flowers which matched the wild crown of them on top of her snow-white head.

'It's the bride's prerogative to be late. Besides...' She

cackled again, enjoying herself immensely. 'It will keep my groom on his toes. It'll do the man good to sweat a bit while he wonders if I'm going to turn up. There should always be some mystery in a marriage.'

Sam gave her his arm and Rose and the others took their seats. Standing at the altar beside his son, the aged groom was indeed sweating nervously. But as his bride entered he beamed, and stared at her with such affection he suddenly seemed ten years younger—which was ironic, because at eighty-five he was a decade younger than his new wife-to-be.

The entire village had been surprised at the haste of this marriage. Rose had known that Mr Anderson and Mrs Fitzherbert were old friends, and that she had spent a great deal of time helping him cope with his grief after his wife had died of a stroke last year, but nobody had realised when love had blossomed. The first anyone had known was three Sundays ago, when the first of the banns had been read.

It had been all hands on deck since then, to get this wedding ready so fast, but none of them had minded. Mrs Fitzherbert was right. At ninety-five, she couldn't afford to hang around making preparations. She wanted to get cracking on her fourth marriage straight away. They were even going on a honeymoon tour of Scotland, because neither the bride nor groom had ever seen it. Both were grabbing life by the horns and living it to its fullest.

Mrs Fitzherbert had finally made it all the way down the aisle to the altar, and it was Sam's big moment.

'Who giveth this woman?' asked the Reverend in his loud, commanding voice.

'I do,' he said, handing her over to her groom.

He stepped backwards and quietly took his seat next to Rose. As he did every single time they sat in this church since the carriage accident, he took her hand, laced his fingers through hers and lifted it to his lips so that he could kiss her wedding ring. Then, in a whisper just for her, with love shining in his eyes, he said what he always said, here in the place where they had taken their vows but not intended to mean them.

'I do—and always will—with all my resurrected heart.'

* * * * *

*If you enjoyed this story,
be sure to read the first two
books in Virginia Heath's
A Very Village Scandal miniseries*

The Earl's Inconvenient Houseguest
His Maddening Matchmaker

*And why not pick up her instalment in our
Society's Most Scandalous collection?*

How to Woo a Wallflower
by Virginia Heath

How to Cheat the Marriage Mart
by Millie Adams

How to Survive a Scandal
by Christine Merrill

Get 3 FREE REWARDS!

We'll send you 2 FREE Books plus a FREE Mystery Gift.

Falling for the Forbidden Duke
EVA SHEPHERD

His Maddening Matchmaker
VIRGINIA HEATH

FREE Value Over $20

Billionaire's Snowbound Marriage Reunion
Naomi Leach

Barcelona Fling with a Secret Prince
Ellie Hall

Both the **Harlequin® Historical** and **Harlequin® Romance** series feature compelling novels filled with emotion and simmering romance.

YES! Please send me 2 FREE novels from the Harlequin Historical or Harlequin Romance series and my FREE Mystery Gift (gift is worth about $10 retail). After receiving them, if I don't wish to receive any more books, I can return the shipping statement marked "cancel." If I don't cancel, I will receive 6 brand-new Harlequin Historical books every month and be billed just $6.19 each in the U.S. or $6.74 each in Canada, a savings of at least 11% off the cover price, or 4 brand-new Harlequin Romance Larger-Print books every month and be billed just $6.09 each in the U.S. or $6.24 each in Canada, a savings of at least 13% off the cover price. It's quite a bargain! Shipping and handling is just 50¢ per book in the U.S. and $1.25 per book in Canada.* I understand that accepting the 2 free books and gift places me under no obligation to buy anything. I can always return a shipment and cancel at any time by calling the number below. The free books and gift are mine to keep no matter what I decide.

Choose one:
☐ **Harlequin Historical**
(246/349 BPA GRNX)

☐ **Harlequin Romance Larger-Print**
(119/319 BPA GRNX)

☐ **Or Try Both!**
(246/349 & 119/319 BPA GRRD)

Name (please print)

Address _____ Apt. #

City _____ State/Province _____ Zip/Postal Code

Email: Please check this box ☐ if you would like to receive newsletters and promotional emails from Harlequin Enterprises ULC and its affiliates. You can unsubscribe anytime.

Mail to the **Harlequin Reader Service:**
IN U.S.A.: P.O. Box 1341, Buffalo, NY 14240-8531
IN CANADA: P.O. Box 603, Fort Erie, Ontario L2A 5X3

Want to try 2 free books from another series! Call 1-800-873-8635 or visit www.ReaderService.com.

*Terms and prices subject to change without notice. Prices do not include sales taxes, which will be charged (if applicable) based on your state or country of residence. Canadian residents will be charged applicable taxes. Offer not valid in Quebec. This offer is limited to one order per household. Books received may not be as shown. Not valid for current subscribers to the Harlequin Historical or Harlequin Romance series. All orders subject to approval. Credit or debit balances in a customer's account(s) may be offset by any other outstanding balance owed by or to the customer. Please allow 4 to 6 weeks for delivery. Offer available while quantities last.

Your Privacy—Your information is being collected by Harlequin Enterprises ULC, operating as Harlequin Reader Service. For a complete summary of the information we collect, how we use this information and to whom it is disclosed, please visit our privacy notice located at corporate.harlequin.com/privacy-notice. From time to time we may also exchange your personal information with reputable third parties. If you wish to opt out of this sharing of your personal information, please visit readerservice.com/consumerschoice or call 1-800-873-8635. **Notice to California Residents**—Under California law, you have specific rights to control and access your data. For more information on these rights and how to exercise them, visit corporate.harlequin.com/california-privacy.

HHHRLP23